SOMEONE FROM THE PAST

Sarah had planned to marry and live happily ever after. It was not to be.

One morning, someone from her past returned and shot her dead. Her friends all became involved in a nightmare of fear and suspicion, some more than others.

Nancy, Sarah's closest friend, knew all the men in Sarah's past, and any one of these four men could have murdered her. Yet the police came to believe that Nancy carried out the murder . . .

SOMEONE FROM THE PAST

Margot Bennett

LS

First published 1958
by
Eyre & Spottiswoode

This edition 2002 by Chivers Press
published by arrangement with
the author

ISBN 0 7540 8604 6

British Library Cataloguing in Publication Data available

Printed and bound in Great Britain by
Bookcraft, Midsomer Norton, Somerset

I

'IF WE DRINK any more champagne,' Donald said, 'something terrible will happen to us.'

'The way I feel to-night, I can't think of anything terrible,' I said.

'Try.'

'We might have to hold the tops of our heads on with wire, like champagne corks.'

'I'm willing to let the top of my head go. Nan, I've something to tell you,' Donald said. He leant forward and took my hand.

While I waited, letting his fingers tell me, I looked past his dark, elated face at the rookery of waiters that flapped by the service door, and on to the china birds that perched in the trellis. They would have a sentimental value, later. Then I felt his warm hand grow cold, it was as if he had been reminded of death. He wasn't looking at me any more, but obliquely, across the restaurant.

I turned round.

She waved to me, from the other side of the room.

I had to wrench my hand away from Donald's, to wave back again. When I let my hand fall, I still had a minute left for retreat. We could all live different lives, if we did the right thing, at the right time. A little dignity is a small part of what we have to lose. She spoke to the man she was with, then stood up and began to walk across the room towards us. She was with us, and the minute of possibility was over.

'Hello, darlings,' she said.

Donald didn't stand up. His hand still lay on the table, and he looked at his fingers. It was a good imitation of a man accosted by a strange woman, until he spoke to her.

'Darlings?'

'It's just a manner of speaking.'

'It's a new manner for you.' He was trying to be offensive, but his voice was unsteady, and Sarah smiled at me, inviting me to share the old secret amusement.

She wasn't smiling at Donald.

'Is this one of your special little places?' she asked, in a voice that knew special little places were always cheap.

'It's a special big place,' Donald said.

'So you're celebrating something?' she asked.

'Sit down, Sarah,' I said quickly, because someone had to say it.

'Thank you, Nancy,' she said in a voice that was wholly friendly.

A waiter rushed with another chair, another glass, another bottle.

'I wanted to tell you I'm getting married,' she said. There was one of those four-second pauses, three seconds too long for comfort.

'Who is it?' I asked.

'He's called Charles Lester.'

'And what is it?' Donald asked.

'He's a company director,' she said.

'We must drink to your happiness,' I said.

'And to your companies,' Donald added. He wasn't looking at me. I had no power over him, at all. I was relieved when he suddenly raised his glass and drank. He smiled at her. It wasn't a good smile, but it restored a little civilization to the proceedings.

'Thank you, darlings. I must go back to Chas. now. But Donald, may I ask you a favour? Just for one minute, I wanted to speak to Nancy.'

'I'll go out and buy a cheap little cigarette I know,' he said. 'They wouldn't sell it here.'

She watched him go, and I watched her. She was twenty-eight, and now she had the clothes to match her looks. I remembered her as I had seen her first, standing in front of the long mirror, jabbing an angry red mouth on to her bitter, beautiful face. She was twenty-two then, but she looked at least two years older. She looked as if she had seen life. It wasn't the way I looked. No one had ever been in love with me, then. A lawyer's clerk had once followed me through the back streets of Cologne, bellowing, 'Nandzee, Nandzee' like a wounded bull, until there were angry awakened citizens swearing at every window; and a Dutch barman with a squint had

6

given me a rose every night until my father had decided to get drunk in a different bar, but I didn't wish to call these incidents love. It was dreadful to me that at twenty I should be plain, poorly dressed, and absolutely without experience.

It was six years since I had first met her. She was more beautiful now; there was more surface to her; she had acquired a background; but between the surface and the background there was still visible the faint, ineradicable scar; the unwanted proof that she had suffered for love.

When Donald had gone through the door she turned back to me.

'Nancy, I haven't seen you for years.'

'Nine months.'

'And once we knew each other so well. You taught me so much, Nancy.'

'Me?'

'You were so full of ideas and attitudes. And you knew all about poetry.'

'Not all. Next to nothing. You make me sound like a blue stocking.'

'Weren't you?'

'Never more than a blue sock.'

'And what are you now, Nancy?'

'A single strand of blue wool. Do you want it?'

'Have you forgotten how we used to talk?' she asked.

'We used to laugh together, too. That's not so easy, now that I'm . . . concerned with Donald.'

'So there's no one I can tell.' She began to look back at the table she had come from.

'What are you doing now, Nancy?' she asked, lingering.

'Writing.'

'Is that all?'

'Most of it.'

'You used to tell me everything. And we used to help each other.'

She smiled at me in the old, hopeful, half-humiliated way, and suddenly I was back in an evening in the past, when I had left her crying by an open window in the dark, while I took a taxi to the ten pubs in London, W.1, where Mike was most likely to be drinking, and then walked him up and down the Embankment for two hours, trying to let him talk his rage out at me before I took him back to her.

7

'Sarah, you'd better tell me what you want me to do,' I said. She gathered confidence at once.

'Guess what?' she said.

'I need a clue.'

'A voice from the past.'

'Someone I know?' I asked.

'Oh, yes.'

'A friendly voice?'

'No.' She was very emphatic.

'Laurence? Peter? Mike?' I watched her as I said each name, but she didn't give anything away.

'Did I say it was a man?'

'Did you need to?'

'I don't need to say anything. I just thought you'd be interested.'

'Why?' I asked. It was the kind of conversation that once had led into a maze of secret history, speculation, and laughter.

'Because you're always so curious about people,' she said.

'But some people repeat themselves, and then I stop being curious.'

'This isn't a repeat.'

'Sarah, are you really worried?'

'I suppose so. But it may be nothing.'

'Explain the nothing.'

She picked up the champagne glass and drank a little, quickly.

'I'll explain it,' she said. 'Someone from the past is threatening to murder me.' She spoke in careful flatness, but twisting her mouth a little as she had always done when she was telling me something dreadful. That didn't prove she was frightened. She wasn't in any way a simple character. She liked all the drama she could get, and was quite capable of copying her own mouth-twisting trick.

'Don't waste time guessing what I'm trying to say,' she said. 'I've said what I'm trying to say. Someone from the past is threatening to murder me.'

'You must go to the police.'

'No.'

'Why not?'

'Because I'm going to marry Charles, and nothing is going to stop me. I've waited all this time for my divorce to go

8

through, and now I'm going to marry him at last. Nancy, we're going to Jamaica for our honeymoon. It's been one of my dreams, to go to Jamaica.'

'Don't eat too much sugar in dreamland.'

'It isn't dreamland. It's a fact, or nearly a fact. But if the police come to the flat, he'll know.'

'Know what?'

'Much more than he does now.'

'Doesn't he know anything?'

'Nothing serious.'

'They keep their ears shut, in the City.'

'He doesn't meet the kind of people we meet. He knows I was married to Mike.' She said the name in a hurt, but unalarmed voice. I saw she didn't think it was Mike.

'Tell your Charles about the others,' I suggested. 'It might be awkward, if he learnt for himself.'

'He won't learn. We shall be moving in different circles.'

'Maidenhead and Deauville,' I said. I laughed. 'Peter in Maidenhead,' I explained. 'I wonder what Peter would do in Maidenhead?' Her face didn't show anything.

'Is it Peter?' I asked her.

She frowned, and gave her head a small shake.

'I don't know. I had this letter. It was typed. I've had some others, too, but I tore them up. I'll post you this last one, if you like.'

'Yes. Is it the same as the others?'

'They've all been the same, the same kind of letter, with different words. I've had about five in the last seven or eight weeks. But I had one two days ago, and this one this morning. The pace is getting hotter.'

'What do you want me to do?'

'See them all for me, please.' She stood up. 'Look, Donald's coming back.'

'You mean see Peter and Mike?'

'And Laurence, too. Please, Nancy, you know them all. It will take you such a little time to find who wrote the letter. It's the kind of thing you like doing.'

Donald was nearly at the table.

'Do I?' I asked, watching him.

'You're so curious about people,' she said. "Bye, darlings.' She gave Donald an affectionate smile, it was remarkable what she could do, and then she began to go.

9

'But I forgot to tell you, Nancy, I'm leaving Diagonal Press in two weeks. I'm working madly to get everything straight. When shall we meet?'

'I'll let you know.'

She nodded, and said good-bye again, and went back to her table. I supposed the man with her was Chas., who was to take her to dreamland. He looked very solid. I wondered what kind of dreams disturbed a company director's sleep.

Donald sat down. He picked up his glass and drank quickly. If there was any food at this meal, I've forgotten it.

'What was she talking about?' he asked.

'This and that.'

'Me?'

'Not you.'

'Let's leave,' Donald said. 'We've done this place.'

'I wonder if I could get some American cigarettes here?'

'Yes. They'll have American.' He signalled to a waiter, and we didn't say anything until the cigarettes had been brought. I lit one. I wasn't thinking about Donald, or having sentimental moments with the china birds in the trellis-work.

'What's so special about Sarah, anyway?' Donald asked.

'I don't want to talk about her.'

'You mean you don't want to talk to me about her?'

'Yes. That's what I mean.'

'I don't want to hear about Sarah and me. I know about that. I want to know about Sarah and you. Why did you like her so much that you still like her, even now?'

'We were friends. Do you think you are going to enjoy working in an agency?'

'It's only three days a week. I saw for myself you were friends.'

'You met us both years ago. I should have thought you knew a lot about us.'

'I want to know more.'

'I should even have thought that you knew more than a lot about us.'

'Not enough.'

I took a little more champagne and considered the glass carefully. I remembered how often I'd told Sarah in the early days that husbands and wives should be totally frank with each other. I expected that Donald and I would soon be husband and wife. There was nothing I wanted to hide from him, even although I had long ago lost my simple faith in frankness and several other virtues.

'I was twenty when we both started work in Diagonal. For five years she was my closest friend. We shared a flat until she married Mike. We helped each other, often. We told each other the things we never told anyone else. We pin-pointed the course of every love affair.'

I stopped there. I wasn't sure how Donald would take that bit, but his face was quite impassive. It would have been better if he'd shown a little emotion.

'Go on,' he said.

'We invented private jokes, and planned impossible futures, and admitted errors we hid from everyone else. For part of the time at Diagonal we worked in the same room. We usually liked the same people, and often went to the same parties and places. We shared everything.'

Donald leant forward.

'Even men?' he said loudly.

I stood up.

'I think I want to leave now,' I said.

He had to wait to pay the bill, but he caught up with me on the pavement outside.

'We'll take a taxi,' he said.

'I'd like to walk.'

'Why?'

'It's raining and it's a long way. Do you want any other reason?'

'No. I'll walk with you,' he said.

We walked a yard or two apart over miles of wet London pavements. I didn't look at him nor speak to him, although I thought I was about to lose him. Love affairs can't be planned with the precision of a military campaign. Not that I think military campaigns are as precise as they say.

When we reached the entrance to the flats, I had no plan at all.

"Will you let me explain?' he said.

'Not out here. You can come in.'

When we were inside I took off my wet shoes and lit the gas-fire. I sat down beside it. It wasn't a cold night, but I was very wet. He stood a little distance away.

'I suppose you'll leave me now?' he said.

I began to laugh. Not much, but enough to annoy. 'It's funny, I was going to ask you the same question.'

He sat down.

'Oh, Nan, why did you go on and on about her?'

That was the question that might have made me laugh, but I didn't, I answered him seriously.

'I wanted you to understand I knew all about her past.'

'No one knows all about anyone's past. You wouldn't know half. You wouldn't know more than a quarter.'

'Much more. I even have a lot of it written down. It was my writing practice,' I said rashly.

'Practice?'

'An editor told me to write something every day,' I said. I looked at Donald dubiously, perhaps not even dubiously. It wasn't possible to tell him the story about that editor and the motor launch—the story that Sarah had thought so funny.

'Do you mean you've something written down about me?'

'No, not about you,' I said quickly.

'That's a lie, isn't it?'

'This is turning into the night of the long knives.'

'You hate me, don't you, whatever you say, you hate me because I was in love with her.'

'Darling, you're twenty-seven. It's not surprising you should have been in love before,' I said, a little too patiently and reasonably. There is a point at which patience and reason lead up the quarrel to Camp Six.

'What is surprising is that you should know so much about it. I suppose you know every detail. What I said to her, where, what I did to her, what she did to me?'

'It's an awkward situation,' I said. 'Let's end it.'

'And she was talking about me tonight, wasn't she?'

He left the chair he was in. Women can argue sitting down, but men aren't so good at it. I suppose they don't feel belligerent enough unless they're on their feet.

'She was, wasn't she? Why did she want to talk to you privately if it wasn't that?'

'If you want to know, she was telling me that someone from the past was threatening to murder her,' I said.

'That's not a bad idea,' he said.

I looked up at him and he didn't even see me. He was standing a yard or so away on the other side of the gas-fire with his arms hanging down and steam rising from his rain-sodden clothes. Misery had taken the colour out of his face.

'Why did she tell you that?' he asked. He wasn't shouting. Everything was being done quietly, as in nightmares.

'I suppose because she thought I knew the people concerned.'

'Did you take them all on after her, or only me?'

'I haven't taken you on,' I said. 'Don't make that mistake. The door's over there.'

'If that's the way you feel,' he said. 'I knew it would end this way.'

He went to the door, and he left.

2

THERE IS A time for melancholy self-accusation, but it shouldn't be extended; when the damage has been inspected, the assessor should withdraw. So, when I was able, I made myself think of Sarah and the men in her past. Laurence, ruined; Mike, angry and implacable; Peter, criminal; and Donald.

Peter was the only one she had known before I met her. Peter had cropped up in her life and dropped out of it like one of these interminable magazine stories, continued through articles and illustrations and thick deserts of advertisements, on pages 35, 79, 82, running thinner on every page, so that it's not surprising that the end, when it comes, is not the end after all, but only an announcement: To Be Continued. She had run away from him and become gradually, gratefully, romantically involved with Laurence and his unreal dreams, but the story had begun with Peter, and gone on with Peter, too.

Peter came from a tough, mean, Birmingham black-spot; close enough to the mean, near-respectable street where Sarah had been brought up by a reluctant aunt who worked in a laundry. He was the reason why Sarah had let her wonderful looks come to nothing.

If a poor girl has the advantage of beauty, she has to use it early. She can go in the chorus at sixteen; or win a beauty competition at eighteen; or train as a photographic model and work up to the pinnacle of displaying clothes for other women to buy. She may even become a starlet. But, like rugby footballers and professional boxers, beauty has a short career. At twenty-eight or so, it ends. Who wins a beauty competition at thirty? Who is a top model, or even an air hostess, at thirty-five? There's nothing much left, then, but to marry into the directory of directors. It's a short summer; if you want to pick the flowers you have to dig hard in the right season.

In the precious years from eighteen to twenty-one, when Sarah should have been cultivating her garden, she was in love with the disreputable Peter. When she should have been learning how to walk, and sit, and dress, and catch the eye of the camera; she was walking through the dark streets with Peter, at night, because they had nowhere to go; she was sitting in the back rows of cinemas, holding his hand; she was working in factories to get money to pay the rent; and throwing up her job so that they could go to the races together. Then she was ill. They didn't have a cigarette in the place, she told me, they were desperate.

The aunt who had never wanted her let her stay on in the back room, although there was no money; but when Peter came to see her the aunt sat and sewed by the open door.

Peter tried working at various manual jobs, but he couldn't keep them. Some guests are prepared to eat what's put before them, without fuss, then they're offered, say, fat pork. They can't eat it. They try and try, but fat pork makes them sick. It's more polite to push the plate away, even to leave the room. Peter was like that about work. He honestly wanted to work, he made many efforts, but he simply couldn't go on with it. His system revolted. Work was like great lumps of fat pork to him. Everyone can't be the same, and there's no special reason why a man should find work more attractive than idleness.

Sarah told me all this slowly, in pieces; sometimes while we cooked tinned spaghetti over the gas ring; sometimes while we explored the streets of Mayfair, looking for indications that society life, the tiara and butler kind of society life, still continued.

We were very romantic. It takes a solid foundation of romanticism to build a good cynic.

On rare occasions, usually outside big hotels, we saw women in expensive furs and jewels. Sarah was convinced she knew a real diamond when she saw it, and I believed I could tell paste at a glance.

'There's not much difference,' I told her. 'Diamonds shine in the dark. Paste doesn't.'

'That's what Peter used to say about me.'

'Do you shine in the dark?'

'Peter said so. He said he'd bring me diamonds one day to shine in the dark beside me. He could only whisper things like that because of my aunt sitting sewing with the door open.'

'Didn't she ever leave you?'

'Only for about ten minutes when she went out to make some tea.'

'What did you do with the ten minutes?'

'We used it.'

'And then she came back?'

'Yes. She came back and sat with her cup of tea. She didn't bring us any. She hated Peter. So we had to whisper again. It wasn't much fun, being ill like that. I'd have died if I hadn't had Peter. Then one night he came in, he was grinning all over. He stood and emptied packets and packets of cigarettes on to the chair beside my bed. And bars of chocolate, and a bottle of wine, too. He said we were in the money. So when I got better I ran away. I ran away to London.'

'Why?'

'Because we were in the money, and I didn't know where the money came from. Because we weren't getting anywhere and I thought it would go on for ever.'

'Did you think you'd turn into your aunt,' I asked, 'and sit sewing beside someone else's open door?'

'That's a funny idea, Nancy,' she said. 'Repeat, funny.'

'You shouldn't say "Repeat, funny." ' I told her, in those early days I was always too ready with my little hard pellets of priggish authority.

'Why on earth shouldn't I say "Repeat, funny?" ' she asked me now.

'The phrase is in its coffin. It's like glamorous.'

'That's what I was crazy to be,' she said. 'Glamorous. I wanted to have the right clothes and long eyelashes and a big car and move in the best circles. So I had to get out. I came to London and worked in a restaurant, I hated it. Then I got a job with a photographer, I wasn't any good as a model, but he let me work in the studio, so I knew about photographs, and

15

when I saw the advertisement for the job on the Diagonal Press I applied and somehow or other I got it.'

'You don't love Peter any more?' I asked.

'I don't want to love Peter any more. I don't want to see him ever again.'

But of course he saw her again. He followed her to London. It took him a long time to find her, but when he did he came crashing into her life with the destructive force of a torpedo. I was glad to be present at the moment of impact: even then, I had a cold-blooded curiosity about people.

I suppose it was partly curiosity that made me write down so much about Sarah, and about myself, too, day by day, as it happened; but there was another reason that seemed pathetic, now. From the moment that I got the job on the Diagonal Press and scrawled out my first paid illiteracies I saw myself as a writer, a great writer, one who kept notebooks and would soon enough be guest of honour at literary luncheons. I was twenty-six now, I had overcome these delusions, I no longer kept notebooks. But they made interesting reading when I was trying to think round my own troubles and into Sarah's. I have a good memory, the notebooks did no more than refresh it, while I read on and on into the small hours that seem so much smaller and more dismal as two o'clock merges into four.

People rarely enter our lives like actors striding on to a brilliantly lit stage. We become conscious of them, like dimly apprehended figures in the muffled hour before sunrise: and not all of them stay with us in the hard light of noon.

Laurence was one of the misty figures; a man we were hardly aware of, until, by imperceptible stages, we knew him well.

He was a round, sad man whose collars were always too tight. Perhaps he believed himself to be thinner than he was.

He was a features editor on one of the Diagonal magazines, and the responsibility hurt him like a thumb-screw. Everything went wrong with his features. They were too short to fill the page; or too late for publication; or devilishly designed by crafty writers for the sole purpose of offending the directors. He couldn't shake off these blows like the other features editors, who were faced with identical problems.

He was often grieved by having to work late in the office. Sarah and I worked late, too, but we did it because we were determined to make a success of the job. They couldn't have stopped us working late if they'd tried, and they certainly didn't try. Laurence would often drift through our room, complaining that he had no cigarettes, or no typist, or no thanks for all the extra work he put in. Sometimes he would stop and join in our arguments about photographs and captions and articles. He knew far more than we did about these things. He liked helping us, and he began to turn into a person.

When Sarah and I heard about the two big empty rooms with a gas ring and a view of the river, we wanted to rent them at once. Laurence offered to lend us fifty pounds to furnish the rooms. We were to pay him back one pound a week each. We could afford that, so we took the place.

Then he came shrinking in, running his finger round his neck until he'd stretched his shirt collar enough to let him speak.

He couldn't lend us the money after all.

We guessed it was his wife.

We were against wives, in a general way. Life was all office to us, and wives didn't enter into it, except as a disquieting rumour. We tried to cheer Laurence up, and he lent us twenty pounds anyway, without asking his wife. We were able to buy two divan beds and some saucepans.

Laurence visited us now and then. He bought us drinks, and lent us books, and showed us the East End of London. He didn't have enough money to show us the West End. And all the time he was falling more and more in love with Sarah.

She was flattered and comforted. His wife didn't exist. We'd never even seen a photograph of her. She was the other side of the moon.

Laurence was more than a lover to Sarah. He was a symbol. He was a pioneer, an explorer, who led bravely on into the jungles of culture. He was the exponent of the good life; the man who knew how to rub the salad bowl with garlic; who could beat time to Beethoven; and mutter airs from Mozart; who could identify the ten best-known English trees, and nearly as many birds; and who rubbed the poets of England round the inside of his head as if they had been cloves of garlic and his head the salad bowl.

His wife, we gathered vaguely and slowly, was different. She had made one corner of the sitting-room into a Tellynook; she had no knowledge at all of the romance that lies in the cobwebs around the cellared wine bottle; her idea of the good life was a three-piece suite that matched the curtains.

Sarah and I were incapable of understanding this kind of woman. She was a bird we couldn't identify. I suppose in a way we were brigands. We were outside society. When Sarah ran away from Peter and the sour aunt who worked in a laundry, she had left everything she knew. I had never known anything worth knowing. I had trailed around Europe for years in the wake of a father who was the international representative of an inferior line of fancy goods. Most of his business was done in bars; we stayed in the cheapest lodging houses; my idea of luxury was to travel third-class instead of steerage on a Greek passenger boat. When I was nineteen he took me back to London. A month later he went into hospital and died abruptly. So Sarah and I shared a deficiency. We had no social background. It wasn't merely that we lacked a rich or respectable background. We had none at all. When we met each other in the Diagonal office we formed our own group and set our own standards, which weren't of a nature to protect poor Laurence and his wife.

As the affair went on, Laurence was letting a lot of romance out of himself. He was like a suburban villa on fire, or a humble little square-backed car that has arrived on a race track by accident, and is determined to give all the fierce Ferraris a run for their money.

He told Sarah his dream was to live on the West coast of Ireland and fish all day and write all night.

'That's safe enough,' I said, when she repeated this to me. 'There's no room on that programme for any woman.'

He asked her to go with him. I knew she didn't have the temperament to enjoy sitting up to the neck in rough water with a fishing-line, so I tried talking to Laurence about his wife. He said he had left her anyway, with a gay good night. I tried to picture the scene, but I couldn't catch it.

So he and Sarah were in love. They were in love all the way. They melted into each other like two ice creams that had fallen side by side on the hot sand.

They didn't set up house together, in London, because they were going to Ireland so soon, but Laurence spent a lot of time at our flat. I occasionally left them alone on Sundays while I went out into the country and grimly learnt to ride horses. For some reason I believed that the ability to ride would give me the respectable background that I lacked. But on week-days I was there, in London, and I inevitably saw a great deal of Laurence.

He was a great reader-aloud. He had this idea that literary people have, that enjoyment can be communicated by the roundly-rolled-out word. We would all sit together, round the gas-fire that is such a feature of London nomadic life, and Laurence would try to inspire us. He even tried with *Paradise Lost*.

'From morn to noon he fell, from noon to dewy eve.
A summer's day; and with the setting sun
Dropt from the zenith like a falling star.'

Laurence would read.

'I think I'll go out and see if the kettle's boiling,' I would say to them. Then I'd go out of the room, and the second I left, Laurence would clutch Sarah in his arms. I'd come back in to ask about sugar, and Laurence would snatch the book, and hastily go on reading:

'. . . Nor did he 'scape
By all his engines, but was headlong sent
With his industrious crew to build in hell.'

Then we'd have the coffee. It was like a kind of night school.

In spite of *Paradise Lost* (a work that didn't particularly appeal to Sarah, as Book Five was succeeded by Book Six, with no end in sight), they seemed determined to go on with their unlikely plans. Laurence resigned from his job, and made arrangements to buy a coracle, a stock of peat, and a gallon of blue-black ink. You'd have thought nothing could stop them except the erosion of the Atlantic coast of Ireland.

There was an evening in the flat when we were having one of those romantic suppers—a bottle of Chianti and lobster salad —while the radio played Tschaikowsky at us. Laurence certainly knew all about the good life. Then the door bell rang. Sarah went down to answer it, and Laurence and I waited, sad and happy by candle-light, drowned in fountains of music.

We were in the third movement before Sarah came back up with Peter, who had found her at last.

The first thing she did, even before the introductions, was to switch off the radio. She was right. Peter and Tschaikowsky were incompatible. Peter didn't fit in with the romantic supper, either. He had the air of carrying fish-and-chips on his shoulder. She introduced him: she was happy and proud to have him with her, but Laurence could do nothing but mutter and smooth back his hair with a jerking hand.

Peter made some remark about the electric light being cut off. Sarah blushed. The candles looked weak and ineffective. She blew them out, and switched on the light. It was the first time I had ever seen Peter, and I saw him clearly then. He had thick brown hair, oiled down too flat; he was a middle-sized man, in a suit of a lighter blue than people wear. He was coarse, he was shifty, but as he stood beside Sarah under the harsh central light, I saw the truth at once. So far as Sarah was concerned, the West coast of Ireland had been washed right away.

Laurence couldn't believe it. He couldn't accept what had happened. He stayed around for a long time that evening, the privileged guest, but in the end he had to go, and Sarah could scarcely take her eyes off Peter long enough to say good night.

Laurence hung about helplessly, for weeks and months, wilting like a broken dandelion. He was jobless and wifeless and Irelandless. He had given up the peat and the coracle and everything else. I suppose life in a leaking cottage in perpetual rain doesn't seem so attractive, when it has to be lived alone. He wrote a book and couldn't sell it. He picked up a few free-lancing jobs: he had been competent enough, in his worried way. He earned enough money to drink, and when he had begun drinking, he couldn't stop. The licensing laws are tough, but the afternoon drinking clubs are tougher.

We saw him on and off, sometimes with gaps of months, sometimes only of weeks. As we moved up in the Diagonal Press, and came to know more and more of the editorial staff, we were often able to arrange outside jobs for him. He had helped us a lot in the beginning: it was a pity there was no easy method of repaying him.

It wasn't Sarah's fault, in any way. She'd never have been good at fishing. The whole thing would have fallen apart, even without Peter. Laurence and his ideas were too flimsy to survive, except, of course, in that part of Sarah's mind that had been waiting for someone like him. People change each other, but not much, unless they are ready to be changed.

Peter got rid of Laurence, but he never got rid of the books and music that Laurence had left behind him. They were

20

enemies that baffled him as completely as if they had stepped off a flying saucer.

There had been other changes in Sarah, too, since I first met her. Instead of arranging her hair in corrugated waves, she now wore it straight. She had softened her voice, reduced her accent, abandoned the purple eye-shadow and the stove-blacked eyelashes. She liked learning, and she was looking for other things to learn.

For the first few weeks of his return, all Peter had to do was touch Sarah's hand, and you could see that for her the world had quivered to a stop and was hanging motionless in space, but that was the best the world could do. It wouldn't reverse for them. They couldn't force it back to the point where she was satisfied to sit in the cheap seats of cheap cinemas with Peter's arm around her. She had a dozen new interests, and Peter rejected all of them.

He never came to live in the flat. He had his own theory of morality, and he was afraid of being kept by Sarah. He blew in fairly steadily, and when he blew in I very often blew out. He had a habit of looking at me as if he was wondering about my chances of winning the 3.15 at Hurst Park.

He stayed around for six months of rapidly diminishing bliss. He did his best to get steady work, but one job after another proved to have insuperable disadvantages. He had very little money to spend on her, and it never occurred to him there was any other reason for the emotional barbed wire that was tangling up between them.

What signs does a man have when a girl is going to leave him? Her attention flickers away from him as he talks; her eyes move about the room, looking for some object more interesting than his face. When he kisses her she stands in patient resignation. She is relieved when a third person disturbs them, and delighted when the third person is followed by a fourth, and a fifth. She is tired, genuinely tired, it's not an act, when he suggests going out together. 'You would,' she says wearily, when he tells her an interesting anecdote about himself. 'It's nothing,' she often says, letting a little irritation out with the words. 'It doesn't matter. Why should it?' She is unexpectedly engaged on Monday: on Tuesday she has to wash her hair. When she meets him on Wednesday, conversation moves slowly against the tide. If he tries to take her hand, she moves it away sharply, amazed that he should attempt such physical familiarity. The silences break over great reefs of time. She begins to study his face with mournful tenderness: she is looking for the spot where the death blow will hurt him least.

Even Peter could read the signs, but he believed, with all the power of his corrupted innocence, that if only he could get in the money again she would love him as unquestioningly as she had loved him in the simple past.

One night he came to the flat, tired and triumphant as if he had climbed some secret mountain.

'Tell her I'm here, Nancy,' he said to me.

'She's lying down, Peter, she's tired. She has a headache.'

'This'll cure her headache.'

He opened the bag he was carrying and banged two bottles of champagne on the table.

'The old Widow Click in person. Get some glasses, Nancy. Have a drink with us before we go out.'

I fetched Sarah. She was too white, too ready to be angry.

He put his arm round her shoulders. It was a possessive gesture, but he needed support, too.

'We're in the money again, Sarah,' he said.

She shook him off, and stood watching, hard and suspicious, while he opened the first bottle. The cork went off with its small imitation of a starting pistol. Froth showered over our new table. She noticed that, too.

Peter poured champagne into three glasses.

'To the good time coming now!' he said.

Sarah didn't touch her glass. It was a raw moment, so I picked mine up and drank quickly. It didn't help. Peter wouldn't have looked at me if I'd been painted purple.

Peter filled his own glass again.

'Get started!' he said to her. 'We're going out for the big-gest night in town.'

She didn't move. He arranged his face into his old three-quarter grin, put his hand into his pocket, and brought out a bundle of notes as thick as the Chicago Tribune.

He fanned the notes out at her.

'Remember the diamonds I promised you? We're half-way there.'

'What have you done?' she asked.

'Maybe I won it at the races,' he said. He kept the grin on.

They looked at each other. They were so still they were like two statues carved in one, with a table between them. Nothing could bring them together again; they were fixed in their separate attitudes. The champagne kept bubbling on. That was the only movement, until Sarah put down her glass.

'Maybe you won it at the races,' she said.

She picked up the unopened bottle of champagne and pushed it into his coat pocket.

'Get out!' she said. 'Out! Out now!'

'Sarah, sweetheart, I didn't get it to spend alone!'

'You won't drag me into this!'

'I'll drag you into what I like, you twisting little bitch!' he shouted at her.

He crashed the bottle and glasses off the table, and before the glass had finished breaking he had his hands round her throat. He could have killed her then, quite easily, but she hadn't even begun to struggle when he dropped his hands. He stood with his head sunk forward. Tears were running down her face, but she wasn't able to speak.

I didn't know what he'd do next. I caught hold of his arm, but he pushed me away and turned and ran out of the room.

The police picked him up late the next night. They could hardly help it. He had spent most of the day describing to all comers how neatly he had knocked the tobacconist out before collecting the day's takings from the till. He was so drunk when they got him he couldn't have fought his way out of a soap bubble.

He was only an amateur, but there had been violence, although not much, in the affair. He was given twelve months.

It was getting on for five o'clock in the morning when I got to that point in the notebooks. I closed the one I had been reading, gathered them all up, and put them away in the drawer where I kept them. There was nothing much in them that I couldn't remember without their help, but I'd had a vague hope that I would find in them some lead on to the man who had been threatening Sarah. It looked like Peter, he had enough violence in him, but I couldn't see him as a man who would put anything in writing before he moved into action. I could have read on, about Mike, and Donald, but I knew these two so well it was hardly necessary to read about them.

I was tired. Donald was still grinding around in my head. I knew I should take a couple of strong sleeping-pills. They would give me four hours' sleep, and a heavily-doped morning that would make work impossible, unless I took a stimulant.

23

After that, a couple of tranquillizing tablets would level me up for the day.

'Love in our time,' I thought. 'I'd like to live in one of those countries where marriages are arranged by the heads of families, and the chairman allows no questions.'

I decided against the sleeping-pills, and I lay awake for the small remainder of the night, thinking of Sarah and Donald, and Donald and me.

The first thing I saw in the morning was the letter from Sarah. I didn't open it at once. I put on the kettle in a hazy way, and ran the bath. I drank a glass of hot water, and took one more stimulating tablet than I needed, while I wondered if Benzedrine would have been better. I had the bath with my mind empty and cross, and while I dressed I thought of my own affairs, and they looked very ugly. I remembered Sarah again as I made the coffee. I had promised to help her. I had other things to do, and it was nearly half-past nine already. She would be a reproach to me. She always got up at eight.

I went to the telephone and tried to ring Laurence. I listened to the double ring for a minute, and then someone at the other end lifted off the receiver, but didn't speak. It wasn't very hard to imagine Laurence stretching out a trembling hand from the bed.

'Laurence, it's Nancy here,' I said hopelessly, but there was no answer, 'I want to see you,' I said, trying to make it sound urgent, although it was like talking into outer space. There's not much to say to a telephone with a receiver off. I hung up. Later in the day, he would remember, and it was almost certain he would ring me back.

I looked up Mike's telephone number, and I was about to ring it when I remembered he'd changed his flat. I couldn't think what to do about that, because I wasn't thinking very well, but in the end I rang his agent.

A very junior office girl answered. It was half-past nine, but the theatrical world doesn't stir early. The girl told me she wasn't supposed to give actors' home numbers without authority, and that there was no one else in the office.

'Oh, damn,' I said. 'You see, I'm from America. I represent the Must Fan Club of New York, and Michael Fenby is our Mustest for June.'

'I didn't know Mr. Fenby had ever acted in America,' the office girl said.

'He hasn't. And if I don't see him today, he never will. I'd be sorry for any actor we awarded the Must-Nottest badge of the year.'

She was so doubtful, she nearly made the telephone wires quiver. But she gave me his number.

I rang, and Mike answered the 'phone.

'Good-morning, Mike,' I said, 'It's nice of you to be up.'

'Oh, Nancy,' he said. 'That's you, isn't it? I've been meaning to ring you. I thought, why shouldn't we have lunch together? Would you like to lunch with me one day, Nancy?'

'Yes, I'd like to.'

'Well, we'll fix it, shall we, make it a date?'

'Yes, Mike.' I waited a second, then asked, 'What date?'

'I'll look up my little book and see when I'm free, and then you look up your little book and see when you're free, and then we'll fix it.'

'I've looked up my little book,' I said. 'I'm free any time, from today on through next week.'

'Oh, Nancy! Has something gone wrong with your affairs?'

'Not a thing.'

'No one gone to prison, or anything of that sort?'

'No.'

'You can tell me all about it when we meet for lunch.'

'You haven't said when we're meeting.'

'I can't find my little book. I'll give you a ring later, shall I?'

'No. Don't do that, Mike. I want to see you to-day.'

'But, sweetie. I'm on Terrivision. That's why I'm up. I'm rehearsing.'

'When?'

'They're the most brutal creatures. Ten o'clock in the great woods. Burnt Oak, or Wembley Park. And you should see, I really wish you could see, the producer. Temperament! He thinks out the sets with a kind of telescope, and when he wants to concentrate, he blows bubbles.'

'With soap?'

'No. He has a tin. He shakes the bubbles off with a bit of wire. They help him to relax. When they burst, they cover the floor with slime, like invisible banana skins. There's practically no one in the cast who hasn't a sprained ankle or a broken neck. You ought to see us, skidding about the place.'

'I will, if you like. I'll come and see you there.'

'No. Why don't we have lunch one day?'

25

'Let's make it today, Mike, please,' I said. 'I specially want to.'

'I've found my little book,' he said. 'I'm free today. And it's only Shepherds Bush, after all. There's a pub called the Blue Unicorn. One o'clock. You can tell me all the gossip.'

I rang off with the faint stirrings of a smile. It wasn't strong enough to be born alive, but even so, I was grateful to Mike.

I flipped around the telephone book, trying to find a lead into Peter. Sarah's letter still lay unopened. I wasn't any more anxious to read it than I was to ring Peter. I knew where he lived, it was in Soho. I knew the street and the number. I could call and see him, later in the day. I wouldn't enjoy that, nor would he.

When I finally opened the letter I found a note from Sarah, hand-written, and a typed enclosure. The note simply said:

'Nancy, here's the letter. Do what you can. Sarah.'

The enclosure was typed on plain paper, thin copy paper, quarto, the kind, a very common kind, that I used for my own typing. It said:

'I haven't forgotten what you did to me in the past. You don't deserve to live, what's a life worth to you? I've watched the road you've taken. Up to a point, any road will do as well as another, for you and for me, too. The trouble it, after this point there's no turning back, we've both passed the fork, there's only one way now. I'm coming for you, one night soon, and until I come you'll never know which of your lovers is going to murder you.'

I read it again and then put it down on the table. It was the letter of a madman, but I'm not at all sure if it's better to be threatened by the mad or by the sane.

I poured myself a cup of coffee and was beginning to drink it when there was a tap, the faintest tap, at the door. The bell worked, I knew that. For some reason the fact that my morning caller had chosen not to ring the bell moved my heart to the wrong place. I opened the door, and Donald came in.

He looked like a man who had been in a ship-wreck. I didn't have time to get my emotions arranged in the correct ranks. He walked slowly past me into the sitting-room.

'Nancy,' he said. 'She's dead. What am I to do? She's dead.'

He sat down by the table. I didn't speak at all for a minute. My mind went dark, as if I was beginning to faint, and when it cleared I could only remember that something impossible had been said. Then I saw Donald again.

'How do you know?' I asked. I was whispering.

'How?' he repeated. He caught hold of my hand and crushed it in his own. 'Because I've seen her. That's what I came to tell you, Nancy. I've seen her. And I'm dead too. As good as dead. I came to tell you, to finish myself off with you, then I've nothing.'

'What happened to her?'

'I don't know. But she's dead. There's blood.' He dropped my hand and turned his face away.

'Oh, Sarah!' I said. I think I began to cry, but I'm not sure. It hurt me to think of her, with blood, from some wound, some painful wound. I remembered how afraid she'd been of any kind of physical pain, how terrified she'd been even of riding a horse. She asked if she could come with me, one week-end. Riding was a social asset, she said. The horse trotted off with her, very slowly. When it reached a pace of about five miles an hour, the strain was too much for her. She fell off. She had only a few bruises, but at first I thought she was badly hurt. She was frozen with misery and terror. I wondered if she'd seen the man who killed her, if she'd had time to be afraid.

'Nancy,' Donald was saying. 'Are you all right? Do you want something, some water, or a drink? Take some coffee.'

'No. Tell me what happened.'

'I've come to tell you what happened. I was there. I wasn't in the room. But I was there. I went in. She was dead.'

'You were there?'

'Nancy, I want to tell you. I was there. They'll say it was me.'

I still wasn't thinking of him. There wasn't anything to think of, but Sarah.

'What did the doctor say?'

'There wasn't any doctor. There wasn't anything for a doctor to do,' he said.

'Didn't you get someone?'

'I wanted to see you. I wanted to tell you I love you. Now I've told you, I'll go."

'Go where?'

'Back to my flat, I suppose. Until the police come.'

'Police? Have you told the police?'

'No. They might not have let me see you.'

'Donald, I don't understand what you're talking about. Don't the police know?'

'No.'

'Does anyone know?'

He shook his head.

'You mean she's all alone?'

'Yes.'

'We have to tell someone.'

'Yes, tell someone,' he said. 'That will be the end of me. It's the end of me, anyway. There will be someone, some old woman, or postman, or milkman who saw me come out.'

'When did you go in?'

'That's what I wanted to tell you,' he said. 'About three o'clock this morning.'

The silence lasted a little longer than the drowning man's last time up.

'I see,' I said.'Then you came back here to tell me you love me.'

'Yes, that's what I did. It's no good trying to explain. I know that. I'm finished. I was finished last night. We were in that place, I was going to tell you what you know, that I loved you and you loved me, and we ought to marry and live together. Everything was all right. Robbie had suggested an exhibition. I had a contract for the agency job in my pocket. I was a man again, with a job, and a girl to love. Then she turned up. She had the knack of turning up. In about five minutes, the time it took to buy a packet of cigarettes, everything was wrong. She made it wrong. Did you expect me to behave like a human being when she was there? You're forgetting what you know, the way she left me. She left me to die, you know that.'

'And now you've left her dead.'

'Yes. I see. No one could think anything else. I'm only trying to tell you. Everything was so bad last night I thought I'd make it worse.'

'And so?'

'And so I went to her.'

'You certainly made it worse,' I said.

I sat and considered. We had left each other, last night, for good. I had asked him to go. I couldn't complain if he had gone to someone else, I thought, and began to complain.

'So you always loved her,' I said. 'You never stopped. When you met her again, you had to go back to her.'

'No. You can't forgive me,' he said. 'You don't have to. I wanted to tell you the truth, that was all.'

I can't pretend I had a quick reaction to any of this. I was

28

thinking very slowly and stupidly. If he'd left me to go to her, even for one night, I wouldn't have wanted him back. Half a man is much worse than no man at all. But now she was dead, and a simple, unpleasant affair had exploded and knocked the horizon apart.

'Now you've told me,' I said, 'one of us ought to go to the police.'

'Yes. They'll think it was me, of course.'

I saw her, left alone for some stranger to find.

'We'll tell the police.'

'Yes. Do that. But, Nancy, you believe me? I wasn't . . it wasn't me.'

'There wouldn't be a lot of milkmen and postmen around at three in the morning. Did anyone see you go in?'

'I don't know.'

'And coming out. When did you come out?'

'I've been walking around. I don't know how long I've been walking around.' He had been standing up, but now he collapsed suddenly, like a man at the end of a long race. I helped him sit down.

'Donald, you have to tell me when you left her flat.'

'Somewhere around half-past eight.'

'Around? Before or after?'

'I don't know. I looked at my watch when I woke up. It was late, I think it was half-past then, or perhaps it was later. I got up. I saw her, then I got out.'

'Were there any milkmen and postmen about when you left?'

'There were people in the street.'

'Did they see you?'

'If they looked, they saw me.'

'Donald, do you want to tell me more?'

'Anything you like. I might as well learn my piece. Nancy, have you a drink in the place?'

'No. I can give you a confidence drug, or a tranquillizer, or a stimulant, or a sleeping-tablet. You look as if you needed them all.'

He roused himself very slightly. 'I had some knock-out pills last night. Perhaps that's why I feel so knocked-out.'

'How did it happen? Was she shot?'

'I don't know.'

'You didn't hear anything?'

'No.'

'Why weren't you—I mean, what room were you in when this happened?'

'I was in the sitting-room.'

'Why?' I asked, with my eyes shut.

'I was sleeping there.'

I didn't say anything.

'Don't look like that.' He suddenly began to shout. 'I spent the night there, but I slept on the sofa in the sitting-room.'

I couldn't look at him. I didn't want to say what I thought, which was roughly what my father's Aunt Julia would have thought.

'You don't believe me, and if you don't, no one else will. She didn't love me. She stopped that a long time ago.'

'Donald, if you're learning your piece, get it right. If you meant to sleep in the living-room, why did you go there?'

'I don't see why I have to explain everything.'

This was too much, even for me in my stunned condition.

'You have a living-room of your own,' I said. 'You could have slept in that.'

'I won't tell you why I went there.'

My terrible, my disastrous curiosity about people, took charge.

'You have to tell me, Donald. How can I help you if I don't know everything?'

'You can't help me, anyway.'

'You must have had a reason for going there.'

'Oh, for God's sake, I'll tell you. I went there to sleep with her. That's what I thought I went for. I didn't give a damn what I did. You'd thrown me out. It was her fault. I hated her. I suppose I thought if—anyway, I thought I could hate her a little more. Then we had a row.'

'Then?'

'Right away, I mean. She'd gone to bed. I rang the bell, and she didn't answer at first. So I banged on the door and then she did.'

'Go on.'

'I don't know how to go on. She told me to clear off, but I suppose she was afraid I'd bang the door down, so in the end she let me in.'

'She'd been in bed?'

'It was three o'clock. Yes, she'd been in bed, all right. She had those wire curler things in her hair. She was wearing a nightdress or something, and she had a green thing, a kind of dressing-gown, over her shoulders. She put it on, I mean put it on properly, and then let me in.'

'And then?'

'And then we had this row.'

'You have to tell me what the row was about.'

'All right, I'll tell you. I asked her something about you. Perhaps that's why I went there. I don't know.'

'I see.'

'And she wouldn't tell me anything about you. She told me where to go. So I told her where I would go. She didn't like the sound of that. And she said—she said she hated, loathed despised me, etcetera, but if I was going to marry you she was —she was—she wouldn't let me go away. Then, I don't know how it happened, we began to drink and talk and in the end she gave me some blankets and I slept in the living-room. I couldn't have slept, even then, but she gave me a couple of these pills, blue things, sodium amytal, I think, that's why I didn't waken this morning, even when . . .'

'It seems we were friends after all,' I said. I began to cry again. Donald came near me, but I pushed him away. I stopped crying. There was no time to spare for tears.

'God, what am I to do?' Donald said.

'Stay here,' I told him. 'I'm going out for an hour. Please, please, don't move out of this flat until I come back. Do you promise?'

'For what it's worth.'

Before I left I went to the drawer where I kept my keys. I'd had the keys of Sarah's flat for a long time.

3

SARAH'S FLAT WAS, like mine, in a respectable, convenient, but undistinguished area. It had taken us both a long time to climb so far. When we had our first jobs together in the Diagonal Press we'd been glad enough to share a squalid double bed-sitting-room, with a bath and a wardrobe right in the middle of the separate cooking facilities. When we had visitors we hid the washing-up in the bath and covered it with the portable draining-board. Neither of us was domesticated, but when Sarah had learnt that it was what she called the done thing to know how to cook, she bought a cookery book, and worked right through it, one dish at a time. I remember we had weeks of soup—Scotch Broth, Bortsch, Lentil Soup, Minestrone. When we had done all the soup we went back to weeks of hors d'oeuvres and then on to months of fish.

It was because poverty made us live so close together that we learnt so much about each other's past and present affairs. It was only what Sarah called the thousand per cent. affair that escaped the hundred per cent. discussion.

Naturally it was Sarah who had the affairs, for although we had so much in common she differed from me in one supremely important respect. She was beautiful. As time passed, my looks straightened out a little, I became presentable, but there was never any prospect of my approaching Sarah's standard of appearance.

I thought of all this, in the taxi. Naturally, I'd taken a taxi as soon as I left my flat. It wasn't a cautious thing to do, but I was in a hurry. I'd spent too long, talking to Donald.

I had just enough sense to get out of the taxi at the corner. When I'd paid the driver I walked quickly along the street. Sarah and I hadn't been able to afford taxis in our early days together. We had only been taken on by the Diagonal Press because one of the editors was engaged in his mad annual search for cheap new blood. We had been paid very little, to begin with. We had often walked home from work to save the bus fare.

I went up the stairs to the flat. I think the valves in my heart were choked with terror as I turned the key and opened the door. There was a bowl of rosebuds on a table. I remembered once, in some other country, I was exploring the woods behind a town, and I suddenly came on a path smothered in flowers. Some of them were roses. I was only sixteen. I thought it was like a fairy tale. I was ankle-deep in flowers, the flowers of early summer, then I was knee-deep, then I could hardly struggle through them. The smell was so strong, it wasn't beautiful, it was a sweet stench. There were too many flowers even for a fairy tale. I turned the corner, and realized in a moment of shock that I was standing behind the local crematorium. They didn't burn the flowers for the dead. They threw them in the private woods. I've never much cared for the smell of flowers, since.

I leant over now and looked at the rosebuds in the vase. A card said: Charles.

I left the roses. I went into her bedroom and saw what it was like to be out of the world. I stared and stared at her, understanding for the first time, in the most savage and painful way, the brutal fact of mortality. A hole was bored into my mind that nothing would ever fill again. So I stood and looked.

We had shared a great many things, but she was dead, dead and cold, even the blood that had come from her heart was dry. She had her death quite alone.

I wasn't an expert. I couldn't tell at first if she'd been shot or stabbed. It wasn't an easy thing to do, but I pulled back the bedclothes. I saw that the blood, although there wasn't much of it, had spread on to the sheets. There was very little blood, I wouldn't have thought that so small a loss could have made her die.

She was wearing a nightgown of the flimsy pretty kind she'd always liked. When I'd looked at it long enough I saw what I thought were scorch marks. So she'd been shot, and the gun had been held very close. She must have seen the man who did it. She would have been frightened, very frightened, and when it was over he'd pulled the bedclothes up again.

I pulled them up now, very carefully. I didn't tuck them in around her. When we'd lived together we'd always avoided these maternal gestures. We were equals, and had never played at mother and child, or big sister, little sister. We weren't equal, now.

I couldn't sit down, but I stood near her. Life is a long affair, and I could spare five minutes to think of the dead.

Later on, these five minutes cost me a great deal.

I went through to the sitting-room. There were some blankets piled on the sofa: an ash-tray lying beside it with about ten cigarette stubs. None of them had lipstick. If Donald had smoked them alone, he'd had a bad night. Then I remembered she'd gone to bed before he came. She wouldn't be wearing lipstick. They'd sat up drinking and talking. She'd certainly smoked.

I took the ash-tray and emptied it in the rubbish bin in the kitchen. After we'd left our first place, she'd taken to reading women's magazines, those that we could get free from Diagonal, and she'd become very domesticated. She always emptied ash-trays before she went to bed at night. I'd picked up the habit from her. I don't like full ash-trays. There must be a reason why she hadn't emptied this one. But there was Donald. If he'd still been smoking when she left him, and that might have been four o'clock in the morning, she wouldn't have taken the ash-tray away.

To wash glasses at four in the morning would demand a high degree of domesticity; she had left the glasses she and Donald had drunk out of, and the bottle, which was nearly empty. It was white wine of some sort, she'd taken to drinking nothing but wine because she thought it was an aristocratic thing to do. I was glad the bottle wasn't empty, because the easiest way to hide it was to put it back with the other bottles, in the sideboard. She didn't keep much drink.

I took the glasses into the kitchen. They were sticky. They would have to be washed in very hot water. I turned on the tap. It was cold. It was the kind of thing these constant-hot-water flats did to you, in June. Then I remembered it wasn't a constant-hot-water flat. She had an electric immersion heater. I supposed it was switched off.

I picked up the kettle from the stove. It had water in it already, so I put it down and lit the gas under it.

I went back to the living-room to clear away the blankets. I was determined there should be no trace of Donald left in the flat.

I folded the blankets carefully, and put them away in the cupboard, and then stood with my hand still on the door of the cupboard, trying to catch a thought that was flicking about in my mind like a nearly invisible insect.

It was something to do with the kitchen, so I went back there. The kettle was nearly boiling. It was hot enough to wash the glasses. I picked up the kettle, still worrying over my fugitive thought, but I had no more time. I washed and dried the glasses and put them away.

I went into the bathroom to see if Donald had left any traces. It was in good order. One of the big towels was damp to the touch, but who knows how long it takes a towel to dry?

There was only the bedroom left, now. Donald hadn't been in there, except in the morning, when he had found her dead. I wondered why he'd gone in at all. To say good-bye? Perhaps.

If the murderer had left the door open, he might have looked in, by pure chance.

I remembered suddenly about finger-prints. Ordinary people aren't finger-print conscious, but for the time being I had ceased to be an ordinary person. With a handkerchief, I wiped the door handles, one by one, so there was nothing left to show he had been in the flat. Or so I thought, until I took a last look in the living-room. There was a scrap of paper on the floor, with two or three names and phone numbers. One of the names I knew—Roberts, the man who had suggested to Donald that he might be prepared to give a small exhibition of his paintings. Donald would never be careful enough to make a good criminal.

I put the paper in the clean ash-tray and lit it with a match. When it had burnt out I ground the fragments with the match, and then emptied them in the kitchen. I was the only living person who knew, or could find out, that he'd been in the flat most of last night. The only living person, with the possible exception of the murderer.

I'd done what I could for Donald, and now I went back to the bedroom to do what I could for her. I suppose I had some idea of setting things in order, of shielding her, so far as I could, from the brutal eye of office.

Her green slippers lay on the yellow carpet. One was just inside the door, the other was near the foot of the bed. She was usually tidier that that, but Donald had kept her up late. I put the slippers neatly together by the side of the bed, carefully not looking at her.

There was a glass of water on the bedside table.

Then I went to her clothes. I'd shared rooms with her for more than three years, from the time we first met until she married Mike, and afterwards I'd stayed with her several times, on and off. I knew her habits nearly as well as I knew my own. We often went to bed late. It was in the mornings that split seconds counted. Long ago we had both developed the habit of arranging our clothes the night before; of seeing that the dress or suit we meant to wear was pressed and complete on its hanger; that the underclothes were in their right order on a chair.

This morning even the clothes were different, although it took me a minute to see why.

I picked them all up, the stockings first. It was important to

35

see in advance that stockings were all right; we had done plenty of swearing, in the old days, about last-minute runs. All the time I was there I kept escaping into side-tracks of memory. Being mixed up in murder doesn't cool the brain. I took the lace nylon slip, it was white. The pants and girdle that lay underneath it were pale blue. I took the brassière last; it was yellow.

I stood holding them all, and worrying and worrying. The clothes were wrong.

I remembered her standing in an old dressing-gown by the ironing board, looking at a mess of melted nylon on the iron and crying in exasperation:

'Oh, why did I have to let the iron get hot! It's my only blue slip. Now I'll have to wear pink with blue pants and a black brassière.'

'No one will see it,' I told her.

'How do you know no one will see it? This might be the day.'

'If the million-pound suitor gets as far as that he won't stop to look at the colour scheme.'

We both began to laugh.

'What a disgusting mind you have, Nancy,' she said. 'But if I ever turn into a millionairess or even a hundredairess I'll spend it all on underclothes that match.'

The conversation was at least four years old. My memory was too good. It must have been because I remembered so much about her that I felt a panic whimpering rising in my throat. I wanted to scream, I didn't know how to stop it. I went to my handbag and took a cigarette and began to smoke. I had to stop it.

She hadn't turned into a millionairess, but she had gone back to Diagonal after the marriage with Mike collapsed. She edited one of their magazines, now—that was, until this morning she had edited one of their magazines. They paid her well: she certainly had enough money to see that her underclothes matched.

She had meant to leave Diagonal in two weeks, and marry Chas. the company director, and go to Dreamland. If she hadn't been killed, she'd be in the office now. It was Saturday, but still she'd be in the office: Diagonal editorial staff always worked on Saturday mornings. Perhaps she'd arranged to have lunch with Chas.

These were unprofitable thoughts, but I had to get my mind

36

steady. I began again to think about the underclothes. She preferred green, and pale yellow. Something about green began to roll about at the back of my mind, a thought that squirmed away like a fish when I tried to catch it. I began to look methodically for a pale blue slip to match the pants and girdle, and suddenly a coloured picture appeared, of Sarah, wearing a green dressing-gown, answering the door to Donald.

I had no idea of being a detective, it wasn't why I was there, the police would attend to all that. I'm not sure why I was so determined to find out about the underclothes. I suppose as usual, even in these circumstances, I was carried on by curiosity. I went through every drawer, every possible place, even the laundry box in the bathroom, but there was no pale-blue slip anywhere. There were plenty of white pants and girdles and brassières: she could have matched everything in white.

I went back to the dressing-table and began to dust it with my handkerchief. I rubbed the mirror over, too: I saw that my face was dead white, with two black blotches for the eyes. I looked as if I'd just been made up for Lady Macbeth's sleep-walking scene.

I remembered I hadn't looked in the wardrobe, so I went to it. She had plenty of clothes, fairly cheap clothes, but carefully chosen. The green dressing-gown wasn't there. I'd looked around the flat enough by now to know that it wasn't anywhere, but it was possible I was having a blind patch.

I'd been keeping my eyes away from the bed, but now I turned back to it in fear. It would be my last sight of her on earth.

The line of her profile was as clean and clear as ever: it had often reminded me of a delicate pencil sketch. I saw with pity that her short, casually waved hair was falling over her pale forehead. I was anxious not to touch her, but I still owed her something for the friendship we'd enjoyed. I leant forward and carefully smoothed back her hair, shuddering as my fingers touched her cold skin. Then I looked at her again, and turned away. At least she wouldn't have to answer any questions. That pleasure would be reserved for the rest of us.

I took the key with which I'd let myself in, and dropped, it into the drawer of the dressing-table where she kept her spare keys. I knew that the key to my flat would be there. We had always had this key-sharing arrangement, since we first lived apart.

I went to the door, remembering there were two things I had to do. The first was to ring the police in an anonymous, impersonal voice; the other was to hurry home and persuade Donald never to tell anyone else in the world that he'd been in her flat that night.

But my timing was bad. I'd lost five minutes somewhere. If I could have had them back I'd willingly have paid for them with all the money I had. I'd gladly have given up a holiday, or promised to do without some future happiness. But there are no bargains to be made with time; the five minutes had gone, like so many other important minutes in my life, and now, when it was essential that no one should know I had ever been in the flat, I heard a step outside the door, and the noise of a key being put in the lock.

Afterwards I saw a lot of things I could have done. I could have hidden in the cupboard in the hall and then slipped out silently; I could have pushed the intruder down and escaped in a flash; I could have accepted the inevitable, and said 'Good morning, she's been murdered.' Instead of any one of these things, I acted quite spontaneously, and, as the key turned, I put the chain on the door.

The door opened for four inches and then was stopped by the chain. I moved back silently. I didn't know if I'd been quick enough; it was possible that part of my face, or of my clothes, had been seen through the crack.

The chained door left enough room for a hand to come through the gap. The hand came in now. It wore a brown fabric glove. It explored the end of the chain, uselessly, because the chain can be removed only from the inside, when the door is shut.

'Miss Lampson,' a voice called. 'It's me. It's Mrs. Dale. Are you there, Miss Lampson?'

I waited, listening to my own gasping breath. The woman was bound to realize that a chain could be put on the door only from the inside. She knew that someone was in the flat. Later, she'd be asked.

The voice was raised to a discreet shout.

'The chain's on the door, Miss Lampson. I can't get in.'

There was a pause, then I heard a grumbling, grunting noise. The key was withdrawn from the lock; there was a shuffling; the noise of footsteps on the stairs. She had gone.

The question now was how long to wait. She had no reason

to know, or even to suspect, what had happened in the flat. A woman who came to daily work and who couldn't get in, wouldn't stand outside, waiting and watching. She'd go away, or perhaps she'd do some of her own shopping, and come back in half an hour. If I waited too long, I'd be in trouble again.

'Four minutes,' I whispered to myself, and waited silently, looking at the red hand of my watch hesitate before each second and then jump.

When the four minutes had passed, I took the chain off the door and went downstairs. The heels of my shoes sounded like hammers.

When I got out into the fresh air again, the world began to turn very fast, while I stayed still in the middle. The trees, the buildings, and a woman with a pram whirled round my head. I had difficulty in keeping up with them. I put one hand against the wall and dug my feet in. It's not an easy thing to make the world stop turning, but I managed it in the end. I was fit to walk again, and the telephone box on the corner of the street was there, waiting. All I had to do was get to it, and remember the number of Scotland Yard. It was Whitehall something, I was sure of that. It didn't matter what it was. I liked standing there, thinking Whitehall something or other. So long as I didn't remember the number I could keep on standing, I didn't have to move.

Then the number came back into my head, I wasn't pleased about it, I would have to move. I let the wall go, I was almost walking, when I saw something that made me feel I might as well lie down and get whirled over the edge. It was Peter, lounging along the street a few yards away.

I was still by the entrance to the flats. It was too late to pretend I'd been anywhere else. I waited, watching him, trying again to understand what kind of man he was.

He was wearing a dirty raincoat and a hat pushed far back on his head. He had the air of false jauntiness laced with bewilderment, that I had seen so often. There was a newspaper under his arm. I wondered if that meant it was late, that the results of the first race were already in the stop press. I hadn't enough energy to look at my watch.

He had seen me already. He put on the old three-quarter grin that would have been a whole grin only if he had a chance to hit a policeman with a bottle. That was what I had once told Sarah.

'Peter,' I said, simulating delight. 'It's months since I've seen you.'

'Hello, Nancy, my love. Don't ask me where I've been all those months.'

'I was going to ask you where you're going now.'

'And where would I be going? I'm going to see Sarah, that's where I'm going. I've a thing or two to say to her.'

'She's not in,' I said. I wondered which of us was the better liar.

'No?'

'I've just come from there. She's not in. I rang. I got no answer.'

'I'll ring harder and get an answer.'

I stood in his way. It was indecent, to let him go up, to ring and knock at a door while the woman he'd loved lay dead on the other side. As my wave of right feeling passed, another wave rolled across my mind. He had been in prison, he might have means of opening locked doors. He mustn't be the one to find her. I had to keep him away from the building.

'Peter, she's out,' I said desperately. 'Come and have a drink with me instead.'

'I wasn't meaning to have a drink with anyone,' he said sullenly. 'I didn't come here to drink with her. Not on your life.'

'What did you want to see her about?'

His three-quarter grin came on again.

'You were always a great girl for asking questions,' he said. 'Maybe I was going to bash her up.'

I had an unpleasant feeling that I was beginning to shake all over. 'Please let's have a drink, Peter.'

'Is there something up with you?' he asked. He looked at me, trying to feel out the situation. 'Did she send you down to keep me out of the way? You two were always teaming up. She sent you down—is that it?'

'No,' I couldn't think of what to say to him. 'Was she expecting you?'

He tapped the newspaper he was holding. 'Maybe she was. I don't know,' he said angrily.

'If I can't have a drink I'll have to sit down somewhere,' I said.

'I don't know if they're open yet. I've flogged my watch.'

'It's half-past eleven.'

40

'Across the road and round the corner,' he said. He always knew where the nearest pub was.

I had difficulty in staying on my feet long enough to cross the road, but I pretended there was a chalk line to follow, and I followed it, past the screaming brakes and the hooting horns. I couldn't add consideration for drivers to my other pre-occupations.

When we sat down in the pub I offered to buy the drinks.

'No woman's ever paid for me,' he said. 'You're not going to be the one to start. What are you having?'

'Vodka.'

That lifted him out of himself.

'Have you turned Commie?' he asked.

I raised a smile.

'I was only trying to think of something powerful.'

'So you need it strong?' he said. He gave me an odd sideways glance.

'I wanted to celebrate our meeting,' I said quickly. 'We'll have beer, if you prefer it.'

'Two vodkas,' he said to the barman.

They didn't have vodka, so we had whisky instead.

I was beginning to breed confidence again. I had given myself away too much to Peter, but now that we were drinking, he'd give himself away to me, as he had always done.

'Have you been seeing much of Sarah?' I asked.

'You know more about her than me.'

'I've seen very little of her myself, since . . .'

'That's it,' he said, 'Since.'

'But I met her by chance last night. She was with a man called Charles. . . . I've forgotten his other name.'

'Charles!' he repeated, with a raging contempt. 'Night-night, Chas.,' he mimicked, in a high, impossible, soprano. Then he dropped down to his normal voice.

'I know the bastard's name.' he said. 'I've got it here.'

He slapped his hand on the newspaper. It was as if we were competing for the annual indiscretion prize.

'That's what I wanted to see her about,' he said. 'Here's the picture! Look at her! Look at him!'

I looked at the picture. It wasn't flattering; she had always been camera-shy. The caption underneath said "Actor Michael Fenby's Former Wife to Marry Company Director."

'That's what it says,' Peter told me resentfully. 'So this Mike bloke she left me for is just a former actor husband now, that's all he is. I'd like to take a piece of him and drop it in an acid bath. And I know what piece I'd take. And is he the only one! Who's she had since then? There was a long-haired artist killed himself for her, wasn't there?'

'No, no, he didn't kill himself, and he doesn't have long hair.'

'You're kidding. She said he was an artist!'

'He is an artist.'

'He'd have been well out of it if he had killed himself. One more drink and I'll tell you what I think of your friend Sarah. I'll tell you the law I believe in.'

'I didn't know you believed in any.'

'You're lucky it's you said that. I wouldn't take that kind of remark from anyone but you, Nancy. The law I believe in, is one man, one woman.'

He waited. I didn't speak. Everything I said was wrong. The first thing I wanted was a sensible working arrangement between myself and my brain, the second thing was a brain.

'Are you feeling all right, Nancy?' he asked. 'What's happened to your line in dirty cracks? I know you well, Nance. You got no ideals. So I'll say it again. One man, one woman. And that's what I'm going to see Sarah about now. She wants a lesson, that's what she wants. I'm not going to stand back and see her marry this . . . bloke. I've got something to say to her. She hasn't got over me yet. We had a lousy spell, that's all.'

It sounded authentic to me; it sounded innocent, but I didn't know. It was possible that danger had given him the strength to act a part.

'Peter, let her alone. It's all you can do.'

He went straight on without listening to me much. He was in an excited state, and the whisky was working on him fast. He was on his second double by now. The first had lasted him fifteen seconds, and he'd ordered again immediately.

'She still thinks a lot of me, I know that,' he said. 'You're her friend, Nancy, you can tell me the truth. Is Sarah marrying this bloke for money, or is she not?' He raised his voice on the last sentence. Anyone in the bar could have heard, but there wouldn't be anyone who was interested.

'Peter, let's not discuss Sarah,' I said in a quiet voice.

That made him angry, at once.

'If we're not here to discuss Sarah can you tell me what we're here for?' he said loudly. 'Tell me that, Nancy.'

'I thought we came here for a drink, Peter,' I said weakly.

'You want another drink, is that it?'

He stood up.

'I'll get you another.'

'Single for me.'

He nodded, and went to the bar. I didn't know if he'd been drinking before he met me, but I was certain he'd order another double whisky. Three doubles was a fair amount for a man like Peter who wasn't a real drinker. I didn't think he was a good liar, either. If he'd had anything to do with what had happened to Sarah, I'd find it out in the next twenty minutes. But I wasn't staying for twenty minutes; I wasn't playing detectives. I had to get back to Donald. All I had to do before I went was to make Peter realize I was completely ignorant of what had happened to Sarah. If he was asked later he'd remember he'd seen me at eleven-thirty, and that I'd talked about Sarah in a way that showed I knew nothing. In the way that he was talking, in short.

Peter came back from the bar with the drinks. I looked at his hands as he put them down on the table. There was a fuzz of black hair on the backs of his fingers. He had very strong hands. I had never liked them, although, in a perverse way, I had often liked him. Everything that had ever happened to him was his own fault and his own doing, but he often had the puzzled expression of the man who had again and again been dealt the wrong cards.

He sat down now, clumsily, so that the table shook and some of my drink was spilt.

'Sorry, Nancy,' he said. 'I had a rough start this morning, that's what. Woke up with a kid throwing a key at me.'

'What kid?'

'Oh, skip it. Here's your health.'

We drank.

'About Sarah, Peter,' I said. 'You've known for a long time you were through.'

'Am I through for good?' he asked. He wasn't speaking loudly now. 'She won't see me.'

'No, she won't see you now,' I said. I tried, but I couldn't make it sound natural. I couldn't even look him in the face as I said it. I looked round the bar, away from him. I looked at a pair of brown fabric gloves in the corner; the right-hand glove wrapped itself around a glass, I think it was Guinness,

43

lifted the glass to a thin, tired mouth, put the glass down again.

She wore a hat and a brown tweed coat. Her face was pale, pinched, and practical. Her eyes thought of herself, not of anyone else. I was sure she hadn't noticed me. There must be thousands of women who wear brown fabric gloves. Even in this district, there must be thirty or forty.

'Nancy, I've always played it straight with Sarah,' Peter was saying.

Brown fabric gloves had raised her glass. When he said 'Sarah' I saw the glass stop on the way to her lips, hesitate, go down to the table again.

I was sitting away from the window. There wasn't much light on my face. Peter had his back to her, but he had gone to the bar, she could have seen him clearly enough then.

'I'm going to settle things with Sarah,' Peter said.

'But not today. You must let her alone today,' I told him. I was in a panic, the woman was sitting by the door, I didn't know what to do.

'You know what I want to get from her, don't you?'

'Oh, God, yes,' I said, 'I'd forgotten that.'

I remembered well enough now, although I had no time to concentrate. I should have remembered earlier. Sex and revenge aren't the only reasons for committing murder. They aren't even the most common.

'Peter,' I said softly, 'you've got to understand, I'm telling you as a friend . . .'

'Whose friend? Her's or mine.'

'Both. But now, as your friend, I want to—advise you. There's an underground station round the corner. It will be better than a bus. Get a ticket out of the machine. Go somewhere away from this district, and stay away all day. Stay with friends, if you can.'

His face altered. He was a man who had experience of living in rat holes, and he had picked up a little rattishness from the rats.

'You're sitting with your back to a woman who might as well not see your face. And if there's another way out of this pub, take it.'

'Through to the Gents, turn left, and out by the Private,' he said in a voice just above a whisper. 'You could do the same by way of the Ladies, Nancy. It's upstairs. Turn left when you get down. Go first, if you want.'

44

I nodded. Then I rose, and without looking at Brown-fabric-gloves, I went upstairs to the Ladies, down again immediately, and out by the door of the Private bar. He knew a lot about pubs.

I took the advice I'd given to Peter and went to the Underground station and bought a ticket from the machine. I went down by the escalator, and stepped on to a train. I knew I still had to telephone the police, but when I sat down in the train the inside of my head felt as if it had been dropped down a chimney. There was nothing I could do but sit. That went on for a long time.

I left the train near the end of the line. I walked through to the other side, and took the next train back. By the time the train reached Charing Cross, the ball of soot inside my head had shrunk to the size of an average brain tumour, so I got out and went to the telephone boxes. What I had to do was ring Scotland Yard in an assumed voice.

I rang Scotland Yard. It was as much as I could do to speak at all. I didn't attempt the extra difficulty of a new voice.

'An accident,' I said, and I was put through to someone.

'What kind of accident?' the someone enquired pleasantly.

'A criminal accident.' I recited her address and rang off.

I knew they couldn't trace a call from Charing Cross. I began to feel like a human being again, immortal, but far from the sin of pride.

It didn't much matter now if I took a train or bus back home. The bus stopped outside the underground station. I lived just at the end of the street. I decided to take a train.

Donald would be waiting. He had to be convinced that the problems of the living were more important than those of the dead. It seemed a logical proposition, I didn't believe anyone could deny it. My spirits were rising. They were nearly up to zero.

As I came out of the station, a man brushed against me.

'Police are waiting for you, Nancy,' he said into my ear, and lurched off again.

It was Laurence.

Even in normal times, I needed a couple of tranquillizers after seeing Laurence. He acted on me like an anxiety pill.

'Come back, Laurence,' I called after him, in a rage, but he walked on, holding out his hand to steady himself against the

45

movement of the pavement. If it had been anyone else, I'd have thought he was only pretending to be drunk.

I had to stop him. I went after him, and when I was close enough, I dropped my handbag. It landed at his feet and burst open.

I went in front of him and knelt on the ground, picking up bits. He had to kneel on the pavement beside me, to help me.

'At the flat?' I asked.

'Yes.'

'How do you know?'

'I've been there.'

'At my place? Today?'

'It's a long time, Nancy, since we lay in the orchard under the apple blossom. A long, long, long, long time.'

I had never lain in an orchard with him. He was thinking of Sarah, or someone out of a book. It wasn't a thing to discuss.

'Why did you go to my flat today?'

'The blossom has turned into hard green apples now. They fall on my head like stones—plop, plop, bang, crash, bang. God, what a head I've got with those apples! I know what Newton felt. I've been through it.'

Drunks have this advantage of being able to conduct a conversational ramble away from the point.

'Why did you choose today to go to my flat?' I asked. We were still crouching side by side on the pavement, pretending to pick up lipstick and keys.

'It was the telephone. When I heard your voice this morning, That's Nancy, I said. I wanted to speak to you, Nancy, but I was tired. You know the way it is, when you've been in bed all night. But you said you wanted me, so I came to your place.'

'When?'

'When I got up.'

'When was that?'

'Why should I ever get up at all? I've got no reason to, have I?' he asked.

His face was very close to mine; I looked at his anguished, reddened eyes; he closed them, and then moved away from me.

'Is there anyone else at the flat?' I asked, thinking of Donald.

'I don't know.'

I wanted to attack him, shake out some facts about the police, but I couldn't risk a quarrel. Whatever he was, he had

46

been part of Sarah's life, so today, even if it was the last day, he had to be treated like an ordinary fellow creature.

'Thank you, Laurence, thank you for warning me,' I said.

He stood up.

'Here's the rest of your money, Miss,' he said in a sober voice.

He handed over the money and went off. This time he wasn't having the same trouble with the pavement.

I didn't believe he'd met me by accident. He must have been waiting by the corner to warn me about the police. It was a friendly action. It was more than I would have expected from him.

I wasn't so sure what his intervention had gained me. I could dye my hair and wear dark glasses and go off to Antibes or Athens or the Aleutian Islands, but I didn't have my passport with me. I could hide in the Cotswolds, or Cornwall, or Cumberland. "Have You Seen This Woman?" the newspapers, or one of them anyway, would demand, and a dozen reporters would be sent to ferret in a dozen reported holes.

I decided that as I wasn't organized for flight, the best thing would be to walk on to the bird-lime.

4

THEY WERE WAITING for me at the flat, as kind and nice a set of policemen as had ever asked anyone to help them with their enquiries. They didn't wear uniform, so their rank was difficult to assimilate. There was a top man to ask unpleasant questions in a pleasant voice; and two lesser men whose job it was to listen without showing emotion. I tried to make that my job, too.

They believed, they said, that I knew Miss Sarah Lampson, as she was known, having been the wife of Mr. Michael Fenby.

'But of course,' I said. 'Do you want to ask me something about her? Do come in, unless you'd sooner talk outside.'

They decided to come in. I'd guessed they would. I opened the door, and we all went in. I was home at last, although home certainly didn't look the same with three policemen in it.

I tried to examine the place quickly, while standing with a pleasant, expectant smile. There was no sign that Donald had been there, only the cigarette ends in the ash-tray. Six, I counted. When he was worried he smoked a lot. Six cigarettes added up to something between an hour and an hour and a half. He had left a long time ago.

'I've been out all the morning,' I said apologetically. I picked up the ash-tray while the back of my neck caught cold draughts of policeman.

The top man, I suppose he was an Inspector, moved around me and looked at the ash-tray in a significant manner, so I put it down casually. I didn't want to be conspicuous, although, with a police Inspector staring at me like a road accident, there were no shadows to shield me.

The best I could do was to sit down with my back to the light.

'Have you known Miss Lampson for long?'

'Six years or so.'

'Would you describe her as a close friend?'

'Yes.'

'You once shared a flat with her?'

'Yes.'

'I suppose you've met most of her other friends?'

'Most.'

The man who was asking the questions didn't seem to me to be a person at all, although he had a friendly, confident surface, like the better type of doctor. Some doctor would be examining her now, probing for the bullet. I had to hurry past that thought, I let my mind take me anywhere, on to a picture of a plumply reassuring doctor. Let's have a look at that heart, Miss Lampson. Nothing much here that a couple of stitches won't put right. Now, a deep breath! That was a splendid try! You're the kind of patient that's not going to cause much worry. If you could see the way some of my other dead patients behave, you'd sympathize with the poor down-trodden G.P.

I laughed aloud. The laugh was too high, it was about to bolt, I hauled it in. I had secret supplies of lovely self-control.

The top man leant forward, politely interested.

'I thought of something funny,' I said.

'What was it?'

48

'An idea I had about a doctor.'

He leant back again. He wasn't satisfied. I suppose his behaviour would have been more predictable if my own had been less peculiar.

'When did you last see your friend, Mrs. Fenby?'

She didn't like to be called Mrs. Fenby, I began to say it. I got as far as 'She didn't . . .' and realized with terror that I had the tense wrong. There was too much hesitation, and then I said:

'She didn't . . . ask you to come here, did she?'

'No, she didn't,' he told me. 'Why should she?'

'No reason at all.'

'We are moderately busy, we wouldn't come here without a reason.'

'You haven't given me any reason,' I said.

'I'm sorry, I wanted to know when you last saw Mrs. Fenby.'

'She doesn't like to be called Mrs. Fenby since her divorce,' I said, triumphantly right.

'Then when did you last see Miss Lampson?'

'I saw her last night in a restaurant. In the Sullivan Hotel.'

'Were you alone? Were you with a friend?'

'I don't often dine with enemies.'

'So this was a close friend?'

'I'm not sure if I have any close friends.'

'But you have described Miss Lampson as a close friend?'

I observed that he was being careful enough with his tenses. With practice, I'd be able to manage it, too, so that every verb left the problem of her existence neither solved nor unsolved.

'I have told you,' I said carefully, 'I first met Miss Lampson six years ago.'

'And you haven't seen her since last night?'

'I'm sorry to seem stupid, but why are you asking me those questions?'

'In the hope of getting an answer,' he said, smiling cheerfully.

'Really, you must tell me what you want to know.'

'I've told you what I want to know, Miss Graham. When did you last see Miss Lampson?'

'I'm sure I have answered that already. I saw her last night in a restaurant.'

'And you haven't seen her since?'

It was a moment of decision. I'd had so many of them, in the last few hours, I should have been good at decisions, by now.

'No,' I said firmly. 'I haven't seen her since.'

The Inspector seemed unmoved, but I saw one of the subordinates shift very slightly in his chair and exchange the smallest flicker of a glance with the other subordinate. I hoped he'd be unfrocked, or whatever they did to plain-clothes men for a punishment. He shouldn't have made me aware that I'd said the wrong thing.

If I had known about this in advance, if I'd had time to prepare myself, I'd have managed better. That was what I told myself, but I knew it was a lie. Laurence had warned me the police were waiting for me. I could have thought up some kind of story in the time. It should have been easy for me. I earned my living thinking up stories.

'When were you last in her flat?'

'I don't know. I can't remember,' I said weakly.

'Don't you visit your close friends often?'

'I haven't seen so much of her recently.'

'An estrangement?'

'Do I have to discuss my private affairs?'

'No, of course not,' he said smoothly. 'We'd like to have a look around your flat, if you don't object.'

'But I do, rather,'

'I have a search warrant,' he said, and showed me.

I watched them. The two subordinates did the searching. They were immensely polite about it. Not at all brutal and domineering like the police invaders one reads of in court cases.

'There's a lot of typed paper, sir,' one of them said.

'It's the first part of a novel,' I explained.

'You are a novelist, Miss Graham?' the Inspector asked.

'I'm the first half of a novelist,' I said, and he gave me the nearest thing to a dirty look I'd had, so far.

I lit a cigarette.

'You smoke American cigarettes?' he asked at once.

'I prefer them.'

He looked at the ash-tray. I wished I had followed my first impulse and emptied it.

'You have had a friend here?'

I stared hard at the ash-tray, and at its exclusively English

cigarette ends. Nothing was going to make me admit that
Donald had been here this morning. Then I had a little flash
of logical thought, the first I'd had in the interview. They
didn't know I always emptied ash-trays at night, they had no
way of finding out that these were today's butts.

'The friend I was with last night saw me home,' I said.
'He stayed long enough to smoke six English cigarettes?'
'I suppose he did.'
'It must have taken him about two hours.'
'Possibly. We were talking.'
'But in all that time you didn't smoke at all?'
'I may have smoked one or two of his English cigarettes,
as I'd run out of American.'
'So you had no American cigarettes last night and you
bought that packet today?'
Donald had bought it for me the night before, in Sullivan's.
Every careful thing I said turned into a lie while I was saying
it. They wouldn't remember one packet of cigarettes in Sulli-
van's. But was it on the bill? Did they keep the bills afterwards,
with table numbers on them? I didn't know. I decided to get
out of that lie quickly.

'I didn't buy them this morning, so I must have had them
last night.'
'But you didn't smoke any while your friend smoked six?'
I nodded, brisk and bright. Words were unsafe.
'Would you mind if we took your finger-prints, Miss
Graham?'
'Would it help if I minded?'
'No. But you understand it's for reference only. We'll destroy
them afterwards.'
Up to that point, it appeared they had dropped in for a
friendly, inconsequential, chat. They must have thought I was
either criminal or insane, not to insist on an explanation. The
finger-print business was carrying it too far. If I didn't refuse,
or demand to know what they were getting at, they would
arrest me on a general suspicion of having done something.
That was the way I felt. I was opening my mouth to make a
great big protest, when the second subordinate approached the
Inspector with a piece of paper. I recognized it at once. It was
the letter, the threatening letter, that Sarah had sent on to me.

The Inspector read it with interest.
'You composed this letter, Miss Graham?' he asked.

51

I decided to make an effort to get back into the habit of telling the truth.

'I had it in the post this morning. Sarah—Miss Lampson—sent it to me.'

'Why?'

'Well, she told me last night someone was threatening her. She said she'd send me the letter.'

'Why should she do that?'

'We were friends. She thought I might be able to help her.'

'You *were* friends?'

'I mean, we used to be close friends.' If I couldn't get the tenses right, it would be better to talk without verbs.

'In what way did she think you could help her?'

'I suppose—she supposed—I might—I could find, who was threatening her.' As a sentence without verbs, this was on the bottom curve of the graph.

'Did you know—do you know, who——" He was getting his own verbs mixed, so he stopped. 'Did she send a letter with this document you received in the post?'

'Just a note to say: Here it is.'

'Where is this note?'

I didn't know, and they couldn't find it.

'You'll let us take a page of your half-novel?'

'If I can have it back.'

'Oh, certainly.'

He took the page, and laid it beside the letter.

'It's the same kind of paper.'

'I noticed that myself. But lots of people who want cheap typing paper buy this kind.'

'You type your novels yourself, on this typewriter?'

'Yes.' I hadn't typed any novels, only half of one, but my hair-splitting mood had passed.

'Take the typewriter,' he said to one of the others. And to me: 'We'll give you a receipt for it.'

'Are you going now?' I asked.

'Just one thing.' He pointed to a bundle of my notebooks. I'd been so engrossed in the contemplation of disaster that I hadn't seen them brought in. I looked at them with a melancholy satisfaction. They contained a great deal of information about the men Sarah had known in the past. The Inspector would have liked to read them. All he needed was a knowledge of my private form of shorthand.

I enjoyed the realization that there was nowhere he could get it.

'What's all this, Miss Graham?' he asked me, frowning over the rolling, jagged lines, interspersed with illegible snatches of longhand.

'Notes for my next few half-novels,' I told him.

He put them down, dissatisfied.

It seemed then that they were really going, at last. The most exhausted hostess at the longest impromptu all-night party couldn't have been more pleased by the thought of solitude. But the party wasn't over yet, it was going to be a long, long party.

'We'd like you to come with us, Miss Graham. We think you may be able to help us with our enquiries.'

'Your enquiries into what?" I asked hopelessly.

'The murder of Sarah Lampson.' He watched my face carefully as he spoke.

It was undoubtedly too late to simulate surprise, but I tried it all the same. At least I chose the safest method, a stunned silence. I maintained it as we left the flat, and in the car I didn't open my mouth.

At the police station I was put in a room by myself. When I complained that I was thirsty, I was offered impersonal cups of tea. No one seemed in a hurry to interview me. Perhaps they were leaving me alone as a crafty way of softening me up. I wondered if they were allowed to offer their involuntary visitors whisky, or gin. Alcohol was one of the great truth drugs. I was sure I would be able to tell a thousand lies on tea.

I finished my tea, and wondered if I could tell a thousand truths. I didn't think I had as much truth as that in me. I had one truth. I loved Donald, and that was why I was sitting now in the police station.

It is untrue to say that we will do anything for love, but sometimes we have to pretend it's true, or we find we have left the open sea and are confined to the narrow ditches for ever.

I knew it was wrong that I should be sitting in the police station because I'd tried to protect Donald, but in another sense it was right. I was in a difficult position, but I wasn't risking anything in a serious way. I might be a little vulnerable round the edges, but I believed that in the centre I was indestructible.

53

Donald was different. If he was accused of the murder it would be, quite literally, the end of him.

He wasn't a lucky kind of man. At the most, he would have two lives, and he had used one of them up already.

I had met him first about four years ago, when I was twenty-two. It was at a party, the kind of party that couldn't be explained to respectable people, possibly because it was a party against them. This one was a musical party. The idea was that everyone should bring a musical instrument and play it at the same time. There were one or two people with guitars, or flutes, but most of the rest brought mouth-organs or dustbin lids. Practically everyone there was under twenty-five; they had a lot of noise in them they wanted to let out.

Sarah and I continually went to noisy, anarchistic parties of this sort, and one or other of us was often sent down to placate the landlord, a distraught man who far too often lived in the flat below, regretting his investment in housing.

At this party I had just returned from one of these diplomatic missions when I saw Donald sitting in a corner. It was the first time I had ever seen him. He looked dark and sensitive and bewildered, and I recognized, with a sudden beat of surprise, that he was someone I had wanted to see. I can't explain what was familiar to me in his face: I suppose he fitted in with some dream, or infant memory, but I knew I was going to like him, I knew it before I heard his voice. It was like the excitement of finding a new island on the lake.

He wasn't talking to anyone, he wasn't doing anything, he looked out of place at this party.

I had a sudden idea about him.

'You look as if you're about to become an ancient,' I said.

He smiled at me hopelessly. I discovered later that one of the nicest things about him was his inability to catch on to any reference. It was a relief, after dealing with people who were all busy capping each other's quotations.

'What do you mean by ancient?' he asked me.

'As if you'd got the dancing and singing out of your system and were going to settle for a lifetime of pure thought.'

'I could still dance and sing for some people,' he said, smiling at me in a different way. He had an air of showing when he was happy, because he'd met someone he liked, and it wasn't the usual Press-Button-A-for-women charm.

I talked to him for a little, then. I decided he'd come to the

54

party through some ill-founded rumour that it had something to do with Boat Race night.

'What kind of party is this?' he asked uneasily.

'It's an initiation party,' I said. 'The weaklings will be carried out on stretchers. The strong remnant will sit on the floor until six in the morning, discussing the decadence of English literature.'

'Really?' He looked simple and puzzled. He was twenty-three or twenty-four then, but he didn't look his age. He had the air of a solemn boy. That's what had made me think of ancients. I had to like him, so I laughed. He looked at me anxiously for an explanation.

'If I picked your pockets I'd expect to find a cricket ball and a Latin crib,' I said. I knew nothing about sixth form boys, I'd only read about them in books.

'Are you keen on cricket?' he asked. I thought he was joking. I'd never before met anyone who would ask such a question. When I saw he was serious, I thought he'd escaped from Debland.

He had an enormous amount of charm. I suppose it came from surplus energy. He was the type of Englishman who is always driving something about the place, cricket balls, or motor-cars, or pheasants. He knew absolutely nothing. He was in the family business, some rural craft like pottery or saddlery. As a boy he had belonged to a pony club and played tennis with the rector's daughters. I envied those girls. I would have loved to be a rector's daughter. I yearned after the respectable background my father had failed to give me, and in the next few weeks, Donald became its representative.

I saw him fairly often. He was a quick learner, far too quick. In no time at all he was explaining to me there was a man called Freud, had I heard? And didn't I think there was something in all this abstract painting stuff?

A few weeks later he was having Freudian dreams and looking for a studio. He gave up saddlery and the rural life. He might have become just another bogus, boring artist, but he didn't lose his simplicity. It flowed through him like the Gulf Stream.

I liked him, even when he met Sarah, and the Gulf Stream slowed down. Both Sarah and I kept on liking him, although she had just taken up with Mike, and I was having a vague affair with a newspaperman who was teaching himself to play the bagpipes. He said it would be a reserve occupation when everyone became illiterate, and even the newspapers had to close down. He lived in furnished rooms; it is not easy to learn about bagpipes. The people in the other rooms kept maliciously ringing the police: he had to take the bag off the bagpipes, and learn to play very wheezily with the pipes alone. He was amusing, as maniacs often are, temporarily. But Donald's charm wasn't only temporary. About nine months after her marriage with Mike had fallen apart, Sarah identified Donald as the man she had always loved.

By that time Sarah was twenty-six, and I was twenty-four. We had stopped going to wild parties, I suppose we were turning into ancients. The process wasn't completed until the day she walked out and left Donald with the gun pointed at his own heart. She heard the shot as she went out, but she didn't turn back.

When my mind got to that point it slewed away, like a bat avoiding a collision with some dangerous structure. I would think of something else. I thought, and fell asleep.

It was, of course, only a half-sleep, it can have lasted only a minute, but when I woke again a man was sitting down at the desk.

'Donald!' I muttered hazily, but it was only the top man again.

'What was that you called me, Miss Graham?' he asked.

'I didn't call you anything. I don't even know your name.'

'I am Detective-Inspector Crewe. I have told you that, before.'

'I can't have heard you.'

'You were thinking of other things.'

'I'm always thinking of other things.'

'But now I want you to think of one specific thing. Why did you go to Sarah Lampson's flat this morning?'

'Why do you think I went there?'

'I am asking the questions.'

'And I'm not answering them.'

He thought that one over.

'We know certain things,' he said carefully. 'A woman who works—worked for Miss Lampson, twice a week, went to the flat this morning at about eleven-thirty. When she had opened the lock with the key, she found the door was on the chain. As you know, the chain can be put on only from the inside. So this morning at eleven-thirty, there was someone in the flat.'

'Perhaps Miss Lampson herself put on the chain,' I suggested.

'By eleven-thirty Miss Lampson was already dead.'

'I meant before.'

'If she put it on before eleven-thirty, she was unable to take it off afterwards. But when Mrs. Dale, the daily woman, returned to the flat, at about twelve, the chain had been removed.'

I felt almost pleased with myself. He had been half-ready to believe that Sarah had put the chain on the door; therefore the woman in brown fabric gloves hadn't realized that the chain was put on only when she had the key in the lock. So she hadn't seen me, or any part of me. She had heard a conversation, or snatches of a conversation, in the saloon bar of the Marquis of Lanchester. That was all. She had only been interested in us because we had mentioned Sarah by name. I'd be a fool if I admitted now that I'd been in the flat.

'Could you give me an outline of your movements this morning?' he was asking.

'It's Saturday, so I got up late and had a slow breakfast. I had to see a friend of mine.' I stopped there, I had to think of a way to explain Peter.

'I had to see a friend of mine,' I said. 'He telephoned!' I added triumphantly. They wouldn't be able to prove anything about the telephone. 'We had meant to have lunch, but I couldn't do it, so we arranged to meet for a drink.'

'Yes?'

'Then afterwards I went to some bookshops. I was trying to find a book that would help me with an article I'm writing on French playwrights. I went to a lot of shops. I ended up in Hatchard's. I found a book there called *Genet v. Ionesco*.'

'Can you tell me what's in this book?'

'If you're absolutely certain you'd like to know, I'll tell you all about it. Where shall I begin? The drama of anti-drama?'

His eyes flickered across the room. He was looking for a life-jacket that would hold his head out of the drama of anti-drama. He was actually a human being; not a great impersonal force like a glacier.

'Why couldn't you lunch with the friend you met for a drink?'

'I'd arranged to have lunch with someone else.'

'And did you?'

'No. I got absorbed in this book. The bit about the Being and the Under-Being of experience.' I knew what I was talking about, I was glad to think he didn't. I had actually glanced at the book in Hatchard's earlier in the week. I had decided to buy something simpler.

'And how long did you stay in Hatchard's?'

'Until after two, I suppose. It was too late to have lunch with my friend. So I had a quiet walk in the Park, Green Park, and then came back by underground.'

'Very well. Shall we just run through the account? You got up late and had a slow breakfast. What did you have for this slow breakfast?'

'Coffee.'

'Then it was so slow you haven't got started on it yet. You left three-quarters of it in the pot. You poured out one cup, and left at least seven-eighths of that untouched. Far from a slow breakfast, I'd say you had no breakfast at all. Next. You went to see a friend to have a drink. Where did you have this drink?'

If I told a lie, brown-gloves would be able to contradict me.

'In a pub called the Marquis of Lanchester,' I said, speaking out boldly for the truth.

'Did you meet there because it was near Sarah Lampson's flat?'

'One meets somewhere.'

'Who was your friend?'

I thought I wouldn't answer that one.

'We know he was called Peter. Do you imagine it will take us long to find a Peter known to both you and Miss Lampson?'

'He was called Peter,' I said. I didn't like the look I had in return.

'Then you went to Hatchard's and read this book, *Genet v. Ionesco*, by . . .?'

'Apfelstein,' I said.

He wrote something, the name of the book, perhaps, on a piece of paper. He rang a bell, and gave the paper to a subordinate.

'You stayed in Hatchard's until two?'

'Yes.'

'It closes at one on Saturdays.'

58

'I wish you did,' I said, from the heart, and he smiled at me. We were getting to know one another, like a headmaster and an erring pupil.

'It would suit me very well if criminals worked a five-day week,' he said.

'You're not really thinking of me as a criminal?' I asked.

'You are an evasive character, Miss Graham. You're a quick liar, but not a good one. Why don't you get it over and tell me the truth now? We'll come to it in the end. You could save a lot of trouble.'

He waited for a minute. Naturally I couldn't tell him the truth, but I felt it would have been nice if I could.

'Did you have any lunch?' he asked.

'No. They brought me some tea, here.'

'You didn't have any breakfast and you didn't have any lunch. Would you like something to eat now?'

'I might be sick.'

He lifted the phone and asked for tea and sandwiches.

I opened my handbag and took out a compact and looked at my face.

'I wanted to see if my hair had turned white in an afternoon,' I said shakily.

'If you'd like to wash, I'll show you the place.'

He took me along a corridor to a door and left me there. Inside there was a lavatory, with a wash-basin and a looking-glass.

While the cold water was actually on my face, I felt a small memory of what life had been like yesterday.

Love is not love which alters when it is hit on the head with a hammer.

I combed my hair.

Love is not love which alters when it is taken to a police station.

I tried to put lipstick on with a steady hand.

Love is not love which alters when it is arrested for murder. Or is it? But I hadn't been arrested for murder. There was no reason why I should be.

When I went back, tea and sandwiches were waiting for me in the empty room. I ate a sandwich. There wasn't much pleasure in it, but I thought I would keep my strength up with another. I didn't know what was going to happen next. I didn't seem to have been asked many questions about Sarah. There was Peter, of course. The Inspector was going to have a lot of fun finding out about Peter.

I tried to analyze what loyalty I owed to Peter, I found I owed him nothing; but still, I didn't want to do him an injury.

There was Laurence. Would they know that he had been concerned with her? They could find it out quickly enough, from any of the old hands on the Diagonal Press. I tried, in a dispassionate manner, to discover my own feelings about Laurence. I was amazed to realize that I had always resented him. He had gone downhill too quickly: the speed of his fall had been an accusation against Sarah, and, to a lesser extent, against me. He had put us in the wrong, even although he'd had to turn into an alcoholic to do it.

And Mike. They would know all about Mike, as the ex-husband, although they certainly wouldn't know how the marriage had broken up. Mike could look after himself, I didn't need to defend him.

Last of all, there was Donald. They would come to Donald in the end: it was my job to see they didn't come to him in the beginning.

The Inspector had left me alone for a long time, even although it was only a quarter of an hour, by my watch. He came back in the room now, and I felt at once he was less sympathetic than he had been before.

'You've had enough to eat?'

'Yes, thanks.'

'What have you been thinking of?'

'Bits of the past.'

'I'd like to draw your attention to a bit of the immediate past. Do you stick to the story that you visited Hatchard's bookshop today?'

'Yes. I had the time a little wrong. I'm weak, on time.'

'And when you were in Hatchard's you looked up a copy of this book, *Genet v. Ionesco*?'

'Yes.'

'Hatchard's had only one copy of this book, and they sold it yesterday.'

I had impious thoughts about book-sellers.

'I'd never have believed anyone would buy it,' I said airily.

'What were you doing when you said you were in Hatchard's?'

60

'I can't see it's important. You've already told me Sarah was dead by eleven-thirty.'

'I want to get your movements straight. You were certainly in the saloon bar of the Marquis of Lanchester at eleven-forty-five, and out of it by twelve. No one saw you before, and no one saw you afterwards, until you returned to your flat about three.'

'But I did exist.'

'Did you? Then prove it.'

I had to put Donald out of my mind. He was the only one who could step forward and say: I saw her before eleven. What time had he seen me? He must have come about ten.

'I existed,' I said. 'I telephoned. I tried to telephone Laurence—Laurence Hopkins—he's an old friend.'

'Of yours? Or of Sarah Lampson's?'

'Of both.'

'You telephoned because you'd promised to get in touch with the men who might have been threatening her?'

'That's it.'

'So you suspected it was this Laurence Hopkins?'

'No, It was just that I telephoned him first.'

'What did he say?'

'He answered, but he didn't speak.'

'Why should he do that?'

'He might have had a hangover,' I suggested.

'Did you telephone anyone else?'

'Yes.' I told him about the agent, and Mike.

'You're slipping, Miss Graham,' the Inspector said. 'Your statement about telephoning Michael Fenby is actually true. He has already told us. So we have to re-organize some of our thinking.'

'I thought you hadn't seen anyone but me.'

'We've seen a lot of people.'

'You haven't had a lot of time.'

'I may have some of them here, in other rooms, now.'

'Is Mike—is Michael Fenby here?'

'You like him?'

'Yes. I've always liked him.'

'Even when he and your friend Sarah Lampson were divorced?'

'Yes.'

'Even when he and Miss Lampson arranged to be married?'

I felt he was watching me very carefully as he asked the question. My heart dropped another inch or two. No one could possibly think I'd had a motive for killing Sarah, but here, away from the normal world, they thought anything.

'Yes!' I said, much too emphatically.

'Why did they get divorced?'

'That was Peter's fault,' I said incautiously.

'Peter Abbott?'

'I didn't tell you his name, did I?'

'We found that out for ourselves. And we know his criminal record.'

'I don't know why you keep me here asking me everything if you know everything already.'

'I'd advise you, in your own interests, to tell me what you know about Peter Abbott.'

'In my own interests?'

'Someone is going to be charged with this murder. It doesn't seem to occur to you it may be you.'

I looked out of the window. There was a very interesting view of a brick wall. I counted twenty-five bricks before I turned back to him.

'Your finger-prints were on the door handle to her bedroom. They were remarkably clear. We don't often get finger-prints like that from a door handle. Too many people go in and out of doors, and touch the handle. The odd thing about this door handle was that there were no prints on it, except yours. And on the other door handles there were no prints at all, even although her fiancé, a man called Charles Lester, tells us that he saw her home last night about one o'clock, that he went into her sitting-room for a nightcap, and that he certainly opened the sitting-room door for her. At twelve o'clock today there were no prints of any kind on the sitting-room door handle. Why did you wipe all the door handles, Miss Graham?'

I couldn't think of a good reason. I saw that he could. I felt that in one more minute I was going to be charged with murder. I knew that if he did charge me, Donald would come forward to defend me, but now I was alone. I was too terrified to think of any way out.

'Your prints were on two glasses in the sideboard,' he said reflectively. 'Someone put the chain on the door at eleven-thirty, just as Mrs. Dale put her key in the lock. You were seen leaving the block of flats five minutes later. She noticed you.

She noticed you again in the saloon bar. What do you have to say to all this, Miss Graham?'

My head cleared a little, although not enough.

'I have to say that you can't even think straight. Because you believe I was there at half-past eleven, you've decided to change the time of the murder to fit in with me.'

'How do you mean, I've decided to change the time of the murder?'

'You said she was dead by half-past eleven.'

'Did I?'

'But surely—can't the doctors tell when she was shot?'

He sighed, and the word I'd used hung between us like a cloud of stupefying gas.

'I have never used that term in this conversation. How did you know she was shot, Miss Graham?'

The hunt was up now. I didn't feel like a fox, or an otter, or some other creature hunted in the open air. I felt like a small animal deep in its own underground tunnel; with a savage ferret scurrying along the black passages after me.

'Please answer my question, Miss Graham,' Detective-Inspector Ferret was saying. His voice didn't carry well, underground.

'Sorry,' I said, 'I was thinking about tunnels.'

'How did you know she was shot?'

'Tunnels. Once in the country I was with some other people. There was a railway tunnel . . .' I couldn't go on speaking. It was too much effort. I went into the tunnel again. It was one of those disused lines with weeds in the middle, but once every few days a goods train was reputed to go through. We all thought it would be fun to walk along the tunnel. There was Sarah and Mike and Donald and me. We went into the tunnel. It was only dusk at first, but we kept looking back to the bright entrance behind us. The dusk thickened, the arched roof of the tunnel vanished into a pressing blackness. Sarah was too frightened to go on. Mike did his best to frighten us all by flapping his arms and screaming and pretending to be a bat, but he was glad enough of the excuse not to go further into the tunnel, and so was Donald. They didn't stay to argue with me when I said I was going on. They were crazy with anxiety to get out of the tunnel. I heard them stumbling away. When I looked back I saw the tunnel had begun to bend. The light was a broken button, then it was chipped off.

I was crushed by the weight of blackness, my heart could

scarcely beat against the pressure. I tried to walk quietly, but there were rough stones between the sleepers. I made too much noise, and the black part of my mind came up to meet the blackness. I began to believe I was disturbing some creature who lived in the tunnel. At first it was an old man who whistled when he breathed, then it was an animal that grunted. I started to run, I tripped over a sleeper and fell. Then I heard the train coming. It was the goods train that came only every few days, and was coming now, at this hour and minute. I got up and ran. I managed to stop myself in time, then I stood flat back against the wall of the tunnel. I was close enough to see the driver's fire-pinkened, smoky face. It was a long train, it moved slowly, and swung every truck at me as it passed. When it had gone I didn't faint, or fall down. I ran after it into the open air.

'To the open air,' I said aloud. At least, a voice something like mine said it.

The Inspector was bending over me. He was holding me up on the chair, with one arm.

'Would you like some water, Miss Graham?'

'I'd like to be in the open air.'

He let me go, carefully, in case I was going to fall over again.

'I suppose I had a kind of black-out,' I muttered. 'I'd like to be in the open air.'

'I'm afraid that can't be managed.'

'No. I was telling you about the tunnel.'

'What were you going to tell me?'

'Only that I get into these tunnels, but I need help to get out of them.'

He gave me a glass of water, and I drank it slowly. Anything for time.

'May I smoke?'

'Yes.'

I lit a cigarette.

'I'd like to help you out of this. Where were you today between twelve and three?'

'I took a train, an underground train. More tunnels. I missed my station. Perhaps I fell asleep. I went on a long way, then I came back and changed on to the right line.'

'At Charing Cross?'

I waited too long to answer, then I could think of nothing better to say than: 'I can't remember.'

64

'Let's see, you're on the Northern Line, aren't you! Where else would you change, except at Charing Cross?'

I wasn't able to think of any station where I might have changed trains. I could see the underground map in my head, but all the lines went on for ever.

'All right, then, it was Charing Cross,' I said.

'And you telephoned Scotland Yard from there?'

I couldn't answer.

'It's a point in your favour, that you telephoned the police,' he said encouragingly.

'All right, I telephoned them.'

'We were looking for you already. Mrs. Dale heard the name Nancy. Everyone we asked knew at once which Nancy had been connected with Sarah Lampson. Are you going to go on denying you were in the flat?'

'I went to the flat, but she was dead already.'

'So that's it,' he said, and sighed.

'How did you get in?'

'I had a key. I'd always had it. We were friends. She had the key to my flat, as well.'

'Really?' he said. He seemed surprised. 'When did you go in?'

'I'm not sure. Between half-past ten and eleven.'

'If you stayed for more than half-an-hour, what did you do?'

'I tidied up a bit,' I said hopelessly. 'I put away a bottle and washed some glasses.'

'And wiped the door handles?'

'Yes.' I suddenly thought I saw a little glimmer of light in the tunnel.

'I'll tell you what I didn't wipe clean,' I said. 'The telephone.'

'Well?'

'I telephoned Mr. Fenby, and his agent, around half-past nine this morning. I telephoned them from my own flat, not from Sarah's. I didn't wipe Sarah's telephone. You may find prints on it, but you won't find mine.'

'I'm glad you thought of that for yourself,' he said approvingly. 'It was the discrepancy we noticed. There were prints on her telephone, only a few, it was very clean, as telephones go. The prints were blurred, they were very possibly hers, but they were certainly not yours. So you weren't there at half-past nine.'

'She was dead before then.'

'I wouldn't say we know that. All we know is that she was shot in bed, and there seems to be general agreement that she was an early riser.'

'She always got up at eight.'

'That may be. You could have gone to the flat twice.'

'Why?'

'Yes, why?' he repeated irritably. He recovered himself quickly. 'If you went to the flat only at half-past ten, why did you stay to wipe door handles and wash glasses?'

I had to get him off that track.

'People lose their heads,' I said. 'I found my best friend murdered. I did all the wrong things.'

He moved his chair a little. I noticed with surprise that I wasn't near the desk now, but at least two feet away. I must have been edging steadily back.

'That letter we found—to her. It was typed on your typewriter,' he said abruptly.

'Impossible.'

'It's certain, beyond a doubt.'

'I don't believe it.'

'Did anyone else have access to your typewriter? Has anyone been alone in your flat?'

'No.'

'We're getting quite a few points against you, Miss Graham. It's a pity we haven't found the gun. Would you have wiped the finger-prints off that too?'

'No.'

'There are only two assumptions we can make, Miss Graham. The first is that you committed the murder. In that case we've nothing much to worry about.'

'No?'

'No. Because if that assumption is correct, I'll establish it beyond doubt in the next two hours. I promise you that.'

'Thanks.'

'But there is a second possibility.'

'And what's that?'

'We'll go into that later.'

We went into everything, then. We went on for hours about Sarah's habits, and switched back every now and then, always suddenly, to my suspicious behaviour. Sideways questions were slipped in about Peter, and Laurence, and Mike. I hoped I gave him the minimum information about all of them, but by

66

the end I didn't know what I was saying, with one exception: I was still saying nothing about Donald.

I didn't know how long I could keep going. If I was actually charged with murder I might crack up. I imagined myself in Holloway. I made up a picture of a wardress in black woollen stockings and varicose veins, with an enormous bunch of keys. I would be in Mediterranean black, with carpet slippers, and no stockings at all.

I had to stay out of that place. I kept coming back to the fact of the telephone, the fact I hadn't been in her flat at half-past nine. I think that was the only thing that persuaded him to let me go in the end. There was just enough doubt in it, to make it unsafe for him to charge me.

He didn't let me go in any very conclusive manner, but by eleven o'clock I was too dazed and tired to answer any more questions at all. I was careful to talk real gibberish, and not gibberish related to the murder. So he told me to be ready for further interviews, and he had someone drive me home.

5

WHEN I WAS inside my own home with the door locked, I tried to work out a plan for getting to sleep. I'd been awake for nearly forty hours. I was afraid I had already lost the habit of sleeping. None the less, I wavered into the bathroom, ran water in the bath, put milk in a saucepan, and sleeping tablets beside the bed.

When the bath was full I turned it off again, and walked around the living-room, staring at nothing much. The nothing finally resolved itself into a real nothing. I was looking at the place on the desk where my typewriter had been. Someone had used it to type the threatening letter to Sarah. I knew it wasn't Donald.

The man who had used the typewriter had the key to my flat. He must have taken it from Sarah, after he had killed her. There was no reason why anyone should want to kill me. I could believe that with my head, but not with the other part of me that made me run to the door now and bolt it.

The telephone rang. I picked up the receiver, hoping it was Donald.

'Nancy? It's Mike here.'

'How nice.'

'Did you see the play?'

'What play?'

'The one I've just been doing for Terrivision. You mean you didn't look at it?'

'I'm sorry. I've been out.'

'I thought you might have been interested enough to watch me on the new medium.'

'It's a fairly old medium by now, isn't it?'

'But Nancy, this was terrific. I'm a brain surgeon, you see, who takes to drink, and just when I'm having a terrible fit of the staggers my former loved one is wheeled in with her brains dashed out. I'm supposed to shake so much, the forceps clash together like a steel band as I approach the operating table. The trouble was that I really was shaking so much I dropped the whole kit of instruments right on her face. It was Sylvia, you know, she's got a shocking temper, I cracked the porcelain jacket on one of her front teeth, she's going to sue me. If I hadn't got between her and the cameras and ad-libbed, the viewers would have heard every word she said. You certainly missed something. It will be in all the papers to-morrow.'

'What will?'

'The Show Must Go On, says famous actor quizzed by C.I.D. But . . . Who Shot His Wife?'

'Mike, have they been at you?'

'I got the handcuffs off just in time to pull on the brain surgeon's rubber gloves. Nancy, why did you stand me up for lunch?'

'I'm sorry. I forgot.'

'I've had nothing to eat all day. Just when I'd finished missing lunch, a very courteous lot of cops took me away for a friendly six-hour chat.'

'It's not midnight yet. Would you like to come over and have lunch now?'

'Yes.'

I put the phone down. I made sure there were a couple of

chops in the refrigerator. I put them under the grill, ready to cook.

There was no time for a bath, but I washed myself quickly, and tried to make my face look more like a face. Mike always expected women to look as if they had just left a team of exhausted hairdressers and ladies' maids in the boudoir. He had the habit of exaggeration.

There was a time when I had worshipped him, five Fridays running, from the front row of the upper circle. He was playing the part of a misunderstood submarine commander. He had done something very shifty in the past, and the crew learnt of it just after the engines failed, sixty fathoms down. They all suspected that he might try to save himself first, and he suspected it, too. In the end he and his nearly unconscious chief-enemy were left alone in the doomed submarine. The enemy wasn't strong enough to use the escape hatch, and Mike stayed with him rather than leave him to die alone. Curtain.

It was years before I discovered that in real life Mike wasn't even remotely connected with the submarine commander. He would have been perfectly charming about it, but he would have been first out of the escape hatch every time. I'd seen it in action often enough.

I was only twenty when I saw the play. When about a year later I was given the job of interviewing him, I was astonished by my good fortune. He was very friendly at the interview, and gradually we came to see each other off and on. I think he looked on me as a capsule, a highly concentrated essence of admiring audience, easy to swallow once a fortnight. When I was with him I felt happy and exalted, as if he'd been my first glimpse of Venice, but I wasn't in love with him. There are romantic conceptions that are the wrong focal length for physical passion.

I had written a great deal about Mike, in my various note-books. I went to one, now, and looked it up, but it was hardly necessary. There were very few things about him that I couldn't remember. I glanced through it, frowning over the passages of adulation, then put it away quickly, and went to grill the chops for his late lunch.

I remembered a night when Mike asked me to drop into his dressing-room after the show and pick up a script. That usually meant that he needed a medicinal dose of worship from me. I didn't object: I liked sitting in his dressing-room while he

69

took off the grease-paint. At that time he was always mixed up in my mind with the part he had just been playing: I felt that I learnt something important just by watching him change back again. I had already noticed that the heroism rubbed off with the grease-paint.

He had a tendency to talk to me freely and maliciously about the people he knew, and, just when I was beginning to enjoy myself, to cry:

'But I'm meeting someone for supper. Pass me that tie, Nancy, before you go.'

Occasionally, when he was in a better mood, he would go so far as to take me out to supper, although he preferred to keep me for lesser lunches and odd Sunday afternoons. Usually I was perfectly contented, even gratified by the attentions Mike could spare, but there were times when I wondered if his malice was all accidental: if it was only by chance that he so often had to dash off to supper with some sophisticated and elegant female when he'd asked me to see him after the show.

I would have enjoyed, for a change, leaving him in mid-sentence, while I dashed off to supper with some other man, but no one ever asked me to supper, except Mike. I went to parties, I was taken out to dinner, but my friends weren't in the supper class. So one night I asked Sarah, who was going to a theatre with a dull commuter, to meet me outside the stage door. I meant to say to Mike I had a friend waiting, I would have to dash.

Things went as usual in the dressing-room.

'Toss over that towel, Nancy. No, not that one, the other one. You'd make a shocking nurse. I can imagine the patients drowning in their blanket baths, while you strolled about, absorbing the photographs on the walls.'

I threw him the towel.

'Who's that?' I asked, staring at the photograph of an alarmingly beautiful woman.

'Bella. Belladonna for short. The most poisonous temperament in the business.'

'Is she new?'

'The pupils of my eyes are still dilated. Give me a cigarette, will you, Nancy?'

'I haven't got any that you like.'

'In the pocket of my coat.'

I went to the coat and found the cigarette case. I looked at the engraved initials: M. F. from B. C.

I lit the cigarette for him.

'Is Bella too poor to buy you a gold case?'

'That wasn't from Bella. She never buys farewell presents. It would be too steady a drain on her income.'

'Where's that script, Mike?'

'It's in the top drawer.'

'Are you sure? I don't want to find myself ruffling through a set of initialled socks.'

I found the script.

'I have to go now,' I said.

'Oh no, you don't. I want you to look at the second scene there and see what you think of the translation.'

'I haven't got the original.'

'It sounds translated. You'll see what I mean.'

'I'll take it away with me.'

'No, I want you to look at it now.'

'Mike, I have to go. I'm meeting a friend.'

'What friend?'

'A girl. She's waiting outside.'

'Bring her in,' he said carelessly.

I went out and brought Sarah in. She was wearing some kind of yellow coat that matched her hair. She looked like the prize the third son gets for being kind to a rabbit.

Mike, who had been sitting covered with grease, giving me orders, not much interested in what I thought of his appearance, stood up with a charming smile of apology. The pupils of his eyes looked normal to me.

'He can't shake hands, Sarah, unless you're wearing your grease-proof paper gloves,' I said.

'I'll have this stuff off in a minute. Nancy shouldn't have brought you in until I had a clean and smiling face to present. Would you like a cigarette, a drink? Nancy, can you see a clothes brush anywhere?'

'I've heard so much about you, Mr. Fenby,' Sarah said. She was very shy.

'I ought to have heard about you,' Mike said softly.

Sarah and I didn't look at each other. She knew all about Mike that I could tell her, and she knew why I'd never brought him round to the flat. Peter had been living half-in and half-out of it for months. There was no chance in the world that

71

Mike would even have endured Peter. But now Peter was in prison: they need never meet; Mike needn't even hear of Peter's existence. That was the way I saw it, but naturally I was wrong.

After that the four of us went about together fairly regularly. The four were Mike, Sarah, me, and anyone else, sometimes Donald, sometimes another actor. I tried bringing along my Bulgarian poet, once, but Mike didn't care for him at all.

I found it interesting, watching a man I knew fall in love with Sarah. Mike talked to me about her in a quite unembarrassed fashion. Sometimes when she was busy he would take me out to lunch. It was a pleasure to him to be with someone who could answer all his questions about her work and how often she had her hair done, and did I think she would like this brooch or that.

Sarah, at the beginning, had a few doubts.

'Nancy, do you mind?'

'No.'

'It's awkward, knowing the same people.'

'It wasn't awkward about Laurence, or Peter, or my Bulgarian threat.'

'But Mike's different.'

'I'm fond of Mike, but I'm not in love. He's been projecting his actor's personality at me, that's all. An actor has to have the kind of personality that can be felt, and I've felt it. I don't like all of it, if you want me to prove that I am really not in love. I truly think there are bits of him that are disagreeable. But he won't show them to you, because he's in love with you.'

'You'd better tell me about the disagreeable bits.'

'Are you going to marry him?'

'Yes.'

'Then it will be a long life together, I'll be outside, I can't tell you anything.'

'Something.'

I didn't want to tell her about his malice, or his determination to be the first to leave any difficult emotional situation. Instead, I said cautiously:

'He doesn't have a Galahad complex. If you hurt him, he'll hurt back again.'

It wasn't much of a warning, because when he and Sarah married they were determined never to hurt each other at all. They loved each other, they wanted to be married, and from what I saw of them at the beginning, they were gloriously happy. It was a short marriage, I didn't see anything of the middle of it, for private reasons I wasn't likely to forget.

What happened was that I had to go into hospital in rather an inconvenient part of England.

I'd always wanted to have a car, a fast car, but I'd never had enough money to buy even a motor-scooter. Then I met a man who had a Jaguar and no conversation. I called him Stony because of his wonderful silence. He taught me to drive. We used to go out at night and keep going on any unrestricted road we could find. We didn't bother about maps, we'd finish up anywhere. We had a plan we'd work ourselves up into a racing team, but I don't think we worried much about any plan.

I've never seen the world look more alive than when it was passing too quickly to be seen; when the villages changed into woods and the woods to fields and the fields to houses that threw themselves at us and missed.

If we finished up by the sea, we would stop and swim; then drive back through the little towns where the lights were coming on in the post offices and the early morning workers rode their bicycles to the stations.

We never talked much. We didn't have anything to talk about except the car. While we were driving we were in a secular state of grace; it was as if we had visions together. We would never have made a racing team. The pleasure was in being alone.

Stony had very little imagination in a general way, it was used up on speed. In the car we thought so much as one that sometimes without reason we would both laugh at the same time, or begin to sing.

After our night drives I would see the events of the next day through an emotional heat-haze. I wasn't entirely sure what Sarah and Mike were up to.

They asked me to cocktail parties. I brought Stony with me. He used to stand still and silent, as fixed as a signpost, in the part of the room in which he'd landed, while bright theatrical girls talked through him at each other. After half an hour or so he would suddenly plough straight through them.

'Let's get out of here, Nancy,' he would say, absolutely ignoring the people whom I was talking to at the time.

'Nancy, we want you to stay on afterwards, have dinner with

us, it's Sunday, it's the only night Mike has free.' Sarah would say in opposition, while Stony listened quite impassively.

'I'm sorry, Sarah, I'm having a driving lesson tonight.'

Then Stony and I would go off.

It was after one of those parties that we had the accident. Stony was driving, it was late, there was nothing on the road, it was our road. A car came out of a side-turning at us, and Stony twisted past it into the track of a coach. It looked like a head-on collision, but he got round it, he was a beautiful driver. We went into a skid: he held it as long as he could; the tyres were shrieking "Gone" at us, and then we came to the corner and we were gone.

When I was lying somewhere with people digging needles into me I shut my eyes, and when I opened them Stony was standing around, covered in slings and plaster.

'All right, Nancy?' he asked.

I went to sleep again. When I woke I was feeling better. Stony was still there.

'All right now, Nancy?'

'It was better than the cocktail party.'

'Yes.'

'But the hangover seems worse.'

'The old Jag has copped it.'

'Oh, Stony. Will you get another?'

'No. My father's been on the buzzer. He's sending me to Canada. To make my own way.'

'I didn't think you'd clear that coach. It was a fast minute, that last one.'

'Yes,' he said.

'You have to get another car, Stony.'

'Yes. In Canada. How about marrying me, Nancy?'

'I'm sorry, Stony, I don't think it would do.'

'I suppose it wouldn't. Not without the Jag.'

He stood looking at me. I couldn't see any emotion in his face at all, but I guessed he was struggling for some suitable words of farewell.

'Then I'd better get along,' he said. 'Anything I can do?'

'People, the firm and so on, ought to be told, and I need some clothes. Tell Sarah. She'll fix everything.'

'Right. So long, Nancy.'

It wasn't a passionate parting, even before he turned at the door to produce his last words.

Sarah came. I was glad to see her, stuck out in the wilds of A30, out of reach of most of the people I knew.

Sarah looked beautiful enough to stop an operation, or even a death. She brought me unhospitalized clothes, and luxuries like eau-de-cologne, and lots of cigarettes. She said she knew the tricks hospitals played.

She was very amusing about Mike and his moods, and how she always lagged one behind, so that she was doing the laundry when she ought to be Juliet; and trying to be Juliet when he was the submarine commander, living alone, a man among men.

'Watch out, if he gets an Othello mood,' I said.

'I've no reason to watch out. I'm serious about being married to Mike. It was terrible when we read about you in the papers. There was a photograph of the wrecked car, it looked hideously dramatic, and it said you were still unconscious. I got ghastly heart-disease at once, it was like being kicked in the ribs. I began to cry. Mike was furious.'

'Furious? What about?'

'He was storming all over the place, declaiming against women. I couldn't stand it any more. I went and locked myself in the bathroom.'

'But you came out again?'

'Not for a long time. I can't bear it when Mike's angry.'

'It's just one of his acts.'

'But he enjoys them so much. And I thought you might be dying. I wasn't in a mood to deal with him. You see, he was furious with you.'

'You haven't told me why.'

'If I tell you it will make you furious with him.'

'No. I'm sold out of fury at the moment.'

'He said he knew it was going to happen and you deserved it because you were gluttonous for sensation. He said you and this maniac Stony were playing a private game of suicide-touching. He said he'd asked you to dinner after the party and your behaviour was offensive.'

'Was it?'

'No. He didn't say a word at the time about your not being there last night, it was only today when the row was on he brought it up. And he said you probably enjoyed the accident. Did you?'

'The middle was all right.'

75

'Nancy! You've picked up those short, short sentences from Stony.'

'It was like being given extra passion to be purged of,' I said.

She asked me if I was in love with Stony, and I told her about his proposal of marriage. She was delighted.

'You mean he just said, "Not without the Jag. I see that," and went away, leaving you in your bed of plaster?'

'There were some last words.'

'Of love?'

'He turned at the door, and he said: "That skid was a hundred and five yards." Then he went.'

Sarah and I both began to laugh. It hurt my ribs, but I couldn't stop. When she was away from Mike, not shedding off loyalty on his side, every situation was as funny, eventually, as it had been before.

I stopped laughing, mainly because it was too painful, and asked her to go on about Mike.

'When your Stony rang up—he used only about ten words— I told Mike I was going down to you. So Mike said I could do what I pleased, meaning the opposite, which is what that usually means, and he would never speak to you again.'

'Does he think Stony and I might have been drunk at the time?'

'He did throw off that suggestion.'

'That's what's worrying him. If I die, there will be an inquest, it will turn out I was drinking at your party, the coroner will make nasty remarks about drunken actors and the wild life. It's a bit unfair. I only drank tomato juice, and Stony had one lager. But Mike's terrified of scandal. If I live on without an inquest it will be all right. It's only if I die he won't speak to me.'

We both laughed, but we knew it was true. Mike would drop me, or any other friend, rather than be involved in a scandal. I don't know if he was having queer ideas about his public, or hoping that an unspotted reputation would help him to an actor's knighthood, twenty years on.

I was in bed for a few weeks, then I was driven sedately back to London in a hired car. The Diagonal Press very decently sent me off to Italy to cover a Society-Drugs-and-Violence case. I was a kind of walking plaster cast; the Italians thought I was another victim, everything went well.

I saw Sarah on my way through London, but I was careful

76

to avoid Mike. I didn't hear from them all the time I was in Italy. When I came back I intended to go right on avoiding Mike, but when Sarah told me the news, I realized I'd have to cancel the row.

Sarah's news was that she had told Mike about Peter when he was in an Othello mood.

'Sarah,' I said, 'you didn't tell him Peter was in prison?'

'You were the one who used to lecture me on frankness between husbands and wives.'

'That was only theory. I should have thought Mike was a special case.'

'That's what he thinks, too.'

'One good thing. You've told him about Peter, and now you'll be able to let the subject wither away.'

'Not yet.'

'Are you still in love?'

'Yes. I'm still in love.'

'I meant, are you still in love with Mike?'

'That's a bitchy thing to say. Yes, I'm still in love with Mike.'

'How much did you tell him about Peter?'

'I told him the truth.'

'That was very rash.'

'What do you think I should do now?'

'Invent a good lie.'

'Seriously?'

'Let the Peter subject drop.'

'I can't. He's coming out of prison.'

'Surely you don't mean to see him again?'

'You seem to forget he went to prison for my sake. There's no one else in the world who cares what happens to him. How can I let him come out of prison with no one to meet him?'

'If that's all that's worrying you, I'll meet him.'

'No. It wouldn't be the same.'

'It would be better.'

She knew I meant it would be better for her and for Mike. But she wasn't looking at it from that direction.

'Would you really meet him?'

'I'd like to.' I was quite sincere. I'd never before met anyone fresh from prison.

'But I've already told Mike I'm going to meet Peter.'

'Now tell him you're not.'

He won't speak to me. He's acting pale and stunned. It won't make it any worse if I do meet Peter.'

'It will make it much worse. It won't be a rift in the lute. It will be a bomb in the orchestra.'

Mike rang me the next day, then he took me out for a drink. For me, he was acting urbane and malicious, but in the end he brought up the subject of Peter.

'One has a reputation, Nancy.'

'A reputation for what?'

'A divorce or two, or even three, won't hurt a reputation, but naturally they have to be divorces of the right kind. If one's wife goes off with the Duke of Kew Gardens, it's a step up in the world, if you look after your feet. But when a wife has an intrigue with a man from Wormwood Scrubs, a man far below the rank of embezzler, then reputation takes to a sordid death-bed.'

'Not if the reputation belongs to a great actor.'

'Thank you, Nancy. But only near-great. There's a very high fence around the great,' he said shrewdly. 'And it's surrounded by the fallen bodies of the near-great who couldn't manage the jump.'

'Mike, you're turning into the philosopher of St. Martin's Lane.'

'I'll turn into the biggest laugh in London if the gossip columns get hold of this. What if a little weasel with a camera is waiting outside that jail to photograph her meeting him?'

'Didn't she tell you I was meeting him instead?'

'Is it true?'

'Yes. Don't worry, Mike. She doesn't mean to see him again.'

'I've warned her if she does, it's caput.'

I thought of telling him it was unwise to threaten Sarah, but I didn't want to overplay my role of friend of the family.

The next morning I waited outside the prison. It was too early. I had nothing to do but look at the walls that contained the prisoners, and wonder if there were any hosts of near-prisoners, trying to get in.

He came out with two other men. I expected to see him blinking his eyes in the daylight. He didn't. I supposed prisons had become so modern that they had daylight inside them, now.

Peter looked jaunty enough until he saw me, and then his smile dropped off.

"Morning, Nancy. Have you come to write a story about me?'

'No. I came to say Hello.'

'Where's Sarah?'

'She couldn't make it, Peter. Come and have breakfast with me.'

'Why couldn't she make it? She said she'd come.'

'Said?'

'In a letter.'

I offered him a cigarette. He took it and smoked it in long, angry puffs. There was about an inch of red tobacco stabbing out beyond the paper.

'Did she send you?'

'I was glad to come. I thought it would be a good idea if you came back to my place and had a long, comfortable breakfast.'

'Is Sarah there?'

'No.' It occurred to me for the first time that he might not know she was married.

'Did she tell you all the news when she wrote?'

'What news?'

He put his hands in his pockets and rocked back and forwards on his heels. I made friendly remarks about breakfast, and talking, and idleness. He gave me one of his old horse-estimating looks. I could see I was still not worth any of his money.

'Did they give you cigarettes every day?'

'That's it, and a bottle of Napoleon Brandy for breakfast.'

'I brought some wine back from Italy, if you'd like to drink at breakfast. Come on, Peter. We'll buy all the newspapers, and you can have six fried eggs with your bacon.'

He was looking all round me, like a cautious rat searching for a trap before it leans forward to take the cheese. Then his face changed. He didn't look like a rat any more, but like a man who has been trapped at the bottom of a cliff, and who sees the rescue party arrive at last.

Without turning round, I knew that Sarah had come.

She went forward and took both his hands.

'I'm glad you're back,' she said.

They kissed each other. The fuse was lit. The blast would shortly take place.

I tried to intervene, but she didn't hear me. What I needed

79

was half an hour to make her understand that Peter out of jail would be no more acceptable then Peter before he went in. I didn't have half an hour. I didn't have a minute, I tried to do it in five words.

'Does Mike know you're here?' I asked.

'Mike can spare a day,' she said.

'A day?'

'Yes, Nancy, only a day,' she said with one of her appealing, guilty smiles.

'Mike?' Peter asked, unpleasantly.

'He's only someone I work for. Nancy's always worrying about work.'

I decided to get out of the way of the falling stones, I said good-bye and left them.

Mike rang me in the evening when he got back from the theatre. I told him I'd met Peter, and that I hadn't seen Sarah all day.

He rang me the next morning. I had nothing to say, except I had no idea, I hadn't seen her.

Sarah rang me, two days later. She'd been home, for a long time. Where could Mike be?

'I think he's got out of the escape hatch,' I said. 'Are you still down in that submarine?'

'Nancy, I'm miserable. Miserable. I don't know what I'll do if I'm left alone any longer.'

I dropped work and went round to see her.

She and Peter had parted for ever, and she wanted to settle down with Mike for the rest of eternity.

'Women do this kind of thing, but they don't do it so openly,' I told her in exasperation. 'Mike can't accept eternity with so many gaps in it.'

'You know him so well, Nancy. Tell me how to explain it to him.'

'It can't be done, Sarah. You wanted someone for forty-eight hours more than you wanted him for a life-time.'

'I didn't want Peter. But for forty-eight hours he needed me more than Mike did.'

Even people who know each other well are driven into telling lies like this, but friendship can't be destroyed by a lie or two. It was Sunday night; I couldn't even ring the theatre. In the end I took a taxi and went on a tour of the pubs. When I found Mike I tried to sober him up for her. We walked along the

Embankment and he told me about the purity of women, and we walked back, and he told me about his reputation. The third time along he told me about the bitterness of being a second-rate actor; and by the fourth he was getting back to normal, with the realization that in certain roles he had proved himself to be one of the greater actors of his generation, and how much he needed a wife to sustain and support him. I stopped him there, with a description of Sarah's beauty and intelligence, and how desperately she needed a husband whose talents she could admire. He said he would go home. I left him outside the door of their flat.

It was wasted effort. I don't know what kind of row they had, but it was permanent. Mike left, and so far as I knew, he never saw her again.

Sarah went back to Diagonal, and they gave her a job as editress of one of their smaller magazines.

I was being sent abroad more and more, as a non-political foreign correspondent. Diagonal had treated us both very well, but I left them in the end, and began free-lancing. For the first few months after the break-up, I didn't see Mike at all, but he dropped into the habit of calling me, when he heard I was in England, and taking me out for meals. He was always very entertaining, but he never mentioned Sarah.

There was one thing of which I was quite certain. Even if it had been in his character, he had no reason to kill her, now, three years after he had left her, when the divorce was through at last.

6

FOR MONTHS PAST I'd been too engrossed with Donald to see much of anyone else, even long-established friends like Mike. It was eight or nine weeks since I'd met him. When he came in the door my first thought was how much older he looked than the man I had once worshipped.

I helped him off with his coat, and he sat down and smoothed his forehead with the back of his hand. All his gestures had a mannered theatrical quality. He looked tragic

F

and miserable, but that was the way he would have wished to look, in the circumstances.

'They took me back to the flat,' he said. 'They took me back and made me look at her. Just routine, that's what they told me. I've seen her in bed, often enough. Why did they have to make me look at her like that, in bed?'

He looked at me desperately, but he didn't wait for an answer. The lines were his.

'They thought I'd shot her. That's why they made me look. Who would kill a woman if it wasn't the ex-husband? Superintendents and sergeants and surgeons, there wasn't a doubt among them. "That's the boy" they wrote in their little books. God, what a gang! You remember I played Raymond in *Death of That Wife?* By tomorrow every newspaper in London will be commenting on the strange coincidence.'

'Not The Times,' I assured him.

'I'll never be able to touch another murder play, that's certain.'

'I've cooked you some lunch, Mike. It's after midnight. You must eat.'

'I brought a bottle of wine. I have to soften you up somehow.'

I made him eat. I really did believe he was desperately unhappy. I saw the bottle of wine was two bottles, and one of brandy.

'Why do you want to soften me up?'

'I want to get you to the point of truth,' he said.

I thought it was an odd kind of remark, but he hurried on, before I had time to give it enough thought.

'Nancy, do you believe it's possible that I shot Sarah? Without hearing a word of evidence, for or against.'

I had been looking at him, of course, secretly (as he had been looking at me), with a surmise floating down my mind like the wreckage that swirls half-submerged in a flooded river. I was glad he'd asked the question. I thought of him, and of everything I knew about him, and the wreckage sank below the surface.

'No, Mike. You couldn't have killed her.'

'Thank you. Now we'll have a drink.'

'Mike. I was in her flat this morning. Before the police. There's a great deal of evidence against me.' I wanted to tell him that I might be charged with murder, but he interrupted me.

82

'They wouldn't suspect you,' he said carelessly. He wasn't interested in my position, only in his. 'They nearly had me, you know, Nancy, but by the most agreeable coincidence my father had come to London on business, and I put him up for the night. He had to catch the eight-fifteen train back north. He wakened me with a cup of tea before he left. It was disgusting; I drank it in a filial spirit only; I loathe being wakened early in the morning. Still, it's enabled him to swear that he saw me into bed at one last night, and that I was still there at quarter to eight this morning. It's a kind of alibi.'

'I hope by another agreeable coincidence the alibi is for the right time. When was she shot?'

'My dear, these experts never know. They think that someone stayed with her all night and shot her early in the morning.'

'They didn't tell me that.'

'Time is the point. It depends what your friend Peter was doing last night.'

'He's not specially my friend. But I don't think—Mike, did you say anything about Peter to them?'

'Naturally.'

'But it might have been Laurence.'

'It might have been your Donald,' he said casually. He looked at me in a sideways manner I didn't like. I began worrying, in case he'd said something about Donald to the police. I couldn't ask him. He was too shrewd. I had to keep Donald's name out of it.

'I wish you hadn't talked to them about Peter.'

'What would you expect me to do? Conceal the fact that she'd left me for a kind of Woolworth's highwayman? They were practically accusing me of murder, you know. I did go out and buy the papers after the old man left. If I was super-murderer, I could have killed her just a minute before her alarm clock went off.'

'Could you?' I asked. I wasn't thinking of him, but of Donald.

'Could I, Nancy? Why would I want to kill her? I haven't dreamt of her. I don't dream. I've thought of her, often enough, at night. I keep thinking, I could have got rid of Peter. If I'd been any kind of man, I'd have got rid of him. When I saw her lying there today, I thought, if I'd warned Peter off, she'd be alive. We'd have been having lunch together, about the time they showed her to me. We always had lunch late, when we were at home. We had breakfast late, too, or at least I did, she always got up too early for me. "Switch that damned clock off," I used to say to her, and I'd go back to sleep. Even that morning he came out of jail, I went back to sleep. When I woke at ten she wasn't there with my breakfast, and at three she wasn't there to have lunch with me. When I came back from the theatre she wasn't there to sleep with me, I had a good night, thinking of her in some back-street hotel, lying with a man who still stank of jail. I could have stopped her all right, but she always got up at eight and I always slept till ten. We might have been married still. What the hell am I to do now? You'll have to take me for a walk on the Embankment soon, Nancy.'

'I will, if you like.'

'No. Can I stay here, for a bit?'

He didn't want to be alone. Neither did I.

'Did you want me to marry her?' he asked me.

'You were in love.'

'Yes. But did you want me to marry her?'

I thought back, until I came to the hump of chagrin.

'No.'

'Why didn't I marry you?'

'Neither of us thought of it. We weren't in love. I just had this unreasonable feeling you were mine. But you never were. And I got over it.'

He leant forward and took my hand.

'We all die. I've had that rammed home. Nancy, I'm in love with your hand, from the honest nail on your thumb, to the shifty nail on your little finger. Your hand is warm. That's half the battle. It's all the battle. Someone I lived with is dead. What's going to happen to me?'

'You're tired. You ought to go home and sleep.'

'The C.I.D. hath murdered sleep. Tonight is the end of the world. No. It ended this morning, when I wasn't even awake. Nancy, I'm in love with your arm, round and brown and soft.'

He knelt on the floor beside me, and rested his face on my arm.

I didn't love him, but when he knelt beside me and needed me I was shaken by a violent pity that seemed a purer emotion than love.

'I need your arms round me, Nancy.'

84

I stroked his forehead with the tips of my fingers.

'Not my arms, Mike.'

He caught my wrist in his hand.

'I love the curve of your eyebrows, and your short, superior nose, and if you took off your shoes, I'd love the second toe from the left.'

I tried to pull my hand away. I didn't like being held.

'These things aren't me.'

'I have to stay with you tonight.'

'It's only because tonight is the end of one part of our world. You want someone. But not me.'

'If you knew you were going to be killed before the morning, if you knew you were going to die, like Sarah, you'd want to spend your last night being loved, wouldn't you?' he asked in a whisper.

I did my best to get away from him, but he held my wrist too tight.

'I don't know what I'd want.'

'People die in the night. It could happen to any of us. If you knew you'd said your last good-bye to daylight, what would you want now? You'd want to give and get all the love you could. Even if you were frightened.' He caught hold of my other wrist. There was nothing at all I could do to get free. 'Even more if you were frightened,' he said. He was gripping my wrists so hard that his finger-nails were white. His face was white, too, and his eyelids were falling over his eyes. 'That's what you'd want.'

'I might want to wander off down Memory Lane,' I said. 'It's the tradition, on the last night. "There's a breathless hush in the Close tonight. Ten to make and the last man in." '

'You're a flippant little beast,' he said, and let my wrists go.

He stood up and went to the table and poured himself a drink. I watched his back, trying to read some truth into the shape of his head. When he turned round, I was already looking the other way.

'Would you like a drink?' he asked.

'Please.'

'Brandy?'

'Oh, no.' I managed to sound shocked by the idea that I might need brandy.

He poured some wine. 'You always bring me down to earth without my parachute, don't you?'

'Only when you're acting too high.'

'It's the fault of this thing I'm in, it opens in three weeks. God, if you could see some of the lines they've given me, they'd have made Sweeney Todd blush. Are you coming to the first night?'

'If alive.'

'Did I frighten you, Nancy?'

'Yes. You're too good an actor to have close-up.'

'I'm sorry. I'm a bit frightened myself. Drink that and have some more.'

I tried to drink the wine. I picked up the glass. My hand was shaking too much. I put the glass down and took a cigarette. Mike lit it for me, and then I was able to pick up the glass.

'It's been a bad day.' I said apologetically. I wasn't going to let him know just how much he'd frightened me.

He poured me another glass of wine. When he'd given it to me he went and sat at the table, a fair distance from me. He leant back in his chair and watched me. I didn't like it.

'Will you let me stay, Nancy?'

'No.'

'You were going to, until I began to act at you. I always spoil it, don't I?'

'It's not that. You're not in love with me.'

'No?'

'No.'

'I've hung around you for years. I know I've stayed away, too. I get so enraged, sometimes, I can't bear the sight of you. Your blood isn't even cold. It's deep-frozen. Why should I droop after you like an exhausted greyhound? I know fifty women who are better-looking than you, and with more engaging personalities, too.'

'Then go to your fifty women. You'll be able to give them six minutes each, before the morning.'

I was nearly crying with exhaustion, but he wouldn't let me alone.

'I'm used to that kind of remark, from you. It's habit. You make the joke, and then we both laugh at me. But when I need you, when I try to get some kind of reaction out of you, you turn round and laugh at me again. You're right I'm not in love with you. And what about you? I suppose you're wallowing deep in love with your Donald?'

86

'I don't even know where he is,' I said. I was determined not to discuss Donald with Mike.

'If you're in love with him, why has he vanished?'

Lights were beginning to flash on and off in my brain. It was unpleasant.

'There's the man with the motive. God, he must have hated her. I think I'll drop Peter and concentrate on drawing the attention of the police to Donald. She nearly killed him, didn't she?'

I felt as if I was being crushed and squeezed like a wet cloth.

'Mike, go away now.'

'She lived with him for nine months. She was right to leave him, wasn't she? I don't know what's missing in him, but it's a big piece. He's like an empty bottle floating in a pond, he's there to have stones thrown at him. It's his existence. She smelt out his emptiness, that's why she left him. He stood there with the gun in his hand, saying he'd kill himself if she went.'

'You don't know,' I said.

I was staring at a segment of the floor, where a match-box and a chair leg were swaying past, anti-clockwise. I tried to catch them with my mind, and make them stand still, but they were out of control, like Mike's voice.

'Everyone knew. She told him to go ahead and kill himself if he wanted to. She heard the shot as she walked out, but she walked out just the same. He shot himself and missed his heart.'

'Everyone doesn't know.'

'I know. That's a good beginning.'

I tried to answer him, but my voice wouldn't come out.

'Perhaps he managed to get her heart, even though he missed his own. Was he the man in her flat last night? Was he, Nancy?'

The coloured lights began to go round my head faster than the matchbox, and Mike's voice buzzed round with them. I thought I saw his face near me, and I tried to get away. Then the lights snapped off, and I dropped into a delicious and complete blackness.

I knew I'd fainted. When I got to the Where-Am-I stage, I was lying on the divan, and I knew where I was. Mike was still sitting at the table. He was resting his head on one hand as though it was the only way he could keep it up. He looked as if he had been dropped into his chair and had no energy to pull himself out of it. I watched him with a weak curiosity. He was handsome, far too handsome. It was all very well on the stage. In private life he was automatically suspected of vanity, of using his professional charm to get his own way, of accepting admiration as his right. Women often avoid the very good-looking man. They want their love to be taken as a gift, not a natural tribute.

He turned round and saw that I was conscious.

'Thank God you've wakened up,' he said. 'If I'd had to get a doctor for you now, at two in the morning, there would have been hell to pay.'

'I'm sorry you've been worried,' I said. I closed my eyes, trying to think of some way to hurt him. I wanted to get the knife back into his ribs. I tried to think of where he was vulnerable, and I remembered he'd never been a success on films.

'I've been worried too. I knew I was going to faint, I was afraid you might take the chance to act out one of your B-class films. I thought you'd bathe my forehead, and undress me gently with averted gaze, and stand brooding over the bed. But not you. You had the big worry. You might have had to get a doctor and some adverse publicity.'

He put on his pained, misunderstood expression.

'I suppose Donald would have done more for you.'

'Oh, yes. People in love, deeply in love, help each other. They don't sit around, worrying about their own position.'

'Has Donald helped you much?'

'Yes.'

'I don't see him as great helper. And I wouldn't like to be in your hands, if I was in a tight spot.'

'I wasn't talking about helping you. I was talking about Donald.'

'Even if I was Donald, I wouldn't like to need your help.'

'I've helped him more than you imagine.'

'I don't imagine anything. I'm not the one with imagination. You are. You've so much imagination you can see yourself and Donald as a pair of self-sacrificing lovers. He's too empty to be in it at all. And you're too cold to help a cripple off with his hat.'

I was beginning to cry with a mixture of self-pity and exhausted rage.

'You don't know anything about love. Why do you think

88

I've been with the police all those hours? How do you think I got in this mess, if it wasn't trying to help Donald? If I'm charged with murder tomorrow, I suppose you'll think I did it.'

'But you don't care what I think.'

'No, I don't. I was in the flat this morning, and if you think I went on my own affairs, go ahead and think it.'

'You went there after he'd gone?'

'Yes. He told me she was dead,' I said drearily. My little burst of hysteria was over. I didn't realize how much harm it had done until I saw Mike's face. He looked as cunning as Shylock, and as triumphant as Mark Antony.

'I knew I'd get it out of you,' he said. He was delighted with himself. 'They told me you'd been there. They were very sweet about it. They wanted me to suggest a reason why you should kill her. They went on about you for hours. I suppose they kept on at you even longer. But they didn't get at the truth. I did.'

'The police have some scruples,' I said. 'They would hardly try to seduce me.'

'But I've no scruples at all, that's it, isn't it? I wouldn't go, I forced you to quarrel, I frightened you, I drove you into an hysterical fainting fit, I'd have made you drunk, if I'd had to. And if you'd like to know, I'd have seduced you, too.'

'A fine piece of great-actorism.' I tried to sound scornful, but I was no actress, I was very frightened, and I showed it. 'And all for nothing. The police know I was in the flat. It's what they've been talking about, all day.'

'They don't know why you were there. That is, they think they know. They think you were there because you killed her. So I had to find out.'

'That's what you came for tonight? To help the police?'

'I came to find out.'

'Because you thought the police were right?'

'I came to find out why you were there. I knew if you'd walked up to your neck in some bog of romanticism, you wouldn't have the sense to walk out again. I didn't know you'd go so far as to get yourself charged with murder to protect that weakling, Donald.'

'And now what are you going to do?'

'I haven't thought that one out yet.'

'I've thought something out. Your behaviour tonight has been so disgusting, I don't want to see you ever again.'

'Disgusting!' he repeated in surprise. 'But I had to find out. I didn't come here with a fixed plan. I had to feel my way. It wouldn't have been any good, just asking you why you were there, would it?'

'You had to find out! Suppose you'd found I killed her. You'd have told the police, wouldn't you? So what it comes round to is, you came here and used the last of our friendship to act as a police spy.'

'I came here to help you. You were making a fool of yourself, for a man who spent the night in her flat. He spent the whole night there, didn't he? Didn't he?'

'Go away. Get out.'

'He spent the night in her flat. There's not a glimmer of doubt, your Donald did it.'

'Is that what you're going to tell the police?'

'It's what you're going to tell them.'

'Am I?'

'Yes. I'll telephone them for you. I'll say you're anxious to go on helping them. You're going to tell them, and not me, because I've had enough of this affair. I don't want to be mixed up in it any more,' he said, with magnificent distaste.

'Out of the escape hatch again,' I said spitefully.

'What do you mean?'

'You always have to be the first to get out of trouble. It's a pathological weakness.'

'You're overwrought, Nancy,' he said in a paternal voice. 'Go to bed. Where's my coat?'

'Over there. I'm not going to tell the police anything. You're the informer. You'll have to do the job yourself.'

His expression was a splendid facsimile of detachment, but it shifted a little at the word Informer. He picked up his coat.

'Good night, Nancy.'

'What pleasure it will be when you get Donald convicted for a murder he didn't commit. I'll think of you often from whatever hideous women's prison they send me to.'

His hand was on the door. He dropped it, and stood for a minute with his back to me. He always had to do things in a theatrical way.

'What do you mean about women's prison?' he asked. He turned round.

'If Donald's charged, I'll be charged too. It's what you've

found out. But you're so damned anxious to stand clear of the gates, you don't care if I'm crushed in them. I'm an accessory. You know that.'

'What did you do?'

'I went to the flat. I had the key. I put away his blankets, and washed the glasses they'd drunk out of, and wiped his finger-prints off the door handles. I had to do it. He was in the flat, and when he got up in the morning she was dead.'

'In bed. With him?'

'No. He slept in the sitting-room. She gave him some knock-out pills, about four in the morning, so he didn't waken up, when—when it happened. Then he did. He found she was dead, and he came away. He left everything. He even left some of the rubbish out of his pockets, with the phone numbers of the art galleries he dealt with. If I hadn't cleared the place up, he wouldn't have had a chance. But it makes me an accessory—you get him arrested, and you'll have me arrested, too.'

'You bloody fool,' he said. He stood by the door, and I watched him, wondering how he'd get out of it gracefully. He put his coat over a chair and came back and sat down by the table. He didn't want to be near me.

'Why did you help a murderer?' he asked.

'He's not a murderer. But if they know he was there, they won't believe that. Now go to the police.'

'Stop dramatizing yourself.'

'I'm not the expert on dramatization.'

'I'm not an expert on murder, am I?'

I began to cry a little, not much.

'What's wrong now?' he asked.

'Sarah. She's been forgotten in all this.'

'She's out of it. We're in. I don't appreciate the death of my former wife, but if you want to know, I'd got over her. It's three years ago.'

'That's a lie. You've been false all night, and now I don't believe anything you say.'

'And what have you been? I tricked you into telling me what happened, but you wanted to be tricked. You'd kept it in all day with the police. I know you. You wanted to let it out.'

It was true enough. I'd been suffering all day from the need to keep everything in. It was painful to endure perpetual

91

attacks without even defending myself, when what I wanted to say was: 'Look, how wonderful I am!'

'Today is Sunday,' Mike was saying. 'Half-past two on Sunday morning. I'm rehearsing on Monday morning. I'll have to get this cleared up by then.'

'Are you going to the police?'

'It's too late tonight.'

'What do you mean to do?'

'I'm staying here.'

'I won't let you.'

'I'm staying here till Monday morning, if I have to. Your Donald will turn up in the end. And I'm going to speak to him before you do. I'm not giving you the chance to fix up anything with him. I'll do the fixing.'

'You can't stay here.'

'I'll sleep in the sitting-room, like Donald. Now go to bed.'

'Yes, I'll go to bed.'

I sat with my eyes closed. There wasn't any way I knew of moving. I had an impression he was standing, watching.

'Go to bed, Nancy.'

'Yes.'

I tried to open my eyes and stand up, but I couldn't do it.

'I'm not going to behave like a B-film,' he said coldly. 'If you can't get yourself to bed, you can damned well sit up all night.'

He left me and went into the bathroom. I heard water running, far away. When he came back he was carrying sheets and a blanket. He arranged everything carefully on the divan.

'I had a hell of a job finding these,' he said, aggrieved. 'I had to get them out of your bedroom. I don't know what I'm going to do in the morning. Do you keep a razor for your male visitors?'

'No.'

'And I'll have to wear the same shirt. If you washed it tonight, it would be dry by the morning.'

I didn't bother answering that one. But I opened my eyes and looked at him. He had his coat and his tie off. He unfastened his cuff links and pulled off his shirt.

'Nancy, you're behaving very badly,' he said. 'Go to bed.'

'This is my flat. I'll stay where I like.'

'Oh, for God's sake!' he said.

He caught me by the shoulders and pulled me up. He

92

pushed me through into the bedroom, and down on to the bed. Then he walked out and shut the door.

I sat for about ten minutes, hating him, before I finally managed to take off my clothes and get into bed. I didn't need the sleeping pills after all.

7

THE ALARM WENT off at eight o'clock. Sarah and I had always set the clock for eight. It was an old habit. I woke up with Sarah in my mind, Sarah as I'd seen her yesterday morning. It was a bad start to the day.

I got up quickly and turned on the bath. For once I hadn't put out my clothes for the morning. I fumbled about in drawers, looking for various things, and remembering that the police had searched through all my belongings yesterday.

In the bottom of the middle drawer, buried under an assortment of underclothes, I found the gun.

It was completely impossible, and there it was.

It was a heavy kind of gun; it looked like a revolver, but I knew nothing about guns. I didn't want to touch it. I shut the drawer and went into the bathroom. The gun hadn't been there yesterday. The police had searched everywhere; then I had gone away with them and left the flat locked up. I remembered how last night, before Mike came, I had worried over the fact that someone had a key to my flat. I had never given the key to anyone, with the exception of Sarah. We'd had that arrangement about keys since she'd left Mike. We hadn't gone back to living in the same place again, but we had both felt, if there was an emergency, a refuge would be useful.

I had the bath quickly. I could see what had happened. The murderer had taken my key from Sarah's flat. He had come back, opened my door, retyped the threatening letter on my typewriter, and destroyed the original. He hadn't brought the gun then. I didn't know why not. Perhaps he hadn't risked carrying it, when he might be seen, coming in or out of my door. But when I went off with the police he was safe. He had let himself in again, and hidden the gun.

I dried myself and dressed. Someone was wholly determined to have me arrested for murder. I wouldn't hang, but I would spend the rest of my life in jail. I felt sick with fear when I thought of it. I didn't know anyone could hate me so much. People don't hate that way.

A man had killed Sarah. He had been angry, revengeful, jealous, drunk, mad. His action had been dreadful, but it was a thing that could be understood in some way. This furtive attempt to destroy me couldn't be understood at all.

I went round all the people I knew, I went round them in a circle, and round again; there were plenty of people who didn't like me, but surely no one who would want me thrown in prison for the rest of my life.

The man who had left the gun with me had to be the man who had killed Sarah. If it really was a man from her past who had done it, there were only four to choose from. It hadn't been Donald: it couldn't be Mike. That left Peter and Laurence: I was sure that neither of them would try to do this to me.

It was quite impossible that this malevolent and murderous enemy should succeed. The police were careful, I told myself in a panic; they arrested the right person; even last night they had let me go. The police would never be deceived by clumsily planted evidence. Then I began to realize that the enemy, with his forged letter and concealed gun, was only reinforcing the case I had already built up against myself. I had done well for him, with my maniac visit to her flat. I had probably wiped away his finger-prints, with Donald's; covered up for him, while I tried to protect Donald; and left signs of my own presence everywhere.

At any moment now some anonymous voice would telephone the police, advise them to search my flat again. I had to get out, take the gun, get rid of it somehow.

I finished dressing, I did my hair, I couldn't have been quicker if I'd heard that a radio-active cloud was rolling in my direction. I picked up the gun and wrapped it in brown paper. I had an outsize handbag that was big enough to hold the gun. I took it, transferred keys and money, and dropped the great clumsy gun in last.

I had to go through the sitting-room to get out. I opened the door, and a chair that had been pushed against it scraped noisily over the floor.

Mike was lying with an arm over his face. When he heard the noise of the chair, he threw his arm back and opened his eyes, but he wasn't really awake. Waking is mostly a matter of habit.

'Go to bed, Nancy,' he muttered. He shut his eyes and rolled over towards the wall. He made a fine sentry.

I went out quickly into a grey, wet day. I didn't have a coat and I couldn't risk going back for one.

The water came up in dirty little waves from the wheels of a passing car. It bounced in pellets from the pavements, and rolled in black streams to the gutters. There were only two other people in the street. They had umbrellas, and they were angry about the weather. I couldn't imagine a detective with an umbrella. I wasn't being watched. There was no one waiting by the bus stop: it was Sunday. A quiet day for the disposal of a gun.

I went to the public call box in the underground station and rang Donald's number. I waited for a long time, but there was no answer.

When I came out of the call box I stood in the entrance to the station and watched the rain. I tried to imagine myself taking the gun to the police. 'I just happened to find it this morning. Someone must have put it there.' 'Really, Miss Graham, do you often find guns among your petticoats?' 'No, no, Inspector. It's more blunt instruments. And darts. I get a lot of poisoned darts in my stockings, and a bow and arrow now and then, but the gun was a real surpise.' 'Get me Broadmoor on the telephone, Constable!'

I laughed, and a man in a raincoat turned round sharply. He was standing like me in the entrance to the station, watching the rain and waiting for something to happen to it.

I decided at once that he was a plain-clothes man and that I was being watched after all. I had the gun in my handbag. I went back into the station in a hurry and bought a ticket. I went down to the platform. A train was there. I stepped into it just before the doors closed.

I didn't know where I was going, or what to do with the gun. The simplest thing would be to walk out and leave it in the train.

Two men were sitting opposite me. One was too young and the other too disreputable to be employed by the C.I.D.

I opened my handbag and laid it on the seat beside me.

Neither of the men was watching me, so I moved the handbag sharply up and tipped out the gun. It should have rested on the seat, but it slid to he floor. The men both looked across at me, and then down to the floor. The object at my feet looked like only one thing in the world, and that was a gun wrapped in brown paper. I bent quickly to pick it up, and so did the disreputable man.

We nearly bumped heads in our common anxiety to reach the parcel. I was close enough to count the pock marks on his face, had I wished. I was certainly close enough to appreciate the magnificent air of gallantry with which he swept the parcel from my finger-tips; and the changing expression of his face as he felt the shape of the parcel. There was no room for doubt; he knew that the parcel contained a gun.

He had it in his hands, now. He sat up, holding it, staring at me. Then he heaved himself over to the seat beside me.

'You going far, Miss?'

'I'm getting out at the next station.'

I held out my hand. He put the gun in it, and said approvingly:

'Nice little packet.'

'Thank you,' I said, in my Harrod's voice.

The train stopped. I gave him a surprised glance of gratitude, like someone in the hunting counties acknowledging a small courtesy from a bailiff, and swept out.

He followed me.

I retained my air of hauteur until we got to street level, and then I turned to him and said: 'Blow off!'

He dropped back.

We were at Charing Cross. I had no idea where I meant to go, but a delicious thought occurred to me. I could drop the gun in the river.

I started to walk quickly. The man from the train had not blown off. He followed me now, and began to talk confidentially about an inch away from my ear.

'You come with me, Miss.'

I shook my head, very correct, never speak to odious fellows.

'What a bleeding shame.'

96

I walked faster, but he kept alongside, always close enough to mutter in my ear.

'What are you going to do with it?'

'If you don't clear off I'll have you nicked,' I said, dropping my Kensington manner.

'You! With that on your hands!' He sniggered.

We walked on. He kept whispering in my ear. It seemed he had a nice little place, but lonely: he was prepared to give me every sexual satisfaction.

'Good Old Joe,' he told me. 'He always hears the girls a-calling, Good Old Joe. They know what I'm good for, see?'

We walked over the bridge in the heavy rain. The way things were, I couldn't drop the gun in the river. Good Old Joe was just part of the general nightmare. He made ghoulish little jokes as we passed a policeman: he knew I didn't dare draw attention to myself.

We were over the bridge now, but the nightmare didn't end. He was still muttering in my ear. As a special favour, he'd look after the whole works for me. Not for nothing, oh, no, but the rod was too hot for me to handle. He'd keep his mouth shut, all right, and never a woman stayed with Good Old Joe who hadn't been licking his boots and thanking God she'd been born before the night was over.

'Taxi!' I shouted, and it stopped. I thanked God for the invention of the taxi-meter cab and the birth of the driver.

'I hope you are carried off soon by some painful disease,' I said to Good Old Joe as I got in and slammed the door.

'Just drive!' I shouted to the driver.

He turned round and swallowed my appearance. Joe was clinging to the handle of the cab. It was no good trying to be inconspicuous.

'Drive me to Southend,' I said, and the driver started. It was about thirty miles. It would give me time to think what to do.

When I had recovered from the impact of Good Old Joe, I tried again to make a plan about the gun. I realized that the best idea was, not to keep it, which was dangerous, but to keep in touch with it. I would leave it in a station luggage office.

I took it out of my handbag and looked at it again. It couldn't be left anywhere, in its present poorly wrapped gun-nish form. It should be put in a box, or a suitcase. I didn't know how to get these things on Sunday morning. There must be someone I knew who lived south of the river. And there was. I remembered Laurence.

I told the driver to stop by a telephone box, then I got out and looked up his address. He lived in Battersea, at seventeen, Woodman's Lane. I told the driver, who turned round without comment. He'd probably realized I didn't mean to drive to Southend in the rain.

I couldn't have had a better idea than going to see Laurence. I would be able to borrow a box or a suitcase from him; find out what had been in his befuddled mind yesterday; and if the police had interviewed him, too.

When we got to Laurence's number, I paid the driver and stepped out into the rain.

Laurence lived in the middle of one of those long streets where even the Victorian builders had lost heart. 'We've done the worst we can,' they said, half-way down the street. It's hopeless. We'll have to go on until we run out of yellow bricks and stained glass.'

I went up the stone stairs. I analyzed the smell as twenty per cent. tom cat; thirty per cent. babies' laundry; and fifty per cent. onions cooked over oil stoves by very old men.

The door was opened by a doleful blonde in a hair net and last night's make-up. I asked her for Laurence.

'He's resting,' she said hopelessly.

'Oh. I wonder if you'd tell him I'm here. My name is Graham. Nancy Graham.'

'Come along in, Miss Graham. Friends of Laurence are ever welcome.'

She took me into a room where last night's supper dishes and bottles waited to welcome the early morning reveller.

'I'll speak to him. Make yourself at home.'

I sat down. I didn't feel I was at home anywhere.

Looking round the peeling, pictureless, hopeless room, I suddenly felt bad about Laurence again.

He had been an unhappy man when we knew him first, but he'd had some kind of flowering when he met Sarah, who was his sun. He'd had a secret repository of pleasure; a multitude of quotations and visions, acquired from books and music and pictures. He had handed them all over to her in a long act of worship. I myself had learnt many things from Laurence, but I wasn't grateful at the time: I remembered the damaging amusement with which I had greeted his suggestion of taking Sarah to Ireland to write and fish.

'You're not a writing and fishing girl,' I'd said to her. 'You'd be happier loving and minking,' and 'Laurence is Wordsworth, without the pension and the poetry,' and 'If you go to Ireland with Laurence you'll end up by being an old woman in a bog grog shop. Laurence will read Ulysses aloud to you, with tears in his eyes, while you swill the floor over with poteen.'

I couldn't worry too much about what Laurence had lost, he was nothing to me, there were people all over the world in refugee camps, I might as well worry about them. That was the correct definition of Laurence. He was a displaced person. He had lost his small-holding in culture.

The blonde came back in the room, half-smiling at me, but with a worried eye on the dirty supper dishes.

'He wants to see you. He's getting up. He's very tired.'

'I'm sorry to disturb him.'

'He can't ever get up in the morning. He works with his brain.'

'Does he?'

'No chance of getting him to bed early. He works with his brain, late every night.'

'That must be exhausting.'

'Other people, you know, they've got nothing *to* them. I meet people in their hundreds every day, but never anyone else like him. He works with his brain.'

'What exactly does he do with his brain?'

'He's writing a book.'

'What kind of book?'

'A history of biographers,' she said, in her flat, whining voice.

'What?'

'A history of biographers. Everyone who's ever written about anyone else, he's writing about them.'

I considered the idea with respect. It would be a long stint, but there was something in it. Laurence would have his imitators. And when a large enough number of writers had written their histories of biographers, someone could write a book about the historians of biographers. It was the way literature progressed.

'You'd like some tea?' she asked, shuffling dirty plates. 'He's getting up soon.'

'If you're making tea.'

99

'I'll put the kettle on.'

When she was out of the room I took a more careful look around. There were a few books, mostly verse. It was as if the poets were limpets, clinging obstinately to the beaten rocks of the room. As well as Auden, Barker, Empson, and Day Lewis, there was a crumbling Milton and a battered Blake. I chose a Day Lewis, thinking that if Laurence and I had nothing else left in common, we still bought the same books, but when I opened it I saw the rubber-stamped sign of Battersea Public Library, half-obliterating the line: 'You walk in a nightmare now, not a dream.' I turned back to the flyleaf, and saw he'd borrowed it a year ago. You get absent-minded, when you keep your poetry in bottles. I put the book back on the shelf and looked for some borrowed biographies. There weren't any. Perhaps he was writing from memory.

She came back, and took a brassière and a pair of trousers from a chair.

'Sunday morning,' she said vaguely. 'It's my day off. I'm in a restaurant.'

'Is that very hard?'

'It's a long day. We start with the breakfasts.'

'I'm sorry to have got you up on Sunday morning.'

'You've come about the murder, haven't you?'

'I—no, I haven't. I thought I'd like to see Laurence again.'

'Now? The day after her murder's been in the evening papers? If you didn't come about the murder, why did you come?'

'I came to see Laurence. It's possible the—murder, made me think of Laurence, I mean, made me think of all the past. You see, Sarah and I started work for the Diagonal Press together, and Laurence was there then.'

'You're Nancy. I've heard a lot about you. You're the one who broke up his affair with that Sarah who's been killed.'

'Oh, no. Laurence—Sarah, they just parted.'

'I've no reason to complain,' she said in a depressed voice. 'If he hadn't left that Sarah, he'd never have come to me. I look after him, that's what I do.' She lowered her voice.

'There's two bedrooms in this house, don't make any mistake about that. I'm here to cook his meals and clean up. We live together,' she said in a fierce whisper, 'but it's only mental.'

'It's nice that way,' I said vaguely.

'I'll see if he's up yet.'

She went out of the room again. I'd have liked to go out too, but I was curious to see how Laurence had reacted to Sarah's death.

She came back again. She had come out of her hair net. Her curls looked like the ridges the outgoing tide leaves in wet sand.

'He's shaving. Putting on an act for you, Miss Graham.'

'He'd have to shave anyway,' I said, rather crossly. I was being made to realize how enormously I had disturbed them. They were putting me in the wrong.

'Not on Sundays. He never shaves on Sundays.'

'We'll just have to pretend it's Monday, then.'

'You're the way he said you were. He's a real judge of character.'

'How did he say I was?'

'Sharp,' she said with enormous satisfaction. 'I'll get you some tea.'

Laurence came shambling in. He looked as if he'd tried to use a razor for the first time, and shown no natural talent. There was a piece of plaster on his chin, and he was bleeding from an unattended spot.

'Good morning, Laurence. I'm terribly glad to see you.'

'If you've come to polish up a story about me and the murder, clear off,' he said. 'Otherwise, have some tea, Dulcie's getting it. Have you met Dulcie before?'

'No.'

'She's a woman,' he said gloomily. 'She's not one of your damned intellectuals who wants to argue the merits of Hindu music. Dulcie's realistic. She gets on with the job of caring for the house.'

I was looking at a pair of stockings hanging out from beneath a cushion. There was no point in blaming Dulcie, she worked for a living, but I didn't like the implied suggestion that I should take lessons from her.

'You've come to ask about Sarah?' Laurence said.

'There's nothing left to ask.'

'It was my fault,' Laurence said. 'I taught her too much. She was ignorant when I met her. Ignorant. I talked to her all the time about poetry and plays. I educated her, and her mind couldn't stand the strain. She got ideas about herself. It turned her into a tart, in the end.'

'I object to that description.'

'A tart. And that's how she got killed. That's why she got killed. That's how they all get killed in the end.'

'Laurence, she's dead. Aren't you sorry at all?'

'Brightness falls from the air. Queens have died young and fair,' he said with his eyes shut. Even his eyelids were trembling. He looked like a man with a terrible hangover.

'Do you remember you used to read *Paradise Lost* to us, Laurence?'

'What are you trying to say?'

'Just talking over old times. Those suppers, with Chianti, and French bread, and the salads you used to make . . . you were part of her life, once, Laurence.'

'I warn you, Nancy, don't throw the past at me. I've battered the past off, it's not hanging on to me. I'm living now the way I live. And Sarah didn't die yesterday. In this house, in this room, she died years ago.'

Dulcie came in with the tea.

'The dead should be forgotten, that's what you think, isn't it, Dulcie?' he asked her.

'Yes, that's what I think,' she said. She was hiding in a corner of her iron thoughts.

'That's what she thinks,' he said to me. 'Dulcie has thought, therefore she is a thinker. Aren't you, Dulcie?'

'Drink your tea and shut up,' she said vaguely. She looked around the room. 'We're in a bit of a mess. It's Sunday.'

We drank tea.

'Have the police been at you?' he asked me abruptly.

'Most of the time.'

'They've been at me too. They'd still be at me if Dulcie here hadn't convinced them, in the most modest and guarded terms, that she had shared my bed all night.'

'There's no need to bring that up, Laurence,' Dulcie said angrily. She turned to me. 'I get up at seven, you see, *from* my own bed, but I don't have to go until half after. I get his breakfast then, of couse it's only tea and a boiled egg, or sometimes a kipper, so there he was in bed at half-past seven, according to the police that's that. He couldn't have got to her by the required time, not without a taxi.'

'I never take taxis,' Laurence said. 'Especially not to death-beds.'

'But he wasn't awake, you see, really, when I went.' Dulcie explained.

'Laurence, I wanted to ask you, how did you know the police were at my flat?'

'You telephoned. I was in bed. I had this damned headache on one side. I couldn't answer. But later in the day, when I'd got dressed and all that, and Dulcie was incommunicado at her place of business, I thought I'd stroll along and have a chat. Then I saw the police car, and I strolled off again and bumped into you.'

'The police would have been a great shock if you hadn't warned me,' I said politely. Then, without thought, impelled by my dreadful, habitual rashness, I asked the question I should never have spoken aloud.

'By the way, Laurence, what did you think you were warning me against?'

The question was too heavy for the air in the room. It lay, large and awkward, between Laurence and myself. There was no chance now of building up any sympathy between us, of acquiring information, or asking for help.

We stared at each other. Laurence red-eyed, sullen, suspicious: myself embarrassed, frightened, and suspicious, too.

'When I saw the police at your door I naturally supposed you'd been mixed up in some shady deal with your criminal friend, Peter.' Laurence said, running his finger round his collar. 'You've touched too much tar, Nancy, to get away with that charitable, whitewashed sneer. What did the police have to say to you about this murder?'

'Routine enquiries. When did you hear about the murder, Laurence?'

'I read it in the evening paper.'

'What edition?'

'I bought two evening papers,' he said. 'They remade the front page to get it in the final edition.'

'Do you always buy two editions of the same paper?'

'Do you always ask such damn-fool questions?'

'I'm sorry, Laurence. When did the police get on to you?'

'About six o'clock last night. That's when I bought the second paper.'

'What kind of time did you have with the police?'

'I couldn't help them in any way at all, except to tell them a thing or two about Sarah—and Peter . . . and the kind of life you and Sarah used to live—parties . . . and men.'

'I should watch out for those plurals,' I said. 'It would have been kinder to have told them how Sarah and I used to live —work . . . poetry-readings . . . and discussions about going to Ireland.' He had managed to make me angry.

'Poor old Sarah,' Laurence muttered. He snatched a cup, and tried to swallow some tea, but tea doesn't go down easily, like whisky. He pushed the cup away. It was a hair from the wrong dog.

'It was Peter who did it,' he said.

'I'm not sure that it was.'

'Then it was that Donald, who tried to kill himself.'

'I don't believe that either.'

'Believe what you choose,' he shouted at me. 'She had too many lovers. That was her trouble.'

'Better the light from one bright fire than the flickering of a thousand candles,' Dulcie said. I think she was quoting from something.

'Oh, shut up,' Laurence said. 'No one's lit even a safety match for you.' He shook his head, as if he was hoping the pieces would fall back into place. 'I'm sorry, old girl,' he said. 'I'm not at my best in the early morning.'

He put his arm round her and kissed her on the cheek. She didn't seem particularly interested. She wasn't an emotional type.

'Don't, Larry dear, not in company.' She began to put the cups back on the tray. She looked down at her feet.

'Have to do something about that carpet,' she said, and drifted out with the tray.

'I'd be lost without that girl,' Laurence said. 'She's done a lot for me. She's loyal. If it wasn't for her, I'm damned if I know how I'd get on with my work on biographers. I've always wanted to do something big. If you can't do something big with your life, it's wasted. I'd go mad if I still worked for the Diagonal Press. What are you doing now, Nancy?'

'I've left Diagonal. I do a bit of free-lancing for them. I go to Italy or Spain occasionally for one of the Sunday's. They don't pay well. And I'm trying to write a novel. I type three pages every night and tear two of them up in the morning. If I'm home early enough in the evening, I tear the third page up too."

'You wouldn't believe the number of biographers there are,'

Laurence said. 'Do you think I could put Gertrude Stein in for her biography of herself, Nancy?'

'She'd liven things up. I'd certainly put her in.'

Just for these few seconds, we seemed to be talking like human beings. I thought I'd better leave before atavism set in.

'I have to go. You couldn't by any chance lend me a small suitcase?'

'I don't possess a suitcase. I never go away.' He stood up and wiped the hair off his forehead with a gesture I remembered. 'I never go even as far as Ireland. Why should I have a suitcase?'

'Or a box,' I said. 'A cardboard box. I want to send a present to my aunt in Cornwall.'

Dulcie wandered in again with a broom. 'Would a shoe-box do?' she asked.

'It would be perfect.'

'I bought a pair of shoes. I have the box.'

'Don't say these impediments on your feet are shoes,' Laurence said, looking at her squashed carpet slippers.

Dulcie didn't seem to notice anything unpleasant in his speech. She went out of the room.

'I'll need a suitcase,' Laurence mumbled. 'I'm going to Italy soon. I could use a bit of the warm South. We'll meet there, one day, the three of us, Nancy.'

'I'd like that, Laurence. I'm sorry we don't see more of each other. It was nice of you to warn me about the police.'

Laurence stood swaying. His red eyes began to water.

'You make me sick,' he said, and lurched through the door.

Dulcie came back with the shoe-box.

When I was going out she said in the same dreary, depressed voice:

'It's been nice meeting you, Miss Graham.'

'And I've been glad to meet you.'

She leant forward. 'But you won't come again, will you?' she said in a quick agitated whisper. 'He's got work to do, he can't get on with it, being upset like this.'

'I'm sorry.'

'Are you? I know what brought you here, Miss Nancy Graham. You came to make trouble.'

'It's not a thing I have to make. It's here already. Thanks for the tea.'

When I was safely out of the flat, I walked around until I

105

found a coffee shop. While I was waiting for coffee I took the string and paper off the gun, put the gun in the box and wrapped the box up with the paper. Then I walked to Charing Cross through the rain, and put the box in the left luggage office. I put the ticket in my handbag and went home.

8

WHEN I GOT back to the flat, Mike was sitting in a chair, reading one of the Sunday papers.

'Nancy, it's after eleven,' he said. 'You stood me up for breakfast.'

'I didn't invite you to breakfast.'

He turned back to the Sunday paper. It interested him more than I did, but it wasn't enough for him to read a paper like an ordinary person, he had to give it all his impossibly elaborate attention.

'I see you've shaved,' I said irritably.

'I bought a razor from the newsagent when I went to buy the papers.'

'Typically inconspicuous. How did you get in again?'

'I left the door open,' he said, frowning, as if he didn't like to be interrupted.

'I don't like leaving the door open.'

'Afraid of thieves?'

'Or the reverse.'

He looked up. 'Nancy, you've been out in the rain!'

'It makes a change, in London.'

'You seem very wet,' he said, examining my appearance with distaste. 'You hair is dripping, and if you had any make-up to begin with, you've lost it.'

'Try to think of me as a fresh-faced country girl, driving the cows along a muddy lane,' I suggested.

'A country girl wouldn't look so exhausted.'

'You forget about all that jiving in the silos.'

'Do something about your hair, Nancy.'

He turned back to the newspapers. 'Listen to this: "Another

Television Disaster: Michael Fenby in 'Surgeon Condemned' staggered across the screen last night in full surgical attire, including, fortunately, a mask. For a considerable sequence of this odd attempt to roll the thousand best-loved clichés into one sickening ball, Mr. Fenby, in his surgical togs, misled us into the belief that this was another play about the Deep South, and that he was a member of the Ku-Klux-Klan. It was only when he shouted: 'A lancet, nurse, and quickly!' that one realized," etcetera, etcetera.'

'That's the intellectual view, Nancy, but listen to this one. "Michael Fenby in T.V. Tops. Fenby, star of stage and screen, master of the sleepy innuendo and the tortured smile, surely jerked a million tears in last night's wonder drama. The story is . . ." Oh, to hell with the story. Here's another one, Nancy: "A dismal week on T.V., redeemed by Michael Fenby's slow, silken, but powerfully conceived . . ." I say, slow, silken, isn't bad.'

'How many papers have you got there, Mike?' I interrupted. 'The lot.'

'I'm going to change my clothes.'

I started to leave the room, then a question came up in my mind, and I stopped.

'It's not like the Sundays to notice a Saturday night T.V. play. They'd have to reset, for London.'

'I haven't been reading you the interesting little news paragraphs alongside. "Actor Michael Fenby's just-divorced wife found Shot in Bed. Police quiz as he rehearses." Thus the interest in the play.'

'I see. Death's quite a good publicity stunt, isn't it?'

'I think you'd better go and change, Nancy. Why didn't you take a taxi, if it was raining?'

'I did. I had to get rid of a man called Good Old Joe. Women lick his boots every night. He thought I'd like to do it too.'

'Is this your usual type of follower? Why was he after you?'

'It was because I was carrying a gun.'

I went out of the room, pleased with my good exit line, until I realized what I had said. I had miserable thoughts about my own indiscretion while I changed my clothes and renovated my face.

When I went back to the sitting-room Mike was still reading the papers.

'Could we have breakfast some time?' he asked.

'I wish you'd go away.'

'I'd like you to iron my tie, after breakfast. I couldn't get the knot right.'

'You wear the wrong kind. You can buy them with a permanent knot. Just slip the elastic over the back of the neck, and it's done.'

'Will you iron my tie, Nancy?'

'No.'

'You're being very disagreeable.'

'I want you to go away.'

'I'm waiting for Donald. Did you see him, when you went out?'

'No.'

'Where did you go?'

'I called on Laurence.'

'I hadn't thought about Laurence.'

'You needn't. He has an agreeably coincidental alibi, like you. He was sharing a bed, until seven-thirty.'

'What's this about a gun?'

'Nothing. I'll make you some coffee.'

I put on the kettle, then I went into the bedroom. The gun wasn't the only thing I had to think about. It was a gun, and nothing more. I put it into an anonymous male hand, and saw it held against Sarah's breast. She'd had simple tastes. All she wanted, basically, was to live further on, a step higher up. She had made several steps, but each time Peter had appeared and called her back. It would have been more reasonable if she had murdered Peter.

She might, in the end, have married this company director, Chas., but I was sure that she would never have got rid of Peter. Even Donald hadn't been able to get rid of Peter. She had walked out and left him to kill himself, because Peter had sent for her. She told me later what had happened. It was almost the penultimate confidence. I'd just come back from one of my foreign jobs, when she told me.

'What did you have against Donald,' I'd asked her. 'I thought he was permanent. You were going to marry him, when I left.'

'I might have married him, if it hadn't been for this three-year clause about divorce. I won't be free of Mike for another year, even now. I couldn't have gone on with Donald. He was

108

too good-mannered. Too anxious about me. He worried too much about what I had for breakfast. He squeezed lemon juice every night and put it beside the bed for me in the morning. If I dropped a handkerchief, he picked it up too quickly. If I had a headache, he offered me too many pills. And I never had to live up to him, like Mike. Donald didn't care if I went to bed smothered in cold cream and hair curlers: everything I did was right.'

She had become restive with Donald, just as two years earlier she had become restive with Mike. But she was older, she knew well enough that she couldn't live with Peter. She had acquired too much veneer to live in a back street of Camden Town and talk small criminal shop. It was impossible that she should ever go to him again. Even if the aunt who had sewed beside the open door had been specially imported from Birmingham, Sarah couldn't have accepted Peter as the brief, ecstatic justification of the long, tedious day.

She enjoyed work, at this period, and adored the life she led after hours; it was only that Donald was too anxious, anxious to make her happy; to share too much of his life with her; to keep her for ever. She told me he made her feel like a prize chrysanthemum, that the gardener had to examine and cherish several times a day. When she wanted to move off and leave him, he was as surprised as the gardener would have been if the chrysanthemum had lifted up its roots, and walked down the road, looking for a better garden.

Donald wasn't like Mike. He hadn't tried to bully Sarah into staying with him. He hadn't issued warnings or given orders. He didn't have any self-protecting toughness that could deny the existence of love, so that pride could be salvaged. Mike had too much vanity to beg a woman to stay with him, Donald had not enough. Mike was outraged by the thought that the woman he lived with should want anyone else; Donald was amazed and grateful that Sarah should have preferred him to other, more attractive men. He was so happy to be with her he was convinced there could be no happiness without her.

Then she had a message that Peter was dangerously ill. She told Donald she was leaving him, and wouldn't come back.

He had this gun, he'd threatened to kill himself before, and he said he'd do it now, if she left.

'It wasn't just a case of someone crying Wolf, too often,' she had said to me. 'It was someone whose only conversation was

Wolf, Wolf, Wolf. I told him that, it was callous, but, Nancy, I couldn't be blackmailed into staying for the rest of my life with someone because he might shoot himself if I left.'

'Did he know you were going to Peter?'

'I told him. I thought it would finish things off completely. Then he was waving the gun about. It's true what they say. I did hear a shot as I went out. I thought it was more bluff, so I just went on. Anyway, the hospital saved him. He didn't die.'

'Happy ending. And Peter?'

'I went to Peter. He wasn't ill, he was wounded. He'd been in some dreadful affair with the police. He'd actually had a gun. He'd have gone to prison for ever if they'd caught him. I took the gun away from him, when I went. I have it now, if I ever want to shoot anyone up.' She laughed. The idea of having a gun was amusing, then.

'The only doctor I dared get was one of those placeless locums, always on the edge of being struck off. It was a change, living in a secret world that even the doctor didn't want to be seen entering. And then Peter was better, and I didn't want to live in that world any more. I'm not like you, Nancy, I have to be in the real world, where everyone wants as much light as they can get. In Peter's world, everyone wanted to hide in the dark. So I left him, and it was final.'

'Is that all?'

'What do you think?'

'I think your finality is unilateral. Peter won't join in the pact.'

'He didn't,' she said, but I was catching a plane. I had to leave her. I didn't hear the next bit about Peter until weeks later.

I was thinking of Peter now, as I stood idly in the bedroom. It wasn't his fault, she'd taken the gun away from him for his own safety. She'd probably made him promise never to use a gun again. I didn't even know if she'd kept the gun, perhaps she'd got rid of it months ago. Ordinary people don't possess guns, it prevents a lot of murder, when trouble breaks out.

I made the bed quickly, then I went to the drawer where I'd found the gun.

I arranged the underclothes by colour, as I usually kept them. I thought of the male hand that had held the gun at Sarah's heart, and saw the same hand, secretly, malevolently, hiding the gun where in the end it would turn against me.

I tried to see this hand. I remembered Peter's short, strong fingers with the fuzz of black hair, closing over innumerable beer glasses; I remembered them, years ago, closing around Sarah's throat. There was violence, in Peter's hands. He had knocked a man unconscious with them, to steal the money that would give Sarah a good time. Laurence's hands were round and soft; I saw him sweep the hair off his forehead; run a plump finger inside his shirt collar; turn the pages of a book with delicate care. Mike's were strong, narrow hands. He didn't waste them when he was acting. I saw the finger nails that had turned white when he had gripped my wrists. I was irrationally afraid when I remembered the scene last night. He had been acting out a melodrama for his own enjoyment. He didn't know I had a pathological fear of being held against my will. If he had known, he wouldn't have cared. I remembered what Sarah had said about the night she'd told him about Peter.

'I know he was only pretending he meant to kill me, but he enjoyed himself more than I did.'

That had been years ago, but I couldn't help thinking now that if Mike had handled the Sarah-Peter situation a little less ineptly, Sarah would be alive, and Donald and I would be safe and free.

I was thinking of hands, and I remembered, with sadness, how Donald had laid his hand on mine two nights ago, at the supper table. I had pulled my hand away to wave to Sarah Donald's hands were square and strong. They didn't look like the hands of an artist, and, whatever Mike said, they didn't belong to a weak or empty man.

Mike came lounging into the room. He didn't knock. He was playing the role of Master of the House. The fact that I, the other member of the cast, was acting in a different play, scarcely interfered with his enjoyment of his own part.

'I thought you were making breakfast,' he said.

'I'm going to clear up first.'

I picked up my bundle of wet clothes from the floor.

'You're not going to wash that lot before we eat?' he asked.

'You do think about yourself.'

'If you want to know, I was thinking that Sarah would never have worn a mixed lot of clothes, like that,' he said. 'If you prefer it, I'll whine about my sorrows, instead of making social conversation.'

'I dressed in a hurry,' I said, looking at the unrelated under-clothes I was holding. 'Did Sarah's things always match?'

'Always.'

'She wanted them that way, when we lived together and we were poor,' I said. 'You were happy together in the beginning, weren't you, Mike?'

'Most people like marriage, Act One.'

'I've never got past the prologue.'

'What about breakfast?'

'I'll get you some coffee now, and clean up the sitting-room.'

I emptied the ash-tray, and cleared away the bottles and glasses. Then I folded the blanket and sheets and put them in the bedroom cupboard. I stacked Mike's Sunday papers to-gether, then I brought in the coffee.

'Someone rang when you were out,' Mike said.

I put down the coffee pot. 'Was it Donald?'

'Whoever it was, rang off again. It might have been Donald, resenting my voice. But I don't know it was Donald, so would you like to go on and pour the coffee?'

I gave him some coffee.

'I'm glad you've managed to dry your hair,' he said.

'I haven't.'

'It looks lacquered now, instead of bedraggled.'

'Do you like women with lacquered hair?'

'I like women who look civilized. That's the first thing. And after that, I like them to be civilized. You're a dreadful little savage, Nancy. Once or twice last night you were ready to kill me. You're a very half-hearted member of society.'

'Would you like some more coffee?'

'Please. The trouble with you is you don't have any respect for authority. This affair now, you ought to be on the side of the police. But you've no consideration for them, no desire to help them, you'll lie to them, deceive them in every way, simply to help that Donald of yours. And yet when I suggest Peter—as the murderer—you won't accept it. Peter's been in prison, so he is automatically innocent. That's the way you think. The other trouble with you——'

'I don't wish to hear about any more of my troubles.'

I wanted to sit still and think, but Mike wouldn't let me. What he wanted was to lick out all my thoughts, like an ant-eater.

'What's this about a gun this morning?'

'Nothing about a gun.'

'You're going to tell me.'

'Mike, I don't want to discuss my affairs.'

'I'm staying in this flat to help you with your affairs.'

'You're staying here because you hope to have a chance of bullying Donald into going to the police.'

'What's this about a gun? Did he leave that with you as well?'

I jumped up and collected the cups and took them out to the kitchen. I put them in the sink and began to wash them. Mike followed me and stood behind me.

'Tell me about that gun. Why were you carrying a gun?'

'I wasn't.'

'You told me that you were, when you took a taxi.'

'Then I was lying.'

'You do a lot of that, don't you? How can I help you if you never tell me the truth?'

'You're not helping me. You're driving me mad.'

'Perhaps you'll tell the truth when you're mad. Turn round.'

'Oh, go away!'

He caught me by the shoulders and pulled me around, facing him.

'Take your hands off me!'

'Tell me about this gun!'

I shut my eyes, I wouldn't look at his face.

'Did Donald give you the gun?'

'What gun?'

He wasn't hurting my shoulders, but he wouldn't let go. When I tried to shake free, he tightened his grip. It wasn't painful to the flesh, but it drove my mind into the beginning of panic. It was an effort not to struggle and scream. I made myself stand still. I even opened my eyes.

'You must let me go!'

'When you've told me about the gun.'

My hands were free. I reached out quickly behind me and snatched something. It was only a cup; I was going to hit him with it, but he dropped one hand from my shoulder and caught my wrist instead. I let the cup fall.

'Now about the gun!'

I didn't say anything.

'So you can't tell me. Now I know that Donald gave it to you. That's the reason you won't tell me, isn't it?'

'No.'

I couldn't stand it any longer. I tried to hit at him with my left hand. He held me away so that I couldn't reach him.

'You can't do anything,' he said. 'So get on and tell me about the gun.'

Then, when it was almost too late, he let me go, and stood back, watching me.

'You frighten easily,' he said.

I turned away. I felt ill. I had to hold on to something. The sink kept me up.

'Donald didn't give me the gun. He's never had the gun,' I muttered.

'Nancy. Turn round.'

'No.'

'I won't lay a finger on you. I promise you.'

He touched my arm, and then took his hand away quickly.

'That was only one finger. It didn't count. Come and sit down.'

I couldn't move. It was as if I'd been swimming the Channel. I was half-way across, and now there was nothing left but to give up and drown.

'Am I allowed to push you,' Mike was saying, 'or shall I get a wheel chair?'

I was terrified of Mike. I could move after all. I went into the sitting-room, and he waited until I had sat down and then gave me a cigarette.

'I'd like one of my own.'

'Where are they?'

'In my bag.'

He fetched the bag and opened it and gave me one of my American cigarettes. He lit it for me.'

'Nancy, you'll get yourself too deep in this. If you go in deep enough, you won't get out again, can't you see that?'

I didn't answer.

'The police aren't very happy about you, already. If you give them anything else to go on, like a gun, it might be curtains for you.'

He waited. I was still getting myself back under control.

'They think you are the only person who ever was in that flat. You know they do. It's what you've made them think. And now I don't know what you're up to, about that gun. I don't know if you're trying to cover up for Donald again.'

I shook my head.

'I'm sorry about that, just now, Nancy. But I had to get the truth out of you somehow. I did try just asking you, first, but I never get an answer out of you. I didn't want to hurt you. I didn't even think I was hurting you. I only wanted to make you angry. You say anything, when you're angry.'

'I won't say anything to you.'

'Why not?'

'After last night. I know you'd tell the police.'

'I haven't told them anything yet. Nancy, can't you understand that if you know anything, the only safe thing is to tell them?'

'They wouldn't believe me.'

'When you begin talking about guns you make me so damned worried. I can't let you wander about London in the rain with a gun. If it was the right gun, and you were caught with it, you might—for God's sake, Nancy. You might be arrested for this murder.'

'I see that. I didn't see anything else much, this morning.'

'Why did you go out so early? Were you carrying that gun?'

'Let me alone, Mike.'

'I had to be asleep,' he said sourly. 'I stay here all night to watch you, and then I'm asleep.'

'You're not responsible for me.'

'Then who is?' he asked angrily. 'If it's Donald, he's not doing very well.'

'I'm responsible for myself.'

'Then you make a shocking job of it.'

'Mike, you don't want to get into trouble. There's going to be a lot of trouble round here. I think you ought to go.'

'What sort of trouble?'

'I think the police will come and search this flat again.'

'Why?'

I couldn't stand any more questions. I was overpowered by the desire to see Donald. I needed to talk to him. I couldn't keep everything to myself any longer.

'I'm going to ring Donald,' I said. I got up and rang the number. He wasn't there. I sat down again.

'Why?' said Mike, inexorably. 'Why will they search the flat again?'

'Someone will tell them to.'

'Who?'

'I wish I'd never tried to give you a warning. I wish I'd never begun this subject. All I said was I thought you should get out.'

'Who will tell them? Go on, Nancy.'

'Oh, I'll go on,' I said. I didn't have any resistance left.

'Who?'

'The person who hid the gun, I suppose. The police searched here yesterday before they took me to the station. And this morning I found the gun among my clothes.'

Mike shut his eyes. He rubbed one finger up and down his chin. He was the perfect picture of the actor thinking.

'Is that the only thing that's been planted on you?'

I told him about the letter that had been typed on my type-writer.

'Bad enough. Even serious. But it won't count for so much when you tell the police the real reason why you went to her flat.'

'I'm not going to tell them.'

'Then I am.'

'I'll never speak to you again.'

'You won't be speaking to me, much, anyway, if you're in prison for life. And I certainly won't go to see you. It would harm my reputation, wouldn't it? If I may be allowed to take the words out of your mouth.'

'Yes, it would harm your reputation.'

'So if I intend to go on speaking to you, I'll have to keep you out of prison. Now tell me what you did with the gun this morning.'

'I won't tell you any more. I'm going out.'

'Where to?'

'Stop asking questions, Mike. I'm going to see if I can find Donald.'

'If you mean to see him without me, I'll go to the police about him at once.'

'Mike, not yet. Let me see Donald first. I must speak to him. I can't stay with you here, waiting, as if it was a trap. I have to see him alone.'

'You're insane. You've got to be stopped. If the police get on the track of that gun, you'll be arrested. The time to tell them the truth about yesterday is now. If you're going out in search of fresh trouble, I warn you I'm going to tell them where Donald was on Friday night.'

'Mike, give me just a few hours. Give me the rest of today.'

'I don't want to be mixed up in this damned thing at all. If I have to get involved, I'll do it when it's some use.'

'Please leave it a few hours. I'll find him, somehow. We'll work out the truth. Then we'll go to the police.'

'You'll work out some lie that will land you in Holloway and let him wander off.'

'Listen to me. What difference does a few hours make? Give me until six, and you won't have to go near the police. We'll go ourselves, and you won't have to do anything. You needn't be mixed up in it at all. You'll be able to save your reputation and your moral position and everything else.'

'Thank you. You are very kind.'

I saw I had made him angry. It would be impossible now to persuade him. He would tell the police. The hunt would be up for Donald, instantly. He would have no chance of getting away.

'Mike, if only you'll give me today to find him, I'll do anything for you. Anything at all.'

'There's nothing you can do for me,' he said. His voice was just touched with the snarl of a dog who meets an enemy in the tiresome heat of summer. 'Nothing at all.'

'Very well.' I went into the bedroom and put on a coat. I took all the ready money I had, it was only about fifteen pounds, and put it with a cheque book and a passport in my handbag, the handbag I usually carried with that coat.

When I went back into the sitting-room Mike was reading one of the papers. He dropped it when I came in.

I remembered I had left my keys and cigarettes in the other handbag, the outsize bag in which I had carried the gun. It was lying on the chair next to Mike's. I walked over to get it. Mike picked it up.

'Do you want your cigarettes?' he asked politely.

He took out the packet and handed it to me.

'And my keys.'

He gave me the keys, and then I remembered the cloak-room ticket. I wanted to take it out, but Mike was still watching me.

'You're going to look for Donald, are you?'

'Yes.'

'Take an umbrella, this time.'

I went to the window, wondering about the rain, and looked

117

down the street. There was a car coming round the corner. I watched it slow down.

'There's a police car at the gate. You have about thirty seconds to get clear, Mike.'

He was at the door with his coat over his arm almost before I had finished speaking.

'How do I do it?'

'Go upstairs. The people above are away. Wait at their door for two minutes, then go down past here, straight out.'

I opened the door on the last word, then shut it softly behind him. I gathered the newspapers off the floor again, but when I heard the men on the stairs I moved near the door. I wanted to open it quickly so that they wouldn't have time to look up to the landing where Mike waited.

The bell rang. 'Regal calm!' I reminded myself, and opened the door.

Detective-Inspector Crewe was there, with two of his extras. I said good morning to them. They corrected me. It was afternoon, they said. They asked if they could come in.

'Enchanted!' I told them.

The Inspector had the easy manner of the casual visitor who would never enter without the welcome which he knew would never be denied.

I was wearing my coat, and he observed this. 'You were going out, Miss Graham? We've interrupted you?'

'Not at all.'

'I have a warrant to search your flat,' he murmured regretfully.

'You had that yesterday.'

'And I have it again today.'

I shut the door with a bang that I hoped Mike would hear from above. 'Are you going to search the place every day?' I asked.

'I hope not.'

'You must have found all the skeletons already. I haven't any new corpses in the cupboard.'

'You won't mind if we look?'

We had been through all this yesterday. I knew it wouldn't matter what I said, so, ungraciously, I said nothing. I sat down and watched the extras go into the bedroom. The Inspector stayed with me, looking idly round the room.

'You buy a lot of Sunday papers, Miss Graham.'

'I write for Sunday papers, sometimes.'

'For all of them?'

'Free-lances never give up hope.'

One of the extras came in and muttered. The Inspector listened, then turned to me again.

'I hear that some of your clothes are hanging up to dry. Surely you weren't out this morning in all that heavy rain?'

'I use what freedom I have left.'

'I wonder why you went out?'

'To buy the Sunday papers,' I said, shortly.

I was trying to keep my eyes off the heavy brown handbag. I couldn't understand now why I hadn't been bold enough to take out the cloakroom ticket in Mike's presence. I thought desperately of switching handbags. All I needed was a six months' course in conjuring, and an indulgent audience.

The Inspector's eyes were roaming. They met the brown bag, and moved up to ascertain that I carried another handbag. I thought, "One minute more, and I'll ask him to arrest me, and it will be over." His hand began to move towards the brown bag.

'Am I allowed to go out?' I asked quickly.

'You will be coming back?'

'Some time this afternoon.'

'Would you think it impertinent if I asked to see what's in your handbag?'

I gave it to him. He glanced through it, not searching properly. If I had taken the cloakroom ticket, I could have hidden it anywhere, inside the compact, between two pages of the cheque book. He wouldn't have noticed. He wasn't looking for a piece of paper. He had only wanted to make sure there was no room for a gun.

'Do you always carry a passport in your handbag, Miss Graham?'

'Yes. I go abroad a great deal. For my work. I'm half a foreign correspondent.'

'And half a novelist. That should add up to all of you, shouldn't it?'

'I think it does.'

'Some people have odd corners.'

'I'm very simple.'

'Do you mean straightforward?'

'I mean transparent.'

The extras came in again. They began to work on the desk. 'It's tiresome to watch this hunt-the-thimble when I'm not allowed to play,' I said. 'May I go out to lunch?'

'If you want to go out, please don't let us keep you. But you won't try to lunch in Paris, or Venezuela, even although you have your passport, will you?'

I took it as a warning that I would be stopped, if I did.

'No. Shut the door when you leave, will you?'

I went out of the door slowly and down the stairs and round the corner as fast as I could. I intended never to come back. I preferred to leave all my clothes, furniture, and general property, rather than answer one question about the cloakroom ticket. I still had my passport. Even if the ports were watched, there would still be some way across the channel.

9

I TOOK A BUS at the corner; there were other people waiting. I was too conscious of them all. They weren't just people, they were people who might give me away to the police, who might be employed by the police to watch me. I was a fox on the run; every dog was a potential foxhound.

On the bus I tried not to meet anyone's eyes. It was important, wherever I was, not to be noticed or remembered. I was convinced that when the police found the cloakroom ticket and collected the parcel I would be charged with murder.

When I got off the bus I walked quickly to the house where Donald lived. I knew he wouldn't be in, but I pressed the bell hopefully just the same.

When I had pressed it long enough I turned away. I walked along the dim street where, even when the sun shone, the shadows had no colours, because the greyness conquered all.

I didn't, temporarily, know what to do next. I had an hysterical vision of myself, walking around London, knocking at every door. When I had finished London I could begin on Sheffield, and Birmingham.

I thought of Sarah, in Birmingham. An undeveloped Sarah,

with hair coarsely waved; rouge and mascara and eye-shadow applied in the raw; and a passion for Peter that grew up with her. He had told her once that he would give her diamonds that would shine in the dark, and in the end he had done it. That was another thing I hadn't been able to tell the cold and logical officials. It had seemed too much like a betrayal of Sarah, and of Peter, too. If they had asked me, if they had said: Did your friend Sarah have any diamonds? Then I might have told them. But that was a question they hadn't thought of asking, and I couldn't voluntarily have laid the story under their stamping elephantine feet.

She'd told me the story when I came back from Budapest. It was winter. I spent the night in her flat, because my own was unheated and unprepared.

'I'm in trouble, Nancy,' she'd told me. 'I don't know what to do.'

'I'm sure you'll manage to do the wrong thing. Both of us are rather good at that.'

'I think I've done it already.'

'Something worse than before?'

'Much worse.'

'You've written the story of your life for a Sunday paper?'

'Do you think it's a joke?'

'I see that you don't. Has Donald come back? He's out of hospital, is he?'

'I think so. But it's not Donald. He won't come back.'

'Then it's something about Peter.'

'Yes, something about Peter. I'll tell you. I'd been out with a man called Lester. Charles Lester. He owns the Stock Exchange, or Lloyd's, or something like that. I'm taking him rather seriously.'

'The City must take him rather seriously, too, if he owns the Stock Exchange.'

'We'd been to the Lemon Grove. Do you know it? It's full of people looking at people who get their photographs in the papers. It's terribly gay and madly expensive.'

'Debland at last! Or is it just stocks-and-shares land?'

'Nancy, I want to tell you. Don't interrupt. I didn't ask Charles up for a drink when he brought me back. It was too late. I'm getting him accustomed to the idea that I don't ask him in, when we're alone. So I said good night at the entrance and went up the stairs and opened the door of the flat. When

I'd opened it, Peter pushed in behind me and shut the door. I thought he might have come—I thought he might mean to do something violent. I tried to get to the phone, but he wouldn't let me. He didn't say anything at first, that's why I was so frightened. Then he turned out the light. He said, not verbatim, I'm not sure exactly, but he said he'd got something for me—he used to promise me something to shine in the dark beside me. And here it was. Then in the dark he put this on my wrist.'

She stopped talking, and held it out to me. It was a bracelet, set with diamonds, the stones with the coldest glitter in the world. I'd never liked them. The diamonds on this bracelet were small, they were only seeds of trouble, but they could grow into a big enough crop to finish Peter, and perhaps Sarah, too.

'What happened then?' I'd asked her.

'And then he said he wanted to see us both shine in the dark together. So I said I'd sooner cut my throat than sleep with him again. And he said one day he'd cut it for me. There was —a lot of trouble. I told him to take the bracelet away. He picked it up and threw it in my face and went out. That's all about Peter.'

'It sounds enough. What are you going to do with the bracelet?'

'What do you think of it?'

'I've seen more diamonds in shop windows, and bigger diamonds in the Crown Jewels, but it's enough. It will serve.'

'Is that all you have to say? Isn't it beautiful?'

'I think diamonds are repellent. Put it away, in case the light shines out of the window into the eye of a policeman.'

She put it on her wrist, and turned it about, admiring it.

'How are you going to get rid of it?' I'd asked her.

'I think I'll keep it for a bit.'

'That's impossible, Sarah.'

'Why? It was given to me.'

'But you know it's stolen.'

'He didn't say he'd stolen it.'

'He didn't have to.'

'So long as I haven't been told it's stolen, I'm all right.'

'You can't keep it, Sarah.'

'You sound very moral. It's just that you don't like diamonds.'

'If it was Leonardo's Virgin of the Rocks, I'd still say you can't keep it. If anyone discovers you have it, you might go to prison.'

'I won't show anyone. I only wear it in bed. I put it on every night when I go to bed, and I lie and look at it, and it's on my wrist when I waken up, then I put it away. I don't show it to anyone. I haven't told anyone, but you.'

'Give it back.'

'Give it back to whom? I don't know where it came from.'

'Then give it back to Peter.'

'No. It's better for him not to have it. He'd do something desperate. He'd only be caught again.'

'I know what you can do. Send it to Scotland Yard.'

'I might do that. Soon.'

'Sarah, I've never tried to make you do anything before. But you've got to do this.'

'You tried to keep me from meeting Peter, that morning he came out of prison.'

'I was right, wasn't I?'

'You were right in the wrong way. You weren't thinking of me. You were thinking of Mike, the hero who couldn't do wrong.'

'We needn't quarrel about Mike now. It's the diamond bracelet, that's what we're discussing.'

'There's nothing to discuss. I'm going to keep it.'

'Sarah, I'm not thinking of Mike, or Peter, or Donald, or anyone but you. That bracelet has to go back. If you like, give it to me. I'll put it in a parcel and send it to Scotland Yard's Missing Diamond Department.'

'You don't understand. You don't know about when I was young, when I was ill, all those months in that place with my aunt. I used to lie back in bed and look at the dirty ceiling and the damp walls and think, it won't be like this always; one day there will be diamonds, the way Peter says. I used to hold up my arms and think of diamonds glittering on them, like this.'

She held up her arm and the diamonds caught more light than there was in the room. I couldn't bear the sight of them.

It was the last time she took me into her confidence, until the night before her death.

The diamond bracelet wasn't the reason that I stopped seeing her, although it might have been enough. I met Donald again. He was miserable, shaken: it seemed to me, half-destroyed.

Sarah had done this to him. For the first time in our history one friendship excluded the other. I fell in love with Donald, not quickly, but slowly and completely, in a way I had never known before. I couldn't, with any loyalty to Donald, continue to see Sarah. Friendship between women is a vulnerable thing.

I had been wandering along streets quite aimlessly, lost in the half-guilty memory of how I'd dropped Sarah at a time when she must have needed me. She had been loyal enough to me, at the end, when she had tried to keep Donald for me.

I saw a phone box. There was one thing I could do, it seemed to be the only thing, and that was to telephone everyone I knew who might know Donald.

I went to a sweet shop and bought a bar of chocolate with a ten shilling note, and asked for the change in pennies.

'It's a lot of change,' the man said sourly. 'That's all right,' I told him. 'Here's a bar of chocolate for your trouble.' He was a jaundiced man; I could see he hated chocolate.

I went back to the phone box and took out my notebook with the numbers and names. I thought I'd begin with the people we'd met at all those furious parties, four years ago—the Bills and Jills and Janets and Toms who had once been my dear friends, and Donald's, too. But it was as if a hurricane had mown them down. Jill had married, I didn't know her new name; Bill had emigrated to Canada; Janet had experimented in love with a random impartiality that had soon caused her disappearance from the London we knew; Tom had gone into a garret to write a book, and had never been heard of again.

There were the people we'd met at more recent parties, respectable cocktail parties, where everyone did such clever balancing tricks with conversation that it was kept right off the ground. One didn't even know the phone numbers of these people. There were the art galleries Donald had dealt with, but these weren't open on Sundays. There were a variety of people from the Diagonal Press who would all connect me instantly with the murder, and be intensely suspicious if I asked them about Donald. It seemed that I had collected a load of pennies for nothing, but in the end I thought of a dozen or so people we had both known well, and worked out a formula. It was important not to sound urgent: I didn't want any of my calls to be remembered.

I began with the friendly maniac who had played the bag-pipes, once, to ask if he was going to the Highland Games, in

124

Inverness. He said he played the flute, now; it wouldn't be heard at Highland Games. I said Donald was a flautist, too; did he know where Donald was? He didn't.

After that I found I could lie into the telephone quite easily. I told people I was going abroad again, could we meet for a drink; by the way, did they happen to know where I could find Donald, who was anxious to have a drink with us, too? They had no idea where he was.

I told others I wanted them to come to dinner, just a quiet little affair, details later; I wanted to get Donald, too, did they happen to know where he was?

They didn't.

I rang a painter called Les. I told him I'd been lunching with an American who bought pictures, who was interested in Donald's pictures; did he know where Donald could be found today?

He didn't, but he was duly sympathetic; it's not so easy to find Americans who buy paintings, whatever they say. He offered to give the American cider and tea-cake, which was all he had about the place, if I cared to bring him along. I said the American drank only Old-Fashioned's, which defeated him, because he didn't know what an Old-Fashioned was. He asked me, but I didn't know either, so I said it was a kind of brown whisky, with slices of cucumber. Then he suddenly remembered there was a painter called Martin who'd gone to Positano, and he had a distinct impression that this Martin had offered to lend Donald his studio. It was just a man called Martin. He didn't know if it was Martin What, or Something Martin, and he wasn't sure where the studio was, except it was definitely in Soho. I was ringing off when he remembered he'd seen Martin give Donald the key, four or five days ago.

That was the only lead-in I could get at all.

It was hopeless. I wouldn't find Donald, I would never find him again. He had left me, he wasn't to be blamed, he didn't know all the things that had happened since Sarah had been shot, he didn't even know that I had been to her flat.

If I was going to be arrested, I supposed I might as well be arrested in Soho as anywhere else. I took a bus that went along Shaftesbury Avenue, and got off and walked through. Soho was quiet. It was too early for the one thing, and the wrong day of the week for the other. The streets wore a lackadaisical air. I walked up and down them, acknowledging the difficulty of identifying Martin's studio, wondering about extra-sensory perception, wishing I was a witch.

I saw a woman I knew coming towards me, her name was Adeline. She was the kind of woman who frightened me; she looked like the vanguard of the enemy. She was the woman whose clothes were always right, she was lofty, with shocked eyebrows, she was manicured and pedicured and sandpapered at great expense; she had private information that the world had been made round so that she could fly to Jamaica for the winter. She was out of the top drawer, and I wished someone had shut it on her in infancy.

She called to me. 'Nancy, Nancy, have you heard about Sarah?'

'What about her?'

'She's been killed.'

'No!'

'Murdered.'

'Quite impossible. You've been drinking, Addie,' I said. 'You've been having one of those long, amorous, nisi-to-absolute lunches.'

Addie didn't like the reference. She was always trying to marry men who hadn't had their divorces made final.

'It's in the papers. One of her lovers killed her.'

'It happens to all of us.'

'What do you think about it, Nancy? Who do you think did it?'

It was pathetic she should have to ask me for anything, even information.

'I think it was that oil man from Mexico,' I said.

'What oil man?'

'That dark little millionaire, surely you met him, Miguel Orinoco; he came to London on a blonde hunt. He and Sarah —I shouldn't be telling you this——'

'I'm as secret as the grave,' she said.

'That's how we'll all be, in the end. He and Sarah—no, I can't tell you, I think it would be contempt of court. Keep it to yourself. Miguel Orinoco. A passionate man in oil.'

She looked confused.

'I'm meeting a friend,' I said quickly. 'Martin, he's an artist, with a studio round here. Do you know him?'

She didn't. She didn't know anything worth knowing. I said good-bye, and went on. I didn't think I was turning into a pathological liar, but I had to keep in practice, for the police.

I wandered into the back streets. Studios could be anywhere. In the end, after a wasted hour, I looked up and recognized the name of a street, and of a number. It was the house where Peter lived. I hadn't intended to see Peter, but I had come to the point of despair. I couldn't walk up and down and round and round any longer. I didn't know if I wanted to see people, or to hide from them. I stood in front of the building for a minute, then I trailed in.

It was a building where a lot of people lived. There was a respectable base of about twenty per cent.—waiters, small-time chefs, their wives and children—and a superstructure of around eighty per cent. of the plankton of the underworld; the lesser tarts; the failed gamblers; the men who had no visible occupation but to talk on street-corners. The superstructure would in the end sink down the building and drive out the respectable foundation. Peter, for instance, had already sunk to the second floor.

I didn't know which room he was in. I knocked at several doors, and was leered at in several languages.

When I found him he was relaxing in his shirt sleeves, as they say, and it was a long time since I'd seen anyone looking less relaxed. He had his shoes off, and I could see from the hollow in the grey blankets that he had been lying on the bed. He stood in the doorway and looked at me, red-eyed, sullen, and unwelcoming.

It was a dark brown room with a dark brown washstand. It looked as if a series of occupants had got rid of the dirty water by throwing it at the walls. There were cracks in the wood-work, and a smell of paraffin suggested a praiseworthy attempt to keep the vermin from coming out of the cracks. If I'd had time to spare, I'd have been sorry that he lived in such a place.

'Peter, I wanted to know if you were all right.'

'Thanking you. I'm all right.'

'Could I come in for a minute?'

'O.K.'

He stood aside, and I went in and sat down.

'Did the police——' I began timidly.

'They picked me up about a couple of hours after I left you. I don't know how they got on to me.'

'I'm sorry, Peter. It was that woman in the pub. She worked

127

for Sarah, she heard our names. Just after, she must have gone to the flat.'

'What I don't get, what I don't get at all, when you met me for that drink, you knew about Sarah?'

He was angry. He was ready to pass his anger on to someone. I didn't think I could endure another attack.

'Peter, I'm sorry about Sarah,' I said dismally.

'That's O.K.,' he said. He sat down on the edge of the bed, looking past me into whatever abyss he had hollowed out for himself.

'Peter, I'd have told you, but when I met you in the street I'd just seen her. I didn't know how to tell you. And that woman tried to get into the flat; I thought she'd seen me. I didn't know what to do. I thought you might be in trouble if you went in and someone saw you.'

'That's O.K.,' he said again. He roused himself a little. 'I've been in trouble, anyway. They picked me up—let's see, I saw you just after opening time—they picked me up about half after one. I was round the corner in the Spade-And-Harrow, fixing my story, but I hadn't got it fixed fast enough.'

'How long did the police keep you?'

'They kept me the whole damned night. They gave me breakfast this morning, and let me go at ten.'

'You'd have been all right if that woman hadn't heard me call you Peter.'

'Would I? What did you say to them about me? What did you tell them about me?'

He stood up and over me, threatening.

'Nothing. Except, when they kept asking, I said you'd been fond of her once.'

'Someone put them on to me. Why did they hold me all night?'

'It was my fault for being with you in the pub.'

'What did you tell them about me?'

I thought he was going to hit me. 'I didn't tell them about the diamond bracelet,' I said, and he drew away from me again.

'That's O.K. then,' he said, and sat down.

'I was in the flat—with her. I looked around. I wasn't looking for it, but I didn't see the bracelet. Do you think someone killed her, for that?'

'I don't think anything,' he said roughly. 'If they get on to the rocks, I'll be nicked, anyway.'

128

'You've had a bad night, Peter. But they've let you go.'

'They let me go because she was killed in her bed.'

'And you can prove something for the night?' I asked, thinking, in a panic, that everyone could prove something, everyone except Donald and me.

He began to walk up and down the room as if he was a prisoner already. 'I had a row with one of these Eyeties downstairs, Friday night, late on. A couple of his friends pulled me off, see. I had a few drinks on, so when one of them tripped me up, the bells went clanging in my head and I was out. They put me back in the room here on the bed. They took my key and locked me in. They didn't want too much conversation in the morning, so they sent up one of the kids to unlock the door. It would be half after seven, anyway, getting on for eight, and this kid took a look and I was still on the bed, knowing nothing. About breakfast this a.m., I began to remember the key being thrown at me, and something about catching a reach-me-down from an Eyetie. So they came along here and asked the Eyeties, and the kid, then they let me go.'

He had been walking up and down all the time he talked, but now he stopped in front of me, glowering.

'Satisfied?' he shouted.

'I think I'll go now, Peter.'

'You wait there, where you are. I want to know, what about you? What were you doing there?'

'She asked me—she asked me the night before—to come and see her.'

'So you found her. Then what? Then you just came away? What were you doing there?'

'Nothing, Peter,' I said, whispering. 'I just got frightened.'

'If I thought you did it—killed her—if I thought you were the one shot her, I'd do you in myself, now. Do you get that?'

'Yes.'

'O.K. then.' He sat down, staring angrily at me with his exhausted, reddened eyes.

'What did you come here for?' he asked suddenly.

'I don't know, I wanted to say how sorry I was, about Sarah, about you and Sarah.'

'You're sorry!' he said contemptuously. 'You're the one who talked her away from me, at the start, when that Laurence bloke was hanging around. She'd have come away with me then, but Nancy thinks this, and Nancy thinks that, and Nancy thinks not; that's what I used to hear. You hated my guts. You thought I wasn't good enough for her. She's got what's not good enough for her, now.'

His voice showed the extent of the disaster. Whatever kind of false hope he'd lived on had been crushed, shattered, obliterated for ever. He wasn't pretending, as Mike might have pretended; he was a man who had really seen the end of his world.

I had stopped being afraid of him. I could only see that whatever I felt about Sarah's death, he felt a hundred times more. Other men had loved her, but not as a permanent part of themselves. Peter now was incomplete for ever, it was if part of his brain had been cut away. Everyone else might somehow escape, but he was an integral part of the catastrophe. I saw, in the briefest flash, it was as if a fragment of magnesium had been lit in my mind, that in his life he had achieved a unity that Laurence and Mike and Donald would never have. Unity is an aesthetic conception: I'd always associated it with tragedy.

I understood there was no point in talking to him, or in trying to offer him sympathy.

'I'll go, Peter. I'd never have hurt her. You know that, don't you?'

'O.K., Nancy, O.K.'

'If you want any kind of help I can give, any time . . .'

He shook his head violently, trying to get rid of words.

I went out. I was sorry I had come, except with that unlikeable part of my mind that was always curious about people, anxious to uncover their emotions and make them partially my own.

In the street I stood hopeless again, submerged in misery that was entirely my own, and not borrowed. How pretentious that I should offer to help Peter, when I had lost all ability to help myself!

I couldn't go around Soho any longer. I wandered out of it, into Leicester Square, where a little Sunday afternoon life was going on around the cinemas. I looked at the people anxiously. I wanted to see someone I knew, now; anyone; I needed someone to help me. London was too big; even on Sunday, here, there were too many faces; they joined into a long pink tangle of tape that hummed and muttered past me; only occasionally there was an unscrambled voice.

'I said to the priest, can you marry us on St. Patrick's Day? Can you wait, he said, or is it urgent?'

I looked vaguely after the Irish girl who had spoken, but she had gone already; I would never see her face. That, and the word, urgent, that she had used, brought me to a stop. No one could ever be found in London, and if they were found they would be lost again. I'd given up the hope of meeting anyone I knew, when George suddenly detached himself from a cinema clump and came over to me.

George was a Bulgarian poet I had once known well. He used to take me to Lyons Corner House to laugh at the English *bourgeoisie*. I wished most earnestly now that I was a member of some such solid section of society.

'Nancy!' George greeted me as rapturously as if he'd thought of no one else for three years, and I reacted at once, put on a smile, pretended I had all the time in the world to speak to him. 'Come and have a drink, Nancy. I've a poem in my pocket I have been wanting to read to you.' He never went out without a poem in his pocket.

'I always meant to tell you, George. I don't understand Bulgarian. I never did.'

'But the music and the rhythm!'

'It's too early for music and rhythm. It's Sunday. The pubs aren't open yet.'

'We'll go to a cafeteria and laugh at the *petit bourgeoisie*.'

'You haven't changed at all, George.' I wanted to cry over the miracle: George hadn't changed. I felt as if I had spent the last three years in the bucket of a mechanical shovel.

'I will tell you the explanation of this poem. There is this girl, and it is raining. If the sun would go on shining she would love this man, but it rains and rains, and she says she goes, so he stabs her in the shoulders.'

'Well, it often rains. George, did I ever have a drink with you and a man called Martin? He paints pictures. I don't know how he earns a living, but he has a studio in Soho.'

'You mean Martin Pericale, the ponce?'

'I'm sure I don't.'

'There's a Martin who is a waiter in the Greek restaurant.'

'No. It doesn't matter.'

He looked at me, and his dark, lively face shaded into solemnity. 'Yes, but it does. You're not well, Nancy. Come with me for a little.'

'George, I haven't any time today to laugh at the *bour-geoisie*.'

'Come to my room and rest. We won't laugh at anyone.'

'I have to find this man, Martin.'

'I have a telephone. I'll read you my poem.'

'No.'

'Nancy, we'll telephone all the Martins in Soho.'

I went to his room, and when we were there he settled down, intensely serious, by the telephone. He knew innumerable Martins, and all the Martins he telephoned suggested other Martins, and one of the other Martins finally suggested a Martin who painted pictures in a studio in Soho, and taught in an art school for a living. He rang the number of this last Martin, and, after a few seconds, he put down the phone.

'There's a man in the studio, Nancy. He says that Martin is away.'

'Could you give me the address of Martin's studio?'

'Yes, Nancy, but you stay here a little while; you are very tired. It's sad that you don't understand Bulgarian.'

'It's a pity you don't write your poems in English.'

'Ah, but it's not only poems. You know I can't make love in English.'

George had a great bargaining instinct. He had done something to help me, and he was beginning to feel he had earned a scene. He liked having passionate scenes: he couldn't write poems without them. I was afraid of the scene, and the time it would take. We'd had so many scenes in the past. I had always laughed him out of them: he rather enjoyed the pleasures of frustration.

'Please, George, could I have that address?'

'You taught me much English once, Nancy, but never English of the right kind.'

'I'll learn Bulgarian, George, if only you'll give me Martin's address.'

'Nancy, for years I have had you in my heart.'

'The Bulgarian or the English side? There's supposed to be a curtain between them.'

He muttered something. 'You didn't understand? It was a line from my poem.'

'The bit where she stabs him? Oh, George, it's so late, it's after seven.'

'He stabs her,' George said.

132

'I do want that address now, please; I must have it.'

'I mean nothing to you, is that it, Nancy?'

I sat with my eyes shut. He talked for five minutes, working up, mainly in spirals, but with a few vertical dashes, and suddenly, through everything, I realized how enormously funny it was that he should sit there, so busy talking about love that he had no time to see I wasn't listening. I began to laugh, and George stopped instantly.

'So you insult me; you came here to laugh at me; you have no heart; you are not fit to love!'

'Give me the address, George.'

He went to the telephone book and tore out a page and crumpled it in his hand. He threw it at me. It gave him a lot of pleasure. I smoothed the page out, and found a Martin Wright on it.

I was so grateful, I kissed George quickly on the way out.

The studio was only seven or eight minutes' walk away from George's rooms. When I got there I rang the bell and kept my finger on it. There was no answer, so I stepped back and shouted: 'Donald! Donald!' It was too late for discretion, now.

The door opened. It was Donald. He stared at me for a moment and then caught my hands and pulled me inside. In the dark corridor we held each other. I had never needed anyone more. I felt I was home at last.

10

IT WASN'T UNTIL Donald took me up to the studio that I was able to see him. His face showed that he'd had a bad time, but he was smiling at me now, with relief and happiness.

'What happened to you, Nancy?' he said. 'I rang you all through yesterday. You didn't answer. I thought you'd cleared off, that you'd left me for good; and no wonder, either.'

'But you didn't ring today?'

His face changed suddenly. The happiness went right out of it, as if it had been drawn in sand and someone had scraped it off.

He let me go. 'I rang this morning. A man answered the phone, so I hung up.'

'That would be one of the police,' I said quickly. I was going to tell him about Mike, but not at this point.

'What was a policeman doing in your place?'

'I couldn't get rid of him. Donald, I'll tell you about that later, but now we've got to go. Have the police seen you?'

'No. I remembered about old Martin's being away; he told me I could use his studio, so I came here.'

'To paint?'

'I suppose I've just been waiting for the police to pick me up.'

'When did you leave my flat yesterday?'

'I don't know. I waited a long time. Then I thought they mustn't find me there, so I came away.'

'Hold me for a minute, Donald, then I'll tell you everything.'

I rested in his arms. I felt as if I'd completed some dangerous mission, and was in sanctuary at last. I wanted to stay where I was, with him. It would have been all right meeting a firing-squad that way, but there wouldn't be any firing-squad; the processes of the English law would be more like a prolonged disease.

I stood away from him. I walked round the room, staring at canvases that had no meaning for me, and told Donald quickly about everything that had happened, with the exception of my session with Mike.

'So now we have to go, Donald. We have to get out of the country. They may be looking for you already.'

'But you said you didn't tell them I was there, in the flat, that night'

'I like this,' I said, staring at a painting. It was an abstract design, it looked like green ropes twisted into some sand dunes, and never getting out. 'No, I didn't tell the police, Donald.' Later on, I'd think of the way to explain that I'd had to tell Mike.

'Donald, I've been doing the wrong thing all through. I've never had time to think. Even now, there isn't much time for it, we have to go. It's no good trying London Airport, or Dover; we have to go somewhere small. If we took the train to Plymouth, we could get to a fishing port I know, where the French fishing boats often come in. Once, when I was about ten, my father took me to France that way.'

'That's a peculiar way to travel.'

'It was cheap,' I said vaguely. 'I think my father was in a hurry. That's how I got the job on the Diagonal Press in the first place, when I was twenty, because I knew about travel.'

'How did you know?' Donald asked, sitting down, as if we'd been allowed an extra ration of time. He was suffering as much from inanition as I was.

'I think you ought to pack something, Donald. I was given the job as assistant to one of their travel columnists. We'd seen very different sides of the same countries, but we worked out an average. Five days' splash in a four-star hotel, two cheap nights in the furnished room of a second-hand shoe-shop, and a quick flick down to the South of France in the back of a meat lorry. Do you know the meat lorries will take you from Les Halles to Marseilles for one thousand five hundred francs?'

'Nancy, you're making it up.'

'It's the truth. When we get to Paris we'll go south on a meat lorry, unless you have plenty of ready money.'

'I have about twenty pounds.'

'Then it's fishing boats and meat lorries for us, until I get a job in Italy. Or do you think we should try North Africa? What about Morocco?'

'For God's sake, Nancy, we can't go like this.'

'Donald, we have to. We can't cash cheques and we must get out of England. Have you got your passport?'

'No.'

'We'll manage without a passport.'

I was trying to make it sound urgent, but Donald didn't get up.

'Why do we have to go?'

'I've tried to explain. They'll arrest you, and me too.'

'But, Nancy, if you cleared up in her flat, I don't see——'

'I'll tell you everything I mean if only we can get on a train to Plymouth. Donald, don't you trust me?'

He put his hands on my shoulders and pulled me to him. He didn't have to say anything in words. I'd had enough of words, too. All my words were wrong. They'd been wrong all day, and all yesterday, too. When I was close to him everything was right again.

He let me go, and I said: 'Now we have to fix up about that train to Plymouth. There's an eight-ten. It's not what you'd call fast. It gets in about one.'

'I don't want to catch it, Nancy. I've made enough trouble

135

for you. If the police are coming, I might as well wait here and let them come.'

'Get your coat or pyjamas or razor or whatever you have here. I'm not going to have you arrested and tried, and I'm not very keen on it for myself, either.'

'You won't be charged with murder,' he said.

'There's that gun.'

'I'll confess to the murder myself before I see you charged.'

'You'll come to Plymouth and on to France and live happily ever after.'

'Go without me, Nan. I'm no good to you.'

'I'll ring for the taxi now.'

While he packed the few things he had, I kept ringing for taxis. The numbers didn't answer. They were engaged. Sunday was a bad night.

'We'll pick one up in the street,' I said.

I ran down the stairs in front of him into the street. It was a restaurant area; there ought to have been a taxi somewhere, but there wasn't.

There was a car by the kerb. Two women were sitting in it, one with a guide book. 'It says this is London's Little Bohemia,' she said, staring in patient wonder at a nocturnal blonde who was doing an early turn of duty in the doorway of a shuttered shop.

'Oh, no, excuse me,' I said politely. 'London's Little Bohemia is down the street and first to the left. You can't miss it.'

They thanked me. I started to walk on, and turned, struck by an afterthought.

'You shouldn't go without looking at the mediaeval building across the road,' I said. 'It's one of the show places of England.'

We all stared across the road. There was a shop that sold kitchen equipment; a few shuttered windows; a pub that looked late Victorian to me, but the light was bad.

'It was the only Trappist monastery in Central London,' I said. 'They're all there, in effigy. I don't know if you're allowed to take photographs on Sunday.'

They thanked me again. 'It won't set us back more than five minutes, Rose,' one of them said. She was wrong. With interested smiles, they left the car.

I looked round. There wasn't a taxi or a policeman in sight.

'Get in, Donald!' I said.

'Nancy, what are you doing?'

I got in and started the engine. I had no time to watch his reactions, but he followed me in.

'Don't worry, Donald. It's only a kind of hitch-hiking. I'll leave the car at Paddington, right in the middle of a crossing. They'll get it back. The adventure will add spice to the tale of their travels.'

'You can't do a thing like this.'

'I can't undo it now. With luck, we'll still catch the train.'

We had the luck. We even had time to buy tickets and find the evasive platform, and we still got on the train with most of a minute to spare.

There was no one in the compartment, except for an old man dozing in the corner. I sat next to Donald, and when the train had run out of London, he put his arm around me and I slept against his shoulder. I woke up once or twice and looked at his face. It was always the same. He was staring straight ahead with an exhausted, almost stunned, concentration. When he felt that I had stirred and wakened, he pulled me back against his shoulder, but without looking at me.

After an hour or two I woke completely. We hadn't bothered to pull the blinds, and I could see the darkening trees skimming past. When we went through the small towns, the lights were on in all the houses, the curtains were drawn on safe people living safe lives. Not one of them could have enjoyed safety as much as I did, leaning against Donald's shoulder in the dark, aware that the world was turning us away from the sun, that we were shut in a little moving box, close together, being pushed away by the past and pulled by the unknown; sheltering each other and rejecting everyone else; two people not afraid of the dark because they were one.

The train stopped at a place, a biggish station. We must be nearly half-way there, I thought regretfully; but, impossibly, it was Plymouth.

The journey was the only thing I'd enjoyed since Sarah's death, but it was more than that, it was the happiest journey of my life. It was far away from the surface of events, it was like being embraced under water by another diver.

It was nearly one o'clock; there was no chance of going to the fishing port that night.

We didn't have much money, so we looked for a cheap hotel.

'How do we check in?' Donald asked me. It was the first time he'd spoken for hours.

'Uncle and niece?'

'Would they believe that?' he asked. He was far away in some dream of his own.

We signed on, at my second suggestion, as Mr. and Mrs. Wright. He didn't know what he was doing.

When we went upstairs we were alone, with time to spare, at last. There was nothing between us and total happiness but a little conversation, but that was enough.

It was an ordinary hotel bedroom, grimmer than most, and cleaner than many. It had the cheap brown wardrobe blocking the chintzy wallpaper; the basin with the crack; the gurgle in the pipes; the bedside lamp with the shade that fell off. It was the kind of room I knew well. I had stayed alone in it, or in a local version of it, all over Europe. This time I was with Donald. It was different from any other room in the world.

He sat down on the bed. In these rooms, no one ever sits on the chairs.

'Do we really have to leave England?' he asked.

'Oh, yes.'

'It's going to look bad, running away.'

'Call it escape. That sounds better.'

'Why do we have to go?'

'You are the only man from her past known to have been in her flat,' I explained, patiently.

'I thought you said it wasn't known. I can't see why they should be watching the ports for me now.'

'Darling, you were actually there when she was killed.'

He looked sullen and puzzled, like a boy given the wrong questions in his trigonometry paper.

'But if they don't know that, then why——'

'Donald, I'll have to tell you. I was terribly indiscreet last night. I let someone else know, in a kind of a way.'

'What kind of a way?'

'I'd been in the police station for about eight hours. When they let me go and I was alone, I didn't want to be. I was glad when Mike came.'

'Mike!' he said with distaste.

'I thought he wanted to talk about her. But he staged an act. I don't know how it was. I just told him—about you.'

'I see.'

'I don't think you do.'

'Then explain it again.'

138

I was silent. It wasn't my fault that a woman can never explain honestly to one man the scene she has had with another. The truth, which made it impossible to tell the truth, was that Mike had worked on my emotions, and I wasn't supposed to have any emotions but those I kept bottled up for Donald's exclusive refreshment.

'You were always very fond of Mike,' he said.

'Not very.'

'Sarah used to say you were.'

'I'm not fond of him now. I don't even want to talk about him.'

'But you talked to him about me. That was a very odd way to behave.'

'I think so, too. I suppose it was hysteria. Let's forget Mike.'

'Yes, we'll forget Mike.'

He got up and went to his suitcase, and turned it round, and put it down again. 'I want to know why you told him.'

'He worked up a scene. First I was sorry for him, then I was frightened, then I was so tired I had a black-out, then he kept on talking about you, and I told him.' It was the nearest I could get to the truth; it was a serious effort to tell the truth, but Donald didn't like it.

'When I telephoned this morning, it wasn't a policeman who answered, was it? It was Mike?'

'Yes.'

'I see.'

'No, you don't. He wasn't there because of me. He was waiting there to see you. He slept in one room and I slept in another. You slept in her sitting-room the night before, didn't you? That's how we got into this trouble.'

'Yes. That's how I got into this.'

'Are you suggesting that I needn't have come in?'

'Well, need you? If you were going to tell Mike what you did, it would have been better not to do it at all.'

It wasn't obvious to me then, but later I saw that at this point I felt I had earned some gratitude, which should be paid. Accountancy is a system that should be confined to offices.

'What exactly did you do when you went to her flat?'

'I swept up some of your cigarette ends, and glasses, and blankets, and little bits of paper with phone numbers on, that you'd left to help the police. And I wiped off your finger-prints and left some of my own by mistake.'

139

'You take murder very calmly.'

'If that's what you think.'

'But you do. She's dead. You don't seem to realize that.'

'I've had it rubbed in.'

'All right. You've had this brush with the police and I've had an easy time. But she's dead. You don't understand that basic fact. Damn it all, it's not decent. You and Mike together the night after. And now here, with me.'

I got up and walked out of the room. I went down to the desk. There was no one there. I put my finger on the bell and kept it on.

After about five minutes a weary man in a half-buttoned uniform appeared.

'I want a room.'

'It's too late,' he said, blinking. 'We're shut.'

'I'm staying here already. I want another room.'

He blinked faster. 'Something wrong with the one you're in?'

'Yes. My husband's in it. I'm divorcing him. Now.'

The man retired into self-protective stupidity. 'You can see the office in the morning. We got no other rooms tonight. The office has gone to bed.'

'Then I'll sleep down here. On one of these chairs.'

'You can't do that.'

'Just try to stop me.' I went and sat down in a chair. He hung around for a bit, then he gave up. I told him to put out the lights again, and he put them all out, except for a faint light over the door, an indication that this was an hotel, although no one would be allowed in.

I sat in the chair for hours. There wasn't any chance of getting to sleep. I clicked over my circular chain of thought like a rosary, round and round again.

When there was a little glimmer of dawn, and the birds, if they'd had anything to sing about in Plymouth, would have been clearing their throats, Donald came down. He was stumbling all over the place, trying to get out. He found a light switch, and saw me.

'I thought you'd gone, Nancy.'

'That's what I've done. I've gone.'

'You mean you're going to leave me?'

'I've left you.'

'I thought that might be it.' He sat down on the chair beside me. Perhaps he was waiting for a conversational opening, so

140

that we could discuss international whale fishing, or England's chance in the next Test Match.

'Nancy. Look at me. Just look at me, and I'll know you're listening. I'm a fool, but it's because I've always expected you to leave me. You see, Sarah left me, though she knew I meant to kill myself if she went. She left me for that—for Peter. She didn't care whether I died or not. She simply left me.' He still sounded incredulous.

'People do leave people, Donald, especially if the people are men and women.'

'But I loved her!'

'No one likes being left. But you shouldn't spend all your time waiting for it to happen.'

'And leaving me for Peter! The man who murdered her, in the end.'

'He didn't. I saw him today. I'm sure he didn't.'

Donald was alert at once. 'Peter! You saw Peter! Really, Nancy—where did you see him?'

'Guess what! I went to his room without a chaperone. And if you'd like to know something else, when I was looking for you I had a long private session with George. You remember George? He ran in sex for Bulgaria, at the last Olympics. If you want to kill yourself and me with this jealousy, I can give you all the poison you need.'

He put out his hand and touched mine.

'What I need is you, Nan. I'm a monster, a vile monster, I don't know why I say these things to you. You don't want me now, you couldn't; I know what you feel about Sarah, but don't sit here hating me. Come upstairs, we won't quarrel any more.'

I let him take me up. He made me lie down on the bed, and stood beside me, watching me anxiously. I didn't have any emotions left; I felt like a piece of cotton-wool that had been crushed in an avalanche, but I could see he didn't want to hurt me. I wasn't the one he was trying to destroy; he had no savagery in him, except for himself.

He brought water, and sponged my face, and dried it carefully, and I began to revive.

He was gentle and kind. It was his bad luck he had to be in love with someone like myself, who was hard enough to see, even now, something funny in a situation where I couldn't sleep with a man who wanted me, in case I forfeited his respect.

When I woke in the morning, my head was resting on

141

Donald's arm, and he was lying fast asleep beside me. He had taken off his coat and tie, and he looked cold and white. I put my head against his chest and listened to the beating of his heart. I remembered about the row last night, but it wasn't important. What mattered was that there shouldn't be another row, that I shouldn't offend his simplicity again. I wondered if there was any way of making myself into one of the rector's daughters, whom he ought to have married. I'd have liked to live in the country in gardening gloves, worrying about Old Blob, the odd-job man.

The rector's daughter would never have got herself into my position; she wouldn't have slept beside a man who had taken off his tie; there would be some conventional ruling about that.

The rules were easy enough to learn. Donald knew them without effort; although when I thought of his affair with Sarah I could see he hadn't always lived by them. His point was that women should keep to the rules. I knew he'd like it better if I didn't sleep with him before we were married. I never had. I'd wanted to make sure he was completely over Sarah, and as totally in love with me as I was with him.

I remembered the first time I'd met him after he came out of hospital. He was trailing along the street in one of last week's shirts. The only thing fresh about him was the morning's hangover. He didn't look as if he'd ever belonged to a pony club, or strolled about under the elms winning cricket matches. He was too shy to talk much to me, at first, but soon we were on a course of black coffee that lasted for months.

This morning was the first for a long time that I had seen him unshaven. I rubbed his cheek with the back of my hand. I wanted to stay beside him until he woke up, but that would be against the rules. We'd get married in France tomorrow. For the present it would be better to try and make myself look more like an English Rose.

I slipped off the bed and undressed and washed quickly. I opened Donald's case. He had a clothes-brush. I did what I could for my suit, and then dressed again. I put some of his shaving cream on my shoes—it was a trick I'd learnt from my father—and polished them with a piece of newspaper.

I had no hair-brush, but I worked on my hair for a long time with a comb, and made up my face with great discretion. When I turned round, Donald was awake and watching me.

'Nancy, come here!'

'Oh, no, Donald. I'm sure you'd sooner be alone to get dressed. I'll go out and get the papers.'

'I'm not specially undressed. Come and say "good morning".'

'No. I'm going to order breakfast.'

'Stay here and talk to me while I shave.'

'Oh, no, Donald!'

'Nancy, what's up?'

'I've joined the Plymouth Brethren.

'You'll play hell with their meetings.' He stood up suddenly and caught me. 'They don't like women with lipstick.'

When he let me go he was very serious. 'I've kissed off the lipstick. They'll let you join, now.'

'Would you sooner I didn't wear make-up? I won't, if you don't like it.'

'What the hell's got into you? I like you as you are, except for the prim look you're wearing. I'd like to do something to shake you up.'

'Don't touch my hair, Donald. I spent hours doing it.'

'Your hair's all right. Did you have secret hair curlers?'

'I don't use them.'

He turned away. He was unhappy again. He began to rub shaving cream over his face. 'Sarah used to set her hair every night,' he said.

"Damn Sarah!" I thought, exactly as if she hadn't been dead. Then I remembered, and for a few seconds I was as miserable as Donald.

'She was wearing them when she let me in that night. And when we were talking; she didn't take them off.'

'It must have been just like old times,' I said.

'What do you mean by that?'

'Only that you must have seen her set her hair a hundred times. You lived with her, and you're not going to let me forget it, are you? When you touch my hair, you wish it was blonde, instead of dark; when you look in my eyes, they're the wrong colour, too. What do you think of when you kiss me?'

'You're indecent, Nancy. A man doesn't discuss that kind of thing.'

'It's sacred,' I agreed.

He finished shaving and washed the lather off his face, staring moodily into the glass.

'Are we ever going to stop quarreling?' I asked, in despair.

143

'I can stop you any time I like,' he said. It was true enough. The moment he touched me, the row was over. I knew he felt the same way.

'I've ruined your face.'

'I'll make it up again.'

'And I'll rub it off any time I choose.'

We went down to breakfast very cheerfully. Waiters were already setting the tables for lunch, although it was only half-past ten. They held a conference against us before they brought the reboiled coffee.

We discussed our plans quietly. Donald wasn't convinced that a French fishing boat would take us. When I described the sleeping quarters to him, from memory, he became set against it. He thought it wasn't the place for someone like me. I still thought it was a good idea.

'Anyway, darling, we're in Plymouth. We could steal a motor-boat from the Navy,' I said, just for the pleasure of seeing the consternation sweep over his face and away again as he realized the alarm had been false.

'I don't think you respect even the Navy,' he said. He actually sounded shocked.

'I'll bet you have an uncle who was an admiral,' I said.

'A commander,' he corrected me. 'I don't see anything funny in that. You have uncles, too, haven't you?'

'I had an uncle. I think he died in prison in Budapest. I.N.T.'

'Politics?' he asked cautiously.

'Nothing so respectable. Illicit Narcotics Traders.'

'Nancy!'

'You'd believe anything about me, wouldn't you? Darling, you'll have to get used to the idea I don't have a family background. I don't even have an uncle buried in Budapest. And I've never been to a Hunt Ball in my life.'

'Lots of people haven't been to Hunt Balls.'

'I'll invent a Hunt Balled past, if you'd like me better that way, And I'll go mayfly fishing with your uncle every night.'

'He'd like that.'

I had asked the waiter for some newspapers, and he came in now, resentfully, with a small selection. I handed Donald The Times. Whether he read it or not, I felt he looked better with The Times, and I myself opened a lesser paper. I looked around quickly. It was lucky we had come down late to breakfast.

144

There was no one else in the room. I hoped the waiters had been too busy to read.

I had always been rather a small-time journalist, doing small, irregular jobs for papers with small circulations. I might have been gratified to find myself on the front page of one of the giants. It was like one of these fairy tales where the wish comes true the wrong way round, and you'd sooner you hadn't wished at all. I was on the front page, all right, with a good double-column picture. *Missing Witnesses in Editress Shooting*, the headline said. And the caption: "Miss Nancy Graham, journalist, and intimate friend of Sarah Lampson, who was found shot in her flat on Saturday morning. Miss Graham, who has been missing from her own flat since lunch-time yesterday, is believed by the police to be in a position to provide them with evidence which may help them in their enquiries. The other missing witness is Donald Spencer, artist. It is believed that both Miss Graham and Mr. Spencer may be on holiday . . ." The rest of the double column went on, all about nothing much.

"Damn Mike!" I thought. I thought far worse than that. I thought things that are scarcely ever said aloud, even in German. If he had heard me there would have been no question of his ears burning, they would have been melted, atomized.

Donald had dropped The Times and was looking at me. I handed him my paper. He had a delayed-action shock when he saw my picture, but when he read on and arrived at his own name, he took the whole impact.

He put down the paper. 'I don't know what my father would have said!'

'Good Gracious!' I suggested.

'And there's my mother.'

'No. There are no fathers and mothers in this,' I said. 'They combed your hair and tied your shoe-laces and gave you cod liver oil and did their duty by you long enough. You're out on your own now.'

'And God knows what my grandfather will say if he sees it.'

'People don't have grandfathers nowadays, do they?' I asked. I wasn't in a mood to discuss his family. I knew we had to move quickly. I took the paper, and folded it with my picture inside.

'My grandfather doesn't like scandal.'

'It seems that no one in this case is in a position to bear scandal, except me. Donald, we have to pay and get out of here. I don't think the fishing boat will do now. It's too leisurely.'

'But if anyone recognizes you . . .'

'I'll buy a scarf and tie it under my chin. I'll look different. It's lucky there isn't a photograph of you. It would be awkward, travelling together, if there was. Now look, Donald, you have to be someone else, not Donald Spencer, if you're asked. Who would you like to be? What about Raymond Buckingham? That's a good name.'

'I don't understand you, Nancy.'

'If you have anything in your pockets, any old letters, driving licences and so on, take them out and tear them up. I'll get some envelopes and some paper, and address a couple of letters to Raymond Buckingham, Esq., with some Dear Raymonding inside. If anyone asks who you are, and you want to prove it, just fumble through your pockets and bring out the letters. I'll be someone else, too. Katie Curzon, I think. Now, you pay off here, and get out. I'll meet you at the station. We'll take a train to Bristol. We can get an Aer Lingus plane from Bristol to Dublin. While I'm waiting for you at the station, I'll telephone Bristol for the time of the plane. We don't need passports to Ireland.'

'But Nancy, I'm not sure——'

I got up. 'I'll meet you at the station,' I said again.

I had nothing to pack. I had nothing to carry but my handbag, and my coat, because it was a pleasant morning. I bought a head-scarf, and tied it hideously under my chin. Then I bought two different kinds of paper. I was sorry I hadn't more time to look at Plymouth. I went on to the station. The worst of it was the long-distance call from the public telephone box, but I got Aer Lingus at last, and found there was a plane at three-twenty. I went out and looked anxiously for Donald. A train for Exeter was leaving in ten minutes, and I was assured there would be a connection for Bristol. I'd had that kind of assurance before, but, at the worst, there would be another plane.

Donald came along in a leisurely manner about five minutes later. He didn't seem to suffer from travel fever. We caught the Exeter train with plenty of time in hand, and in Exeter station buffet, over undrinkable cups of tea, I wrote the letters

146

that were to give us new, nebulous personalities. One of the letters to Raymond Buckingham was a rather touching little love note, from Sukey, and the other was curt and stiff, from his grandfather. I remembered about the postmark and stamp at the last moment, so I tore the top of one envelope away, and gave him grandfather's letter without the envelope. It was signed Geoffrey Buckingham. I thought that was fair enough. I imagined him as Sir Geoffrey Buckingham, Bart.

We travelled in different compartments to Bristol, and at the station we took different taxis to the airport.

I went into the reception office a minute ahead of Donald. A pleasant girl told me the fare to Dublin. It was six pounds something. I was worried for a minute in case I didn't have it, but when I opened my handbag it was there. I was counting out the notes when I developed a nasty feeling that I was being scrutinized. I turned round, and it was true enough. I knew a plain-clothes man by now, when I saw one, and in this case I saw two.

'Miss Graham?' one of them asked politely.

I picked the money up again from the desk. I would have liked to make some last-minute memorable remark, like an admiral: "There's something wrong with our damned passengers, today," for instance, but I didn't have the nonchalance. I just said: 'Yes, I'm Miss Graham,' because there didn't seem any point in pretending to be Katie Curzon, when I had my own passport in my handbag.

They went through some sort of formula, about evidence, and London, and did I object? I scarcely listened. I'd learnt already how much weight my objections carried, with the police, and I was trying to will myself not to look for Donald. He was in the office already, I knew it.

'I don't mind going back to London with you,' I said loudly to the plain-clothes men. 'Not if it's important.'

Donald went past us and up to the desk. 'I've a seat reserved by phone,' he said. 'My name's Buckingham. Will you look it up?'

I went out of the door with the plain-clothes men, and then into the car that was to drive us back to London. I had brought it on myself. I was a fool. The police knew that the first thought of any criminal dolt without a passport was to get to Ireland and then think out the next move. Bristol Airport was an obvious place to watch.

147

It seemed bad luck that I should have had to admit who I was, precisely because I did have a passport.

Most of the way back in the car I thought of Donald. I was surprised that he had displayed so much resource.

II

AT HALF-PAST FIVE that afternoon I was in the police-station again, in the room that I had been in two days ago. I was waiting to see Detective-Inspector Crewe. It was a circular form of nightmare, but on this, the second time round, the circle cut deeper. I felt like a piece of soft metal under a machine tool in a factory. The diamond-hard point would spin around and around me until the segment dropped neatly out of my brain into the Inspector's hands.

When I had been here on Saturday, I'd had two simple aims: to conceal the fact that Donald had slept in Sarah's flat; and to deny that I had been there at all. I had succeeded in the first and failed in the second. Now, two days later, I was in an infinitely worse position. There was the gun; there was my attempt to escape from England. Worst of all, they knew about Donald. I realized, with the faintest stirring of hope—it was as if hope was an unfeathered bird trying to squeeze out of a hard shell—that they had no proof even now about Donald. They would have Mike's word for it, and mine against it. Donald himself was safely away.

Detective-Inspector Crewe came in now, and said "Good afternoon". He was full of regrets that they'd had to call me back from Bristol. He seemed anxious for my comfort—he was a very well-mannered man. I was offered tea again, and a bun.

'I'm sorry,' I said, 'permanent out-patients like myself get past the point where they can be placated with a cup of tea.'

'But surely you prefer to be an out-patient, Miss Graham?'

'It might be more restful inside,' I said weakly. For a minute I almost believed it. This was a dangerous state of mind. To conceal it I opened my handbag, looking for a cigarette. The packet was empty. It was too great a blow. Everything was

148

against me. I was filled with irrational self-pity; not about the gun, and the police, and Donald; but because the packet of cigarettes Donald had bought me on Friday night was finished.

I took out the empty packet and crumpled it in my hand. It was something to be thrown away; it was like the last relic of the simple past. At any moment now I would begin to cry, and the inspector would sit, watching me curiously. He probably had a tear-gauge, to measure the exact emotions of hysterical witnesses. Perhaps criminals could be identified by their tears, as they could by their finger-prints.

'Would you like a cigarette, Miss Graham?'

'I'm sorry. I only smoke American,' I said, as I'd said to so many people in commonplace circumstances. "I only smoke American." It was affectation, and habit, but affectation and habit were the two things I lived by; I would have to drop both of them, in prison.

'I have some American cigarettes here.' He held out the packet. He was too kind. I had to be careful that his kindness didn't soften me, didn't make me try to respond by being kind to him, and telling him the truth.

He lit the cigarette, and we sat and looked at each other through the smoke, two adversaries disguised as ordinary people.

'Miss Graham, we've brought you back from Bristol because we received some information that throws light on your presence in Miss Lampson's flat two days ago. The information is that a friend of yours, a Mr. Donald Spencer, was in the flat at a relevant period, and that when you discovered this, you went there to remove all traces of his—occupation. Is this correct?'

'No.'

'Is that all you have to say?'

'I'd like to know who your informant was.' The question wasn't necessary. I knew it was Mike; I'd have liked to kill him for it.

'That's not a thing I'm obliged to tell you.'

'It doesn't matter. It's just that I dislike spies. And whatever he told you is untrue.'

'It does provide an explanation—the first we've had—to account for your presence there, and for your very peculiar actions. Why did you cover up for Donald Spencer? Is he your —are you in love with him?'

149

'No.'

'We have information to the contrary.'

'I'm the only one who'd know whom I was in love with.'

'We have heard—from various sources—all about this Spencer's past connection with Miss Lampson. Now, if we suppose, what is not necessarily true, that Donald Spencer is criminally involved, then your own position will be very difficult. These difficulties can be reduced, they can even be removed, by co-operation with the police. Would you like to tell us the truth now?'

It was becoming impossible to lie convincingly. 'Donald wasn't in the flat,' I said. It sounded like a recitation, delivered from a distant platform.

'Wasn't he?'

'Why don't you ask him, instead of me?'

'Oh, we will, you know.' Listening to the inflection of his voice, I was sure they couldn't ask him, they hadn't caught him. He'd got away; perhaps he was in Ireland already, and safe.

'Until you do, you'll just have to take my word for it, he wasn't there.'

'Then who was? Who killed her? Let's have your suggestions, Miss Graham.'

'I haven't any.'

'Was it your other friend, the man you had a drink with, so soon after? Was it Peter Abbott?'

'No, it wasn't him. I'm sure of that.' My head cleared suddenly. I began to think again, in a logical manner, the way people ought to think, not emotionally. 'I can prove that,' I said firmly, 'if you'll tell me first—is it true you had him here before two o'clock on Saturday, and kept him till the next morning.'

'Unfortunately, that's true. We don't usually hold people so long, but he has a criminal record; we had a lot of questions to ask.'

'Then you see, this gun, you know about the gun—I suppose you thought I'd been hiding it, but it wasn't mine—it was put in my flat. It was planted there; it must have been after you searched on Saturday—was that three o'clock?—and before Sunday morning, because I found it then. So you see, it couldn't have been Peter. He was with you all that time. He couldn't have been hiding the gun with me.'

'You're asking us to believe that this gun was hidden in your flat by the murderer?'

'That's the truth.'

'And that he hid it with you after we searched your place on Saturday?'

'It was among my clothes in the drawer on Sunday morning. You'd have found it if it had been there on Saturday.'

'I'm sure we would.'

'So it proves that Peter didn't do it, didn't kill her.'

'That's what it seems to suggest.'

There was something strange about his manner; I wasn't able to analyse it. He was a smooth talker with a well-controlled face. Most of the time you can find out something from people's faces, if you watch them, but in this place I was not the watcher, but the one who was watched.

'I hope that you don't think I'm lying, that I'm making it up about the gun being hidden. It wasn't my gun, it really wasn't; I'd never seen it before.'

'I wonder if you expect me to believe that?'

'Yes, I do. You have to believe it. It proves that Peter is innocent, that is, if it's the gun that shot her. And, of course, it has to be that; it can't be any other gun. You've found out all about that already, I suppose?'

'We have a ballistics department. Now, Miss Graham, tell me why you didn't let us know at once when you found the gun concealed in your room.'

'I thought you wouldn't believe me.'

'But when you discovered Peter Abbott had been kept here all day, then you decided we would believe you?'

I was silent. It wasn't the first time he'd twisted my words round into the wrong channel.

'Tell me about your movements on Sunday morning, after you found the gun.'

'I was frightened, so I rushed out. I took a train. I went to see Laurence—Laurence Hopkins, I mean—to borrow a box. Then I went to Charing Cross Station and put the gun, in the box, into the cloakroom, where you found it. I was mad to leave it there, but it would have been safe enough if only I'd taken the ticket out of that handbag before you came.'

He smiled at me, it seemed to be in pure friendship; my heart began to sink before I heard his words.

'That's very factual, Miss Graham. But the account is wrong in one particular at least. We haven't found the gun.'

I stared at him, I was appalled. It was impossible. 'You mean it wasn't at Charing Cross cloakroom?'

'I mean we haven't looked there for it.'

'But you had the cloakroom ticket!'

'We haven't found any cloakroom ticket.'

'But you've just told me you had the gun. You said it was with your ballistics department.'

He smiled at me sympathetically, and I sat, sunk in chagrin. He'd known nothing about the gun; he'd trapped me into telling him everything. I needn't have said a word about it; I was in deeper than ever, now.

Deeper and deeper and deeper, I kept on telling myself, while I answered questions, explained how I'd left the ticket in the handbag, described how the parcel had looked when I left it in the cloakroom. Constables were sent to my flat for the handbag. Sergeants were despatched to Charing Cross, to search the cloakroom. The results were clear enough. There was no gun, they thought I had made up the whole story.

We went back to the subject of Donald. He believed I knew where Donald was now; I had to convince him I didn't. In no time at all, I was in difficulties again. I couldn't explain how it was that I had vanished from London on Sunday, and not reappeared until Monday afternoon in Bristol. I made the mistake of suggesting that I had spent the night in Bristol, but I didn't even know what the town looked like; I didn't know the name of a single hotel in it. Had I spent the night in London with some friend, and travelled to Bristol by day? Yes, I'd done that, but I didn't know the day trains. I ended by describing my departure from Victoria, but there weren't any trains to Bristol from Victoria. We agreed that I'd travelled from Paddington, but when? I began to worry about the car I'd borrowed the night before. It seemed likely that the women had described me to the police, and I had left the car in a prominent position by a crossing outside Paddington.

'The fact is, I did travel from Paddington, but it was last night.'

'What train did you catch?'

'It was about eight; it was after eight.'

'There's a train to Bristol at seven-fifteen. Was that the train?'

I began to say that it was, but I had to stop. It had been well after that when I borrowed the car.

'No. It was after eight.'

'But the next train to Bristol on Sunday night is a long time after eight. You must surely remember when you caught the train.'

I'd had enough of railway time-tables. There were no more trains I could invent.

'I caught the eight-ten from Paddington,' I said stupidly.

'But that goes to Plymouth.'

'Yes, it goes to Plymouth.'

'Where did you stay in Plymouth?'

'In an hotel. I don't remember its name.'

'Alone?'

'Naturally.'

'Not with Donald Spencer?'

I was worn out. I was exhausted by my own inventions The only thing I wanted now was to tell the truth, all the truth, and get it over. But it was too important to conceal the fact that Donald had been with me. If they knew he'd been with me in Plymouth, they'd guess he'd gone to Bristol Airport with me; they'd look for him in Dublin. He wouldn't be any good at hiding himself; he'd been too well brought up to have an instinct for the obscure room in the back street. He'd be staying at one of the expensive hotels. That was the trouble with having a private income.

'I was staying alone,' I repeated. We hadn't checked into the hotel in our own names, that was something, but I remembered that my conduct in the middle of the night had been conspicuous. The police in Plymouth would be asked to investigate the hotels; the night porter would certainly remember me.

The Inspector was indefatigable. He didn't shout or bully, he scarcely raised his voice. He considered every one of my answers, then turned them around to give the results he wanted. He was like someone doing one of these children's puzzles, where little silver balls have to be rolled into the right holes. Then, when I'd got to the point where I would have been glad to confess that I'd killed Sarah—killed Hamlet's father; assassinated all the Grand Dukes left in Europe; when I'd have admitted anything to put an end to the questions—the questions suddenly ended.

'You can go home now, Miss Graham.'

I couldn't believe it I couldn't see the reason for it, unless he had someone else waiting in another room, to be questioned as I had been.

'Have you found Donald?' I asked stupidly.

'I said you could go home now. I'll see you again tomorrow, perhaps. You will remember we know the different routes to Ireland, and to other places, like the Channel Islands, for instance, where passports aren't required?'

'Yes, I'll remember.'

I knew I still had my passport. He knew it, too. He suggested that I should leave it with him. He'd give me a receipt, if I wished. I gave him the passport. If I was to be sent to prison, I'd hardly need it.

He offered to send me home by car. He was very considerate, I suppose. I accepted the offer. I was afraid there might be some crime reporters waiting outside the police station; I had to get away from it quickly.

It was still early. I hadn't been in the police station very long, but time isn't always measured by clocks.

I asked the police driver to set me down by the corner of my street. I said I wanted some fresh air. I waited until the car had driven away, then I walked slowly along the street, away from home. There was a fugitive idea I had to catch, a way of proving to the police one thing, anyway, that I had really had the gun that it had been left with me, that I hadn't been lying about that. The idea succumbed in the end. I took a taxi and gave the driver the address of Laurence's house in Battersea.

When I had paid the driver I walked up the crumbling steps and knocked. Dulcie opened the door. She was respectably dressed, this time, although all her clothes drooped, as if they'd been made for someone with wider shoulders. Her hair was arranged in iron ridges, and there was a suggestion of iron in her face, too, as she looked at me.

'Miss Graham! Did you want something?' she said. She came out of the door towards me, almost shutting it behind her. She gave the impression that she'd sooner deal with me here, on the landing, than invite me in.

'I wanted to see Laurence.'

'I'm afraid you can't. He's lying down. He's resting.

'Oh. May I come in for a minute?'

154

'I'm cooking supper,' she said, still blocking the way.

'Please. I would like to sit down.'

Reluctantly, she let me pass. I saw the open kitchen door as I went in. There was no supper cooking there; there was nothing much happening, unless the unwashed breakfast dishes could be counted as an event. She saw that I had looked into the kitchen; she shut the door quickly; it didn't develop our friendship.

'I was on the point of cooking supper,' she said. 'Sit down, Miss Graham. What was it you wanted?'

'I really wanted to see Laurence. I wanted to tell him I've been with the police again.'

'He's upset enough, with things the way they've been. You put him right off his work, Miss Graham, if you want a home truth, when you came yesterday.'

'I'm sorry. I came here because I don't want to put him off work. I thought it would be the easiest way, to ask you myself, not to tell the police.'

'To tell the police about what?' she asked in a kind of shrill whisper. 'He's seen the police already. He's finished with them. They're satisfied. Don't you begin bringing the police into it again, Miss Meddler.'

'I'm not trying to meddle. It's really about me. I wanted him to tell the police that I came here yesterday morning, to borrow a cardboard box. Or you could tell them, if you wanted . . .'

She stood, frowning. 'You'll have to explain yourself a bit more.'

I didn't know how to explain myself to her. I wanted to talk to Laurence, even if he was drunk. I could make him understand, somehow; I wasn't able to communicate with this woman.

'It's just that the police didn't believe something I told them. If they knew about the cardboard box, it would be different. I thought that Laurence, you and Laurence, wouldn't like them to come, asking more questions, and I wanted to be sure you remembered about the box.'

She didn't look inclined to remember anything that would help me.

'You're trying to drag him into that murder again. It's not good for him, Miss Graham. He upsets easily. He has to get on with his work. It was bad enough with the police, but seeing you yesterday, it's turned him moody.'

155

'If I could see him now, we could be moody together,' I suggested.

'You tell me what you want, about the cardboard box, and I'll tell you what I think, Miss Graham.'

'I'll tell you,' I said, in a kind of exhausted rage. 'Someone left a gun in my flat on Saturday, on Saturday afternoon or evening. I wanted to leave it somewhere, and I didn't have a box. So I came along and borrowed it from you. The gun has gone, now, and I just wanted you to say about the box.'

She patted her hair into position, although it was there already, and went through some mental process that made her face blank and empty.

'I'm not sure if I remember about the box.'

'But you must. It was only yesterday morning.'

'We don't want anything to do with guns. Not in this house.'

'Will you phone the police for me and tell them I borrowed the box?'

'No, I won't. And that's that. There's no reason Laurence should get himself mixed up in all this trouble.'

I was shaking with fury. 'Then I'll phone the police and get them to come along and ask you. That will be more trouble, and you'll have to tell them the truth.'

'Now you're turning nasty, Miss Graham. Let me tell you, I'm not obliged to remember the box, it's a thing anyone might forget; and another thing, nothing that's happened between you and Laurence makes me want to help you now.'

'You mean you're going to lie to the police, say you never gave me the box?' I was shocked. I saw afterwards that it was the last thing I had the right to be.

'I'm not going to let you make him worse than he is now. Is that all you came for, Miss Graham? Or did you come to ask more questions? Because if you're curious to know what Laurence was doing on Saturday afternoon, he was here, here with me; it's my afternoon off, he was here. I did the shopping. I was back before four, and Laurence stayed here working on his writing, till he had this message from the police. When he came back from them we had our supper, see; he was very upset.'

I wouldn't have believed the blonde had so much fight in her. I had none left in me, I was sure of that.

I stood up. 'I wish I could see Laurence.'

I waited. She didn't answer. She was implacable, the female

156

defender. It was useless. She'd never let me see Laurence again.

'I think I'd better go,' I said.

She went to the door and opened it for me; we didn't have any more words. We understood each other fairly well. There are many situations between women that don't need words at all.

I went to the nearest main road. I took a bus until I got into an area where I could find a taxi. All I wanted now was to get home. I'd had enough of the day, enough of the week-end; for the first time in my life, I'd had enough of life. I tried to think my way out of it; it was only a mood. What I wanted was a good brain-washing. I could go back to the police station: Please, Inspector, could you wash my brain; do you do that here? Yes, thanks, I'd like to have it done now. You'll look out for those spots in the middle, will you? And let me have it back by Wednesday? It won't be quite dry? Then leave it till Thursday, I wouldn't like to have my brain back wet.

I got home then. I got out of this other taxi, and this time I decided to go in. There was nothing else to do but to go into the beautiful silence, the unpleasant emptiness. It was cold, and dismal—an English summer evening straight out of the refrigerator. I sat down in a chair, wondering if I had the strength to light the gas fire. It seemed I hadn't, because some time later I was still exploring the creases in my crumpled mind when the door bell rang. I dragged myself up and opened the door. Mike was standing there.

I absorbed his appearance slowly. There were a lot of things I had to say to Mike. I was still thinking them out when he began to speak.

'Nancy, you should have told me you were back. God, I'm exhausted!'

He pushed past me and went into the sitting-room and sat down. He looked flat-out. He looked as if he'd just finished running a mile in three and a half minutes, and needed a trainer to hold him up for the press cameras. After a minute, he spoke again.

'Have you ever felt you can't go on, Nancy? That's the way I feel tonight.'

'What's happened?' I asked, in an unsympathetic voice.

'Liz has cracked up,' he said.

'I'm sorry. Who is Liz?'

'Nancy, I've told you a hundred times. She's playing opposite

157

me in this ghastly thing. You know we began rehearsing today. Liz is no actress—Sarah Bernhardt's wooden leg could give her lessons—but at least she can speak her lines, she has a voice. Then today, absolutely without warning, she dashed into one of these nursing homes. Appendicitis—at least, that's the story. And do you know whom they've given me? Kitty! Kitty—the rock on which Shakespeare's mighty barque foundered. Even Stratford gave up Shakespeare after Kitty's Lady Macbeth. Do you know that this play we're rehearsing was written, specially written, for Liz and me?'

'Who wrote it for you? Shakespeare?'

'Some oaf in a grocer's shop. He wrote it on the back of one thousand five hundred paper bags. That's the hand-out, anyway. The customers had to carry home their rice loose.'

'Mike, I've got something serious to say to you.'

'This play's got more holes in it than the paper bags. I'll tell you the story.'

I gave up. I didn't have the energy for a row. It was going to be a big row. It wouldn't do to fall asleep in the middle of it. I'd get rid of him quickly, and have the row later.

'Don't tell me the story, Mike. I'm busy.'

'What are you busy at?'

'I'm busy at wishing you'd go away. I can't understand how you can sit there and talk about yourself after everything that's happened.'

'Has something new happened?'

'The police brought me back from Bristol, that's all.'

'Is that why you look so dishevelled?'

'I wish you'd go away and associate with Liz, or Kitty, or Sarah Bernhardt's wooden leg, and leave me alone.'

'Did you sleep in these clothes?' he asked, in an interested, pleasant voice.

'Yes, I did.'

'Really, Nancy, you're incredible. What will Donald say, when he comes to take you out to dinner?'

'He's not taking me out to dinner.'

'Then we can eat together and I'll tell you about the play. I'll give you half an hour to get ready.'

'I'm sorry. I can't come.'

'You said Donald wasn't taking you out. Is he coming here?'

'You know he isn't. You know he can't. You're the one who's made it impossible for him to come back at all. Mike, how

dare you tell the police about him! I'm so angry, I—I never
hated anyone—so much.' I wanted to go on with the row, I
wanted to say things that wouldn't be forgiven, but I was too
tired, my voice was fading away.

'If he's not coming here, you'd better get ready for dinner.'

'Go away, Mike,' I said. I was hardly able to whisper it. 'I
simply don't want to eat. That's the position.'

'Did I tell you that I'm on a diet that I invented myself?
It's a warning, more than a diet. They give me a mess of grated
carrot and cucumber skins; they put it in front of me, and I
look at it for a long time, and I think, if I'm very careful
with no potatoes, I can still eat a real meal and not be reduced
to this anti-food. Then I wave away the cucumber skins and
concentrate on meat, or roast duck, and nothing to drink,
thank you. What did you have for lunch, Nancy?'

'I was on a train without a restaurant car.'

'What did you have for dinner last night?'

'I was on another train without a restaurant car.'

'Did I ever tell you about my journey to Aberdeen?'

'Not now. Don't tell me now. I want you to go away.'

'I will give you an account, station by station; it will be like
a T.V. documentary without the jokes—unless you tell me what
you've had to eat since we had coffee here yesterday morning.'

'I had breakfast this morning.'

'You mustn't let yourself go like this, Nancy. You'll turn
into one of these premature old crones; you'll spend half your
life having scented fat rubbed into you from outside because
your stomach's shrivelled away. There will be nothing left of
you but two painted eyebrows and a mauve neck; a horrible old
hen scratching away in Bond Street. Now get ready and we'll
go out to dinner.'

'No, thanks.'

'You don't seem to realize that it's only when I'm rehearsing
that I'm able to eat dinner at a dinner hour.'

'I'm not coming, Mike.'

'Doesn't it occur to you that after the kind of day I've had,
I might be hungry?'

I didn't bother to answer. I knew he'd go away in the end.

He took a notebook out of his pocket and looked through
it, sometimes flicking straight through the pages, and at others
stopping with a reminiscent smile.

'Did you ever meet Addie Blair, Nancy? There's a beautiful

159

woman. What a profile! She'd get a job as a model any day, if she needed the perks.'

'I met her yesterday in Soho.'

'Really? May I use your telephone?'

'Certainly. There must be some woman who is aching to hear the story of your journey to Aberdeen. I'm going to wash. Shut the door when you leave.'

I went out of the room. I washed my face with a lot of hot and cold water, turn about, and changed into the first clothes that were easy to change into. I gave the minimum attention to my hair, remembering how hard I'd worked to be the rector's daughter such a short time ago.

I collected a few of my early notebooks. There were some things I wanted to look up about Laurence, and about Peter and Mike, too. I meant to go through it all carefully when my head cleared a little.

I went back into the sitting-room. Mike was still there.

'You look a bit better, Nancy; like a ghost in a clean shroud. Where do you keep the glasses? I sent out for some food. Cold chicken and some white wine. Could you rake up some salad, and some brown bread and butter? Cut it thin.'

'If there's any bread in the house, it's stale.'

'Get some plates, anyway.' He sat down again.

'I don't want anything to eat.'

'Then do you mind if I start?'

'I prefer to invite my guests.'

'I'm not exactly a guest if I provide my own food. I can see I'll have to fetch a plate as well.'

He came back from the kitchen with a plate and a knife and a fork. One plate, one knife, one fork. He had an easy, natural interest in his own welfare.

'I rang up Addie. She was fixed for dinner, already. She always is. That girl knows everyone. She told me she saw you yesterday.'

'Even.'

'Who is Miguel Orinoco?'

'Someone she doesn't know.'

'She said he was a Mexican millionaire and that he'd been Sarah's lover.'

'And she asked you not to tell anyone?'

'She doesn't like gossip.'

'It's one of the only two things she understands.'

'Did you tell her about this Orinoco?'

'I may have done. It would have been unkind, not to tell her something.'

'Do you know what I think about you, Nancy?'

'I don't wish to hear it. Are you going to the police—about Orinoco?'

'No.'

'That's funny. I thought you were working for them.'

'Why are you in such a bad temper?'

'I don't want you here at all. What right had you to go to the police about Donald?'

'I told you I would, if you went out to see him alone.'

'That's not a reason.'

'Try to think about someone but Donald, for a change. Where is he, anyway?'

'You've come here to get at me again. I knew you had. I'm not going to tell you anything. I distrust you absolutely. I despise you.'

'Where is he?'

'I'm not going to answer any questions.'

'You told me you helped each other? How is he helping you now? Well-wishing from a distance?'

'He's having dinner with Orinoco.'

'If they're both eating, there's no reason why you shouldn't. I'll get you a plate.'

He went out to the kitchen and came back with a plate and some buttered slices of bread.

'The bread's so hard, it rings when you hit it. You're a rotten housewife, Nancy. I'm afraid I've had most of the chicken, but here you are.'

He passed me the plate of chicken. I tried to eat some, and began to cry.

'For God's sake, what have I done wrong now?' Mike asked.

'I hate you for telling them about Donald and then coming here being kind to me, because I'm too tired; I just don't have the energy left to get rid of you. I don't want your kindness, I don't want to accept it, and I don't want this damned chicken.'

'I don't have to be kind. I have great reserves of malevolence. You know that. But I don't want to waste time talking to a woman with starvation-hysteria. So go ahead and eat, I'll look the other way; we needn't be collaborators in food. I'll get on with learning my lines.'

He turned away from me, and brought a roll of typescript out of his pocket. He began to read it over to himself, stopping now and then to mark it off in pencil.

I began to eat. I wasn't hungry, but of course it was true, I ought to eat, if I had to see the police tomorrow; I didn't want to begin crying in front of the Inspector.

'Have some wine,' Mike said over his shoulder. 'Half a glass will give you the strength to kill me. Like Tosca. You be Tosca and I'll be Scarpia.'

'I don't know what you're talking about.'

'You're illiterate, Nancy. I'm talking about opera. The villain Scarpia tortures Tosca's lover, so that when she hears his groans she'll do anything to save him. Tosca agrees to become Scarpia's mistress. Scarpia calls the torture off, then Tosca doesn't want to be his mistress after all. She sees a knife on the table. Can she kill Scarpia? No. She is only a weak woman, she has feminine scruples. Scarpia turns away. She seizes a glass of wine, knocks back two sips; it gives her strength for murder; she stabs Scarpia, he dies. Here's the wine. I'll pour it for you.'

'It doesn't seem an exact parallel. Are you Scarpia?'

I took the glass from him.

'Have two sips. That's a good girl. I'd like to be Scarpia. It's a magnificent part—brutal, lecherous, powerful. I'd be Scarpia all right, if I could sing. Shall I hum it for you?'

'Please not. I didn't know you had time to go to opera.'

'When I'm resting, or rehearsing.'

'I've never been to an opera.'

'That's exactly like you. You're an ignorant savage, disguised as an intellectual. You think because you've heard Mozart and Beethoven on gramophone records that you have covered the field of music. And it's the same everywhere. Have you read the plays of Ben Jonson?'

'Who has?'

'I got involved in Bartholomew Fair once. What a disaster! Have some more wine, Tosca. You need strength for the dagger.'

He poured another half-glass of wine. I ate some chicken and bread while I drank it. I was beginning to revive now that the conversation was safe and abstract.

'I'd like to play a good villain, but if you move out of Shakespeare, you haven't a chance, today. Villains are supposed to be slightly comic, now; they daren't write plays with a villain in the centre. Everyone understands too much about everyone else; everything can be excused and explained; there are no evil people any more, only psychopathic personalities. But some men are bad, evil—I'd like to play one of them. I could do Scarpia all right. Donald could be the tortured lover, and I'm out there in front, in a black and silver scowl, saying "Be mine, or your lover dies." '

'You'll have to find another grocer to write it for you. He could use the butter paper, this time.'

Mike took out his cigarette case. 'Do you want one? Or would you sooner smoke your own?'

'I've run out. I don't have any.'

'I'll make sure for you.' He took my handbag. I wasn't watching him carefully, I was thinking of some of the other things I had to think about.

'What's this letter to Miss Katie Curzon?'

'It was my false identity for Bristol Airport, when I was going to Dublin. I didn't use it, they recognized me.'

'And Raymond Buckingham, Esq.?'

'That's—what are you doing, looking through my handbag?'

'I was looking for cigarettes. The Raymond Buckingham letter isn't a letter. It's an empty envelope.'

I remembered I'd taken one of the letters out of its envelope, because of the stamp and postmark difficulty. 'It's an empty envelope; throw it in the waste paper basket, and let my handbag alone.'

He shut the handbag. 'Are you sure you don't want to write to Raymond? What's his middle name? Donald? Was it Donald's false identity? He got away with it, did he, and you got caught?'

'It's a letter I was writing to a friend.'

'I'm sorry, Nancy,' he said insincerely, 'I shouldn't have looked in your handbag. Will you have one of my cigarettes?'

'I think perhaps I will.'

He lit it for me. 'Go on about Scarpia,' I said. He was safer when he was talking.

'Where would you like me to begin? Where you kill me?'

'That would be interesting. But I can't do it. I have to see a dagger on the table before I have a chance to kill you.' I hadn't eaten much for two days. I was a bit light-headed, like

Tosca, on a very small quantity of wine, or I'd have seen that Mike was leading up to one of his theatrical climaxes.

'Where's the dagger?' I asked.

'Here's the dagger,' he said, and laid the gun on the table.

I looked at it with about twenty-four conflicting thoughts in my mind. It wasn't affected by my thoughts. It lay there, black and lethal and threatening, in the worst way—the impersonal way.

'How did you get it?'

'I took the cloakroom ticket out of that bag of yours, yesterday. I saw the ticket when you asked for one of your own cigarettes.'

'If you give me a minute, I'll think of something I can say about you, in English. I don't swear well enough, except in Dutch and German.'

'Nancy, I was trying to help you. You got me worried about that gun. I didn't want you to touch it again. Then you warned me the place might be searched. I thought it was safer if I took the ticket.'

'I can't understand why you didn't hand the gun over to the police right away, and say, "She had it, she's the one who had the gun." You're so keen to help them.'

'I was trying to help you. I was trying to keep you from getting into extra trouble.'

'You haven't kept me out of trouble. You've got me into it. I told the Inspector about the gun today. I thought it would make them see Peter couldn't have done it—couldn't have killed her and left the gun with me—because he was at the station, with them, all the time that I was. Then they looked for the gun in Charing Cross; it wasn't there. Now they think I was lying about it, that I was a kind of accomplice, making up a gun-story just to give Peter an alibi.'

'But you are an accomplice, Nancy. You're not Peter's accomplice, you're Donald's.'

'Whatever I say, whatever I tell that damned Inspector, I'm always in the wrong.'

'That's because you tell so many lies about Donald.'

'You hate him, don't you?'

'I don't like men who live on women. I don't mean money, he's all right there. That's what he is, the amateur with a little money; he's not like the rest of us, who have to work or die. He's an emotional parasite. Kiss me good night and love me

164

for ever, or I'll shoot myself. Save me from the police, go to prison for me, or something terrible will happen to me. He's got no life of his own. He's left you, hasn't he? He's got away, that's the truth. It's important to him. He has to get away. And you're still here, telling lies to save him, lies that are going to land you in prison. You're the fall-guy, Nancy. That's your role.'

'You make me so tired, I'd like to get to a nunnery. One of these places where they put the needle down quietly, in case it shatters the silence. I'd like to be somewhere where no one talks.'

'You mean the grave?'

'Mike, let me alone now. I want to be alone.'

He picked up the gun and held it in his hand.

'You don't want to be alone with this. Where's Donald, Nancy?'

'I don't know where he is.'

'Where's Donald. Come on, you're going to tell me. Where is he?'

'I have no idea.'

'He went to Bristol Airport with you, didn't he? Let's see, now. You'd be careful to arrive separately. Did he see the police pick you up?'

I tried not to listen to what Mike was saying. I was a good non-listener, I had a talent for it. All I had to do now was exercise my talent. The best thing would be to recite a long narrative poem to myself. I couldn't think of one, I couldn't think of a single line of verse. It wasn't the time for poetry.

'Did he see the police pick you up?' Mike repeated. 'You can answer that. It's unimportant, isn't it? What happened between you and the police was your affair, not his.'

'Yes. It was my affair.'

'So he tossed you to the police. While they were worrying you to death he had a chance to get away. Then he went to Dublin, because it wasn't his business. That's what happened, isn't it?'

He waited. He couldn't make me answer. I'd abandoned poetry. I was trying mental arithmetic. No one can listen to anything when they are absorbed in the beauty of multiplying 493 by 49, in their heads.

'Do you think he's trying to help you now?' Mike asked.

I looked away from him. He went on talking. I made the first line 4,437.

'You seriously think he's in love with you?'

I tried to see the numbers. Four nines and one, thirty-seven.

'He's deserted you. You'll never see him again.'

It was remembering the two lines and adding them together that was difficult.

'He had to get away. Can't you understand? Peter, Laurence, even me—we all had alibis for the time.'

Seven, five, one.

'You and Donald are the only two people in it who could have killed Sarah.'

The sum snapped out of my head. It was true enough. I hadn't had time to look at it before. The other three couldn't have done it. Even the police believed that.

'So I'll tell them he's in Dublin, and very possibly calling himself Raymond Buckingham.'

I didn't remember admitting anything about Donald, but all the damage was done. I hadn't told Mike, but he knew everything. Suddenly I couldn't endure any more. Milke's voice was a torture, it was like having a hole drilled in my skull. When Mike stopped, the Inspector would begin again. Between them they had sent me back into my nightmare tunnel. The blackness was pressing on me. I was terrified. I was alone; Donald had deserted me; poor Sarah had been killed; Mike was an enemy who had hunted me into the middle of the tunnel. When I tried to run. I fell down. I was in the tunnel for ever.

'The Irish police will find him before the morning,' Mike was saying. His voice hadn't stopped. It wasn't going to stop.

'I killed her,' I said, from the depths of the tunnel.

Mike had been shifting the gun about from hand to hand, but now he suspended every movement.

'That's what happened. I killed her, and that's the end of it.'

'Did you, Nancy?' he asked softly.

'Yes. Now you can let me alone.'

'Can I let Donald alone, too?'

'He has nothing to do with it.'

'Why did you kill her?'

'You've found out what you wanted to know. Now you have to stop. Tell the police. They're going to arrest me, anyway. I'm tired of waiting for it.'

'Is it the truth you killed her?'

I covered my eyes with my hands. 'Go away. I don't want to

see you. I'd be in Ireland now, with Donald, if you hadn't interfered.'

'You're unbearable!' Mike shouted. I was afraid he was going to attack me. I took my hands away from my eyes. Even on the stage I'd never seen such hatred on his face.

'Someone ought to kill you,' he said. He looked ready to do it himself. I pushed back in my chair, away from him. As well as everything else, worse than anything else, I was afraid of him. I reached forward quickly and snatched the gun from the table. I didn't know anything about guns. I didn't know if this gun was fit to be fired. I had to defend myself somehow.

He turned and caught my wrist and bent it back until my grip loosened; then he wrenched the gun out of my hand and dropped it on the table.

He stood with his head down, looking at me. If he was calmer than I was, it was by a very small margin.

'I'll leave you alone with it,' he said, then he walked out of the room. He had more self-control than I thought; he was able to shut the doors quietly.

12

WHEN HE HAD gone, what I wanted to do was sit, all night and the next day too, and cry and cry, but I had no time for it. I waited until my heart had settled down to its normal beat, then I went back and forwards in my tunnel, looking for the gleam of light that would lead me into the open again.

I tried to think of Donald; he had been my comfort and my strength, but he had gone. Everything that Mike had said was true. There was no more comfort, no more strength to lean on. Worst of all was the bitter, established fact. Mike, Laurence, and Peter had their alibis for that morning when she had died. Either Donald or I had killed her. It was a narrow field.

I picked up the gun and looked at it, not idly, but fascinated. I'd never had less to live for. When they charged me with murder, and put me in prison, I wouldn't find it easy to come by a gun. I'd stay there, in prison, for ten or fifteen years. I hadn't a mind that would endure injustice quietly. I'd be burnt-out before they let me go.

I tried pointing the gun at my head. When I felt the touch of the metal, I knew I hadn't the mind for self-destruction, either. That meant I had to find some way out, some way of fighting back. I couldn't be neutral.

I thought of Mike, and the Inspector, and of Donald, too. It was an effort to push them out of my mind, but it was done. It was my life, I'd find a way of keeping it, I didn't depend on anyone, I told myself.

It was the right thing to believe, when I'd no friends left. Sarah and Donald and Mike, the people I'd loved in very different ways, had gone. The lesser friends would go, when I was charged with murder. There wasn't much left for me, but independence. It had a sour taste, but when the telephone rang my heart went down again. There was no voice I wanted to hear. Everyone was an enemy.

I picked up the receiver.

'Nancy? It's Stony here. Back from Canada.'

'Stony! How lovely to hear your voice! How was Canada?'

'Cold.'

'Are you back for good?'

'No. Two months. I've bought another Jag. Want to see it?'

'Yes.'

'I'll come round now.'

'No. Wait, Stony, I'd better tell you, Sarah's been killed. Everyone thinks I did it.'

'Did you?'

'No.'

'I'll be round.'

'No, Stony, not tonight. Tomorrow. Ring me tomorrow.'

'Don't you want to come out in the Jag?'

I had a beautiful vision of the whole dark world hurtling past, and prison left for ever in some pit behind me. But I had gone too far over the edge of the pit. I'd better leave Stony out of it.

'Tomorrow, Stony. Thanks for ringing.'

I put back the receiver. I couldn't use Stony, I saw that, but I wasn't alone any more in the hostile world. There was Stony. There would be others. Even the Bulgarian George wouldn't desert me. He'd come and read unintelligible verse through the grating on visitors' day.

I picked up the gun. I wouldn't have dreamt of turning it on myself now. I would put it away. The police could have it in the morning.

I flicked the bullet chamber around. I knew nothing about it, but there was a space for six bullets, and there were only four bullets left. Two shots had been fired. Then I saw how the murder had been done. It wasn't only Donald or me, after all. We weren't out of the running, but Peter and Laurence and Mike were back in.

I laid the gun down on the desk. Everything was happening in my mind, at speed.

I saw her room as I had found it. The green slippers lay separately on the yellow carpet. It wasn't the way she'd have left them, when she went to bed at night. The underclothes hadn't matched. That had worried me from the beginning, but as I remembered them now I saw that more than the colour was wrong. There was a glass of water by the bed; the green dressing-gown was missing. And on the bed lay Sarah, with her fair hair falling over her cold forehead.

There was nothing in all this to convince the police. If I gave them the gun, with two shots fired, would they believe me? I had told so many lies, for Donald. They had no reason to trust me, now. They might say I'd fired the second shot myself. Bullets didn't carry a date stamp.

I thought of her again, remembering the cold touch of her skin as I had lifted the pale, softly waved lock of hair from her forehead. Even her hair had changed so much since I first met her. She had worn it coarsely waved, for Peter, in Birmingham. When she came to work for the Diagonal Press she'd had a reaction, and kept it short and completely straight. I wasn't sure when that had happened. Before Laurence's time, anyway. There would be something about it, in the notebooks. I remembered her well enough, her straight hair golden in the yellow light of the candles, while the radio played Tschaikovsky, and Peter, who had found her again, stood staring at Laurence.

When she'd married Mike, her hair had been beautifully, discreetly waved. She'd had to spend a lot of time at the hairdressers. Mike wasn't the kind of man to endure a wife who pinned her hair up every night, or went to bed covered in cold cream. He wouldn't know that she'd ever had the habit of setting her hair at night. Donald—she'd never had to live up to Donald. He'd thought she looked beautiful whatever she did. She hadn't bothered to conceal hairpins from him. Why should she? She looked pathetic and charming with her hair pinned up. She'd opened the door to him, on that last night, with, as he said, those wire curler things in her hair. She hadn't taken them out for him. Surely she wouldn't have left them in for anyone else.

My thoughts had been racing; I tried to stop them, to reach out and catch an idea. Everything wasn't lost. If I could find one point, one single irrefutable point, to add to the fact that two shots had been fired from the gun, then I would be out of the tunnel again, safe, in the free and open air.

I stood by the desk, looking at the gun. It was lying where the typewriter had stood, until the police had taken it away. It was a poor exchange, I preferred the typewriter. They had taken it away because someone had re-typed the threatening letter on it, someone who had known already that she was murdered, someone who had murdered her. The man who had retyped the letter was the man who had written the original letter, with its odd phrasing, I was sure that Peter wasn't literate enough to have composed that letter. There was nothing else in that line of thought. They had taken the typewriter away on Saturday. This was only Monday, half-past eleven on Monday night. Only two days, and the road had changed under my feet.

It saw it then, at once. I left the gun, and went quickly to the bookcase. I was kneeling beside it, I'd found the book and opened it at the right page, when the doorbell rang. I took the book and dropped it open over the gun. Then I went to the door.

I ought to have expected someone to come that night. I wasn't surprised now to find that it was Laurence.

I couldn't find a reassuring phrase to greet him with, as he stood in the doorway. He was red-eyed, and shaken, but not shaking. He was sober. There was no comfort in that.

'I thought I'd drop in,' he said. 'Dulcie's working late.'

I didn't think it was true, even Dulcie wouldn't have had to work as late as this, but I wasn't after the whole truth, only a part of it. I was anxious to have that part, and it seemed that chance for once had been on my side, by obligingly sending Laurence to the door.

'Come in, Laurence,' I said, very brisk and pleasant. I held the door open, and he came in. I shut the door behind him. It was time to leave the plane and take to the parachute. I didn't have any confidence, but excitement was chasing around inside me, pushing against my heart.

Laurence was mumbling something about having come to borrow a book, Aubrey's Lives, I knew I didn't have it, but I said I'd look.

'Have a drink, Laurence?' I didn't want him sober, I didn't care for the look of him, sober.

'I'm on the wagon.'

'You don't mind if I drink?' I poured myself half a glass of wine from the bottle Mike had left. I began to laugh, but I stopped, it didn't sound right.

'We'll have a literary evening,' I said. 'We'll talk about plays and poetry. It will be like old times, Laurence. It will be as if we'd never been on our long journey. We're years away from the start. Do you remember the scene from Chekhov's "Seagull" when the mother and her lover travel across Europe by train into Russia—it must have been a hell of a trip—and a minute after they arrive, without even taking off their coats, they sit down and begin to play cards?'

'Yes, I remember.'

'And the son shoots himself. Do you remember that?'

'Yes.'

'So in spite of everything that's happened, in spite of our long journey, we'll sit around and talk about the things that solid respectable people discuss over coffee and biscuits twice a year, when they've been to the play. It's not only civil servants and school teachers who read, even bus conductors and jig-and-tool setters read books. We mustn't give up.'

It was talking at headlong speed. I wasn't sure where I was going. It was like driving along a dark road with Stony in the Jaguar, it was like the night we had swerved and skidded and crashed. I remembered what I'd told Sarah about that last minute—"It was like being given extra passion to be purged of." Tonight I mustn't crash.

'Do take off your coat, Laurence. Don't be too Chekhovian.'

He looked confused and haggard, but he took it off, his fingers trembling on the buttons.

'You're not expecting anyone else?' he asked me. His voice was shaking as much as his fingers.

I wished I were. I knew that Donald wouldn't come, and

that Mike had gone for good. I was sorry now that I'd told Stony not to come. It was too much, being alone with Laurence. I'd have welcomed even the police. Then I thought, it was easy enough. The telephone was there, they'd take only a few minutes to come.

'About these biographers,' Laurence said. He was staring at me wildly.

I went to the telephone. 'We'll have a party. I'll ring Tom. You remember him? He's a publisher, he might be interesting on biographers, he used to know Lytton Strachey and Gertrude Stein well.'

Laurence smoothed back his hair with yellow fingers. "An unlikely combination,' he muttered.

I laughed, I laughed too much, and stopped too suddenly. I felt for the nines on the dial with my fingers.

'How old is this Tom?'

I tried to think how old Tom would have to be. I couldn't remember when Lytton Strachey had died. It was the kind of thing Laurence would be sure to know.

'Old Tom,' I said vaguely. 'Getting on for seventy, I suppose.'

'If you're thinking of having a party,' Laurence said heavily, 'I shouldn't bother with Tom. He may be past the party years.'

'I'll get someone else.'

'No. Don't telephone.' Laurence said. We looked at each other. We were both aware that something was going to happen, but neither of us was certain which way the road would turn.

'If you don't want anyone else, I won't ring,' I said. I put the receiver down. 'Have a drink, Laurence.'

'No.'

'If I told you that you were frightened to drink, would you pick up the reference?'

He shook his head.

'Hedda Gabler. First she drives him to drink by telling him he's frightened, then, when he's lost his manuscript, she drives him to shoot himself. I'm sorry. All my literary references end in guns. Have a drink?'

'No.'

'Are you really frightened to drink, are you afraid you can't stand it?'

I drank some more wine. I tried to look as if the spectrum had more and better colours, down Wine Alley. He sat staring blackness at me. I wanted him to drink. He looked as if he hadn't had a drink all day, and for an alcoholic that's a desperate way to look.

'You're not worrying about Sarah, are you, Laurence? It's two days, it's fifty-eight hours since she died. Some time it will be fifty-eight days, and she will be quite forgotten. It was terrible to see her with that red hole in her heart, but already it's turning black, in my mind. It doesn't look red any more. Have a drink!'

I pushed the bottle and glass towards him and he picked up the bottle and poured wine until the glass was full and drank it, then he filled his glass again. The bottle wasn't going to see us through. I remembered Mike had brought wine and brandy on Saturday night. I went to the cupboard quickly. I felt like walking backwards. There were two bottles of wine; one unopened, the other almost empty; and most of the bottle of brandy. I brought back all three bottles and put them on the table. For the time being, I was the opposite of alcoholics anonymous. I had to get him drunk. Drunk and garrulous first, then drunk and incapable.

We had another drink. I wasn't ready to leave Wine Alley for Brandy Corner. It took careful manipulation to see that Laurence had the brandy; and didn't turn suspicious because I had wine, and very little of that.

He drank two glasses of brandy as if he knew there was a hole in the bottom of the glass and if he didn't empty it quickly the brandy would run out. He banged the glass on the table, and I filled it again. I thought another glass would do it. He'd be ready to talk, and still fit to understand what was said. I waited for him to pick up the glass, but he left it on the table.

'When did you see Sarah?' he asked.

'Friday night.'

'I meant when did you see her after she was dead.'

'I—the police made me look.'

'Is that all?'

'All for the moment.'

'They didn't make me look.'

'You were lucky, not to see her dead.'

'I suppose I was,' he said. He picked up the third glass of brandy and drank it. I thought that would be a good point to stop, but he poured another glass from the bottle.

'I've been on the wagon today,' he said apologetically.
'Is it painful to fall off?'
'Sometimes.'
'Is it the road that changes, or the wagon?'
He sat blinking, trying to catch the allusion that I hadn't meant to make so soon.

I spoke quickly. 'Let's drink now—to Sarah—to the Sarah we both knew, four years ago.'

I raised my glass and drank, watching him, and he drank too, scowling, as if he couldn't bear the taste of the brandy.

'Will you let me talk about Sarah to you, Laurence?'
'I damned well won't.' He tried to stand up.

'Sit down, Laurence. I want to talk about Sarah to someone. There's no one else now. It has to be you.'

'She was a——'

'Oh, no, she wasn't. She was good and generous and beautiful and that makes her ninety per cent. better than the rest of us. She was beautiful, wasn't she, Laurence?'

He shook his head violently, trying to get rid of a picture.

'And she was generous. She's helped me with her last shilling; she tried to help me with her last words. And she was good, too. She didn't have a lucky start. She lived in poverty, with an aunt who hated her. She could have escaped, and lived like other people, better than other people; she had loyalty and kindness and ambition, but when she met Peter, the road went wrong. Roads can change under our feet. The road has changed under mine in the last two days. It's not the one I started on.'

He was leaning forward, staring at me. I had all his attention and I knew now that I was right. It was all I really wanted to know. I should have broken away then; I couldn't get to the telephone, but I could have reached the door and been half-way down the stairs before he followed me. But indiscretion was as much a part of me as heart and lungs. We were going into the long skid; I couldn't stop now.

'She wasn't promiscuous, Laurence. She was never that. She meant to be loyal to you; when she married Mike, she meant to stay married; eighteen months later she meant to marry Donald. She wasn't aware she couldn't do any of these things, because of Peter. You can never see the point where the road goes wrong, until after you've passed it.'

'Why do you keep talking about roads?' Laurence asked. He

174

took another drink; his face was anguished; he wasn't enjoying his alcoholic session.

'Sorry. I was thinking about a night when I drove too fast with a friend. We crashed. But I was talking about Sarah. When she met you, she knew nothing, and she wanted to learn. I don't think she'd ever been to a theatre, until you took her. She'd hardly heard of Shakespeare. She used to say you were her university, Laurence. And that she owed you more than any other man on earth.'

'That's enough about Sarah.'

'You knew her so well, Laurence. I suppose you knew all her habits then, four years ago?'

'I suppose I did.'

'But some habits get forgotten, and some habits change.'

'Not all of them,' he muttered. 'She always got up at eight.'

'Yes. You and I and Donald and Mike and Peter and her alarm clock all come together on that one point. She always got up at eight.'

'Dulcie brought me breakfast at seven-thirty. I couldn't have got there in time. The police are satisfied.'

'But only just satisfied.'

He was getting angry, now. His face was taking on redness and solidity.

'You could have got there by twenty-past eight, Laurence. Easily, by half-past.'

He tried to loosen his shirt collar. 'She'd have been up by then.'

'Yes, she would.' I took a sip of wine, and he had another gulp of brandy. I was worried about the brandy, now, he was having too much.

'When you lived with her she was poor. She couldn't have all the clothes she wanted. You didn't know that later on she always bought her underclothes in expensive sets, that she would never wear clothes that didn't match. It's a thing that any man might forget, but I haven't forgotten.'

'Is there anything else you haven't forgotten?'

'She always arranged her clothes in the order that she put them on. So she didn't put out those clothes on the chair. They were in the wrong order. The stockings and slip shouldn't have been on top.'

'You've a good memory, Nancy, a good memory.' His voice was very thick.

175

'There was a glass of water beside the bed. For years now she's drunk lemon juice when she wakens in the morning. You're out of date, Laurence.'

'Is that all—you've got nothing else now, have you, Nancy?'

'Her hair was straight, when you knew her. She's had it waved, for a long time now. She slept with it pinned up. She kept the pins in until she'd had a bath and begun to dress. But when I saw her, Laurence, there wasn't one pin in her hair.'

'She was shot in bed,' he shouted.

'I'll tell you how it happened, Laurance. She got up at eight. When she'd had a bath, she began to dress. She took the pins out of her hair. When the door bell rang, she put on a green dressing-gown, and went to the door. It might have been the postman. She opened the door, and let the murderer in.'

'She was shot in bed, and you can't prove anything else with your damned nonsense.'

'Where is the green dressing-gown?'

'You're mad, Nancy, you're raving.'

'And the blue slip and brassière? Where did you put them, Laurence? It must have been hell for you, getting her out of these bloodstained clothes. Where did you do it. In the bathroom?'

'That's enough, Nancy. I'm warning you. It's enough.'

'Then you had to shoot a hole through her nightdress. It was clever of you, to get it in the right place. I didn't know your hand was so steady.' I looked at his hand. It wasn't steady now. 'What happened to the second bullet?'

'The green dressing-gown might have been rolled in a bundle behind the nightgown,' he said. 'Like a sandbag. You didn't think of that, did you.'

'And then you had to put her in the nightdress. She was only just dead, and you had to do that.'

He pushed his chair away from me, and away from the table.

'I put her in bed, first,' he said, with a sigh that didn't finish quickly. It had taken a long time to escape, and he was glad to let it out now. He looked at me, thinking of how he'd put her in bed, but he didn't see me. I was a stranger, I was anyone he'd met in the night. He began to talk rapidly, letting it all out, but it wasn't much more than a mutter, sometimes it was less. I could scarcely hear.

'It wasn't meant to happen that way, I'd been drinking. No

sleep without drink, that's how it is. I've lain awake too many nights. When I sleep, I sleep, but when I lie awake I can't stand it. I've thought of killing her, often and often, it's what she earned, for killing me. I've seen myself with guns and knives, but I'd never use them, I'm not that kind of man. I've seen how to throw her out of windows. I've wakened Dulcie in the morning, mornings and mornings, again and again. I've told her I killed Sarah, I killed her last night. You get these ideas, when you lie awake. That morning Dulcie came in with the tea and her ill-timed remarks about money. She threw the paper at me and went away. She's a good girl, Dulcie, she's stood by me, but she gave me the paper and went away. It was in the paper. Sarah was going to marry a rich man. I hadn't the price of a drink in the house. Hell, I'll see her, I thought, see her before she goes to work, or I didn't think at all. I don't know. I got there, and she opened the door.'

He stopped and had another gulp of brandy. I waited. I knew he had to finish the story now.

'She opened the door. She had something on her wrist. I could see these things shining. Diamonds, I thought, Sarah with diamonds.'

His voice sank lower and lower. I couldn't hear him at all, except for snatches about Cities of the Plain, and women who had been stoned to death. He was very drunk by now. I wasn't sure if he knew I was there, even as a stranger, or if he was talking to himself, like a lonely drunk in the corner of a bar.

She hadn't wanted him to come in, then she said she'd make some coffee, and he could wait in the kitchen while she dressed.

I could believe in that scene. He'd been on her conscience. She'd never turned him away. A dozen times at least I'd seen him asked in for an uneasy coffee; an unhappy drink; a mumbled conversation. I'd asked him in myself, now and then. He'd had enough bad luck, without being pushed away from doors.

He hadn't stayed in the kitchen. He'd followed her back to the bedroom. She wasn't wearing the bracelet. She'd just put it away in the drawer.

His voice began to vanish again. I couldn't understand more than half of what he was saying. I think he tried to take the bracelet out of the drawer. The gun was in the drawer, too She'd told him to clear off. I didn't catch the sequence of the row. Something about the letters, she guessed he'd written them, she said she'd sent the last one on to me. He didn't, he couldn't remember, but the gun had been fired, and she was dead. It wouldn't have gone that way if she hadn't kept the gun in the room.

The monologue suddenly finished. We sat in silence for half a minute, then he poured some more brandy. There was only half a glass. It was the end of the bottle.

'And what did you do then, Laurence?' I asked softly.

He didn't want to tell me. Perhaps he was beginning to see that I wasn't, after all, that mythical stranger it's safe to talk to. The stranger that comes out of books. When a man's committed a murder there's no one in the world he can talk to safely.

Laurence spoke slowly and jerkily now, he left words out of sentences. It seemed he'd had a kind of black-out, but he came out of it with his mind in action. He realized his only chance was to pretend she'd been shot at a different time, a time when he couldn't have been there. He knew that with Dulcie's help he could prove he'd had no chance of getting to Regent's Park before eight.

'Did you go in the sitting-room?'

'No. Not the sitting-room.'

He stopped and wiped his brow. 'Brandy?' he said.

'It's finished, Laurence. Have some wine.'

I took the corkscrew and began to open the bottle. I hoped he'd be unconscious soon.

'What did you have against me, Laurence?'

He was sitting, staring vacantly at the wine bottle. As I got the cork off the bottle he roused himself with that violent shake of the head that was so painful to watch. It was as if he was trying to move an obstruction.

'Someone had to do her in. Peter was the one I wanted, but the hell of it was, it couldn't be Peter. If I'd known where he lived, I'd have planted the gun on him. I thought of Fenby, but when I suggested him to the police, they said he'd had his father with him. I knew there was this Donald Spencer, but I didn't know enough about him. Someone had to do her in, so I left the gun with you.'

It seemed funny he hadn't known where Donald was, when Donald had lain in the next room, doped by too-strong pills, wakened, perhaps, by the shots.

178

'But you copied the letter first, before you knew about the others. You copied the letter on my typewriter. That was unfriendly.'

He stood up. He was holding the edge of the table with one hand, while the other waved about, maintaining his precarious balance. I was astonished he could stand at all. I didn't like the way he was looking at me. I pushed him a glass of wine quickly. It was better when he was sitting down.

He began to mutter and shout at me now, with his eyes shut. I guessed the world was moving, the way it does, and it hurt his head. Drunk or not, he could say the things that reached home. He gave me a picture of myself I didn't enjoy, and some of it was true.

Then he sat down again. 'I've been raving, Nancy,' he said in a voice that was half-sober. 'Apologies and all that. I've been having these damned waking nightmares. I get this pain in my head, it's on one side, I don't know what it is. What have I been telling you? What have I been saying? Last night—last night was hell. I dreamt I'd killed Sarah. But it's not a dream. It's when I'm awake. I haven't slept for a month.'

'You should see a doctor, Laurence.'

'Yes. I'll do that.' We looked at each other warily.

'Those dreams—it's lucky for me she was killed in bed,' he muttered.

'But you've admitted——'

'I've admitted nothing!' he shouted. 'I had a dream, that's all.' He stood up, leaning against the table. It rocked towards him, the bottle of wine began to slip. It fell sideways, with its neck over the edge of the table; wine flooded on to the floor. I tried to clutch the bottle as it slid right off the table, but it was too late. When I picked it up, it was empty. There was nothing left to drink, and no chance of getting Laurence unconscious now.

'I've been raving, Nancy,' he said. 'Maybe you're right, she wasn't killed in bed. Then Peter was able to get there. He killed her. Peter!' he said again. He snatched the empty bottle, and tilted it into his glass. Only a few drops came out. He swallowed them.

'No. The murderer wrote a letter to Sarah. Peter's illiterate. He couldn't have written that letter.'

'Then Fenby.'

'Mike's not interested in poetry, unless it comes out of a play.

And Donald hasn't read a line of poetry since he left school. It's you and I and Sarah who like poetry.'

'You're talking of her as if she was alive. I won't put up with it, Nancy.'

'Then it's you and I who like poetry.'

'What's poetry got to do with it, anyway?'

'Do you remember the letter, Laurence?'

He shook his head again, with the same violent, tortured gesture.

'I do. It worried me at the time, but I had other worries. I didn't see the connection until tonight. The letter begins and ends with a threat, but in the middle it says: "Up to a point any road will do as well as another, for you and for me, too. The trouble is, after this point, there's no turning back, we've both passed the fork, there's only one way now." Do you remember it, Laurence?'

'No, I never saw it.'

'But you remember a verse by Day Lewis. He's one of the poets both you and I like. You have his poems at home, and I have them here. But this isn't in his collected verse. It's in a later book. You borrowed it from Battersea Public Library, and it's a pity you didn't return it. I saw it in your flat yesterday. I opened it at the page. "You walk in a nightmare now, not in a dream." That's the verse you quoted from. I suppose you didn't even remember you were quoting. It's a poem with a good idea. It gets inside your head, and stays there, and like other good ideas, it can come out at the wrong time.'

'I don't believe you,' Laurence said. 'I didn't quote anyone. Show me the book.'

'It's on the desk, over there.'

He went to the desk. He picked up the book. It was open, as I'd left it. He looked at the page. He was reeling, he could hardly have seen the print, but he began to read aloud, as he'd so often read to Sarah and me in the past. He had a feeling for poetry, and a good voice. He read now:

> ' "Besides, for such travellers it's all but true
> That up to a point any road will do
> As well as another—so why not walk
> Straight on? The trouble is, *after* this point
> There's no turning back, not even a fork;
> And you never can see that point until

180

After you have passed it. And when you know
For certain you are lost, there's nothing to do
But go on walking your road, although
You walk in a nightmare now, not a dream." '

I think he'd have read on, he'd have finished the verse, if he
hadn't looked up and seen my face. It was I who had told him
to pick up the book: there was no reason why I should have
forgotten what had made me put the book there, on the desk,
when the bell rang. While he read I'd been waiting, transfixed,
helpless, hopeless. He closed the book and turned unsteadily
round, and saw the gun that the book had hidden on the desk.

I was someone else, now, I was outside the whole thing. It
was as if it was happening in a strange house, and I was looking through the window. There wasn't much to be seen. A
man closed a book, turned slowly round, and uncertainly,
clumsily, picked up something from a desk. At that point I
would walk on, I wouldn't know what happened next. I looked
back. Laurence had taken the gun in his hand, and suddenly
I wasn't outside any more. I was in, everything was out of
control, the crash was coming at last.

He twisted the gun in his hand. He seemed horrified by the
sight of it.

'You've got no right,' he said. 'You've got no right . . .' His
blurred, whispering voice died away. I didn't know what I'd
no right to do, but I was afraid, and, like a fool, I showed it.
I might have done something to stop him, all I needed was an
easy, confident manner, the kind that is recommended for
putting savage dogs at their ease. Laurence was worse than
savage. He was mad, ferocious, diseased. I recognized that now.

I backed away, and Laurence moved forward.

'Shouldn't have a gun, Nancy. You shouldn't.'

'Laurence, I'll find you another drink, I'll get one somewhere.'

He hesitated, and I tried to get to the door. He swayed
forward, blocking the way, and I went back again.

'Came here tonight, Nancy, came as a friend,' he said. He
was staggering on his feet. The gun was pointing, not so much
at me, as round me. I watched the wobbling barrel. It looked
big enough to blow off my head, but it was only an ordinary
gun.

'Not treated as a friend,' he muttered. He looked down at
the gun. He seemed surprised to find he was holding it.

181

I was close to the bedroom door. I moved along the wall, still facing him, and tried to turn the handle.

'Away from the door,' he said, and I came away from it.

'You, Nancy, always gone your own way, always to hell with everyone else, you'll go my way now. Sit.'

I couldn't do it. There was some kind of hope while I was on my feet. Then I thought if I could make him talk, if I could keep him talking, he might forget what he wanted to do.

'You don't want that gun, Laurence, you don't want any more trouble, drop it.'

'You sit down, or you're going to have it now, Nancy.'

'You don't want to hurt me, that's not why you came here, it isn't.'

'I came to give you this.'

He put his hand in his pocket and pulled out the diamond bracelet. He held it in the palm of his hand so that we could both see it. All the light in the room went into his hand and flashed off again.

'Passage to Italy,' he said. 'Six months in Italy. You can go to Italy any time you like, but not me. But still, I'm giving it to you.'

He threw it on the table. It landed on the empty brandy bottle with a ringing noise, like a small handful of pebbles. I hardly looked at it. I was watching the gun in the unsteady hand.

'Pick it up,' he shouted.

I put my hand out towards the bracelet and snatched the brandy bottle and threw it at him. It hit him on the side of the head, and while he was spinning round I ran past him. I reached the outside door, I had it open when he turned and fired. It got me on the shoulder, it didn't feel like a bullet, it was like being hit by a half-ton rock.

I don't know exactly what happened next, but somehow he caught me and pushed me back in the room. He'd been smoothing back his hair, he had a bloody forelock now.

He had the diamond bracelet in his hand. He stood close beside me and waved it in my face, shouting and cursing at me. I didn't listen, I couldn't hear it, I was telling myself it had come, it was the final crash, and trying to think of something for the end. Donald's face wasn't there. It was only Sarah's I could see. She was terrified. I tried to tell her it was all right, there was nothing to be afraid of.

Then there was someone else in the room, I didn't know what was real and what wasn't, but the gun went off again. I saw Laurence, there was another man with him, but I knew the bullet had gone straight into my heart. I didn't know how I was still able to stand, with a bullet in my heart. I put my good hand to my left side, and it was true enough. There was a lot of blood.

When I looked up from that, Sarah's face wasn't there any more. It was Stony's.

'Hello, Nancy,' he said. He was searching for words, and he got them at last.

'I've brought the new Jag round. Want to see it?'

13

IN HOSPITAL I kept opening my eyes and seeing Inspector Crewe's face floating over the bed. He had a nasty, disembodied appearance, I was glad to shut my eyes and get rid of him. That happened so often he got mixed up with the whole thing, he was part of the situation. I just accepted it in the end, I realized this was hospital, and he was there. I soon gave up hoping the nurses would send him away. He was always there. Sometimes when I opened my eyes the electric light was on, then it was night, and sometimes it was off, then perhaps it was a different day. I didn't have any way of measuring the time.

There were consultations round my bed, when everyone spoke very quietly. I didn't like that at all. They asked me questions that I couldn't hear. I tried to guess what they wanted to find out. 'No next-of-kin,' I said. They have morbid minds, in hospitals.

I didn't like to open my eyes, much. I was worried in case I died and everyone thought the Inspector was my next-of-kin. It didn't seem respectable to die with only a policeman sitting beside the bed. I tried to send him away, but the words didn't work out well. So I stopped trying to speak. I lay quiet, and thought of the next-of-kin I'd like. The best I could do, in my low condition, was my father, the High Court Judge, and my uncle, a shady but rich art dealer in New York. With these two behind me, I could die in comfort anywhere.

When I woke up again the Judge was trying the Stratford Shakespeare Company for indecent language; and the art dealer had just discovered twelve Rembrandts in an Amsterdam coal cellar. So neither of them was able to sit beside my bed, but the Inspector was still there.

I heard his voice this time. It was something about making a statement. Whatever he called it, he meant he was going to ask more questions.

'I knew he'd killed Sarah, so he took a couple of shots at me,' I said. I rather liked hearing my own voice again, after all that time, but I didn't want to go on hearing it. I hoped I'd told him what he wanted, so that he'd go away.

He wasn't a man who liked going away. He probably enjoyed hospital life more than I did. He wanted to know how the gun had arrived back in the flat; where the diamond bracelet had come from; how I'd known she wasn't shot in bed. I couldn't answer the first two. I tried the third, and got involved in underclothes and green dressing-gowns. How did I know about the green dressing-gown? It was too late now to bring Donald into it. I didn't have the strength, or even the inclination, to lie. I took refuge in a very high temperature and a faint, irregular, pulse. After that, they wouldn't let him see me, for days. But, when I was better, he came back.

'This is an unofficial call, Miss Graham.'

'I'm not allowed visitors.'

'I thought you'd like to know. We've been holding him on a charge of attempted murder, against you. But he's confessed to the other.'

'Poor Laurence.'

The Inspector gave me a queer look, but I wasn't going to explain to him. Sarah had always been unhappy about Laurence. She had no malice in her. She wouldn't have wanted him to suffer any more, because of her.

'The woman he lived with was persuaded to tell us a few things. He came home with that dressing-gown and the underclothes, in a bundle. She threw them in the river for him. So that seems to be cleared up. You wouldn't like to explain to me now why you told so many inconsistent lies?'

184

'I can't explain. You're so official. It's not like talking to an ordinary man. The conversation's too one-sided.'

'You were covering up for someone. We know it wasn't for Laurence Hopkins. Just whom were you protecting?'

'A Mexican oil millionaire, Miguel Orinoco. I'm sure someone's told you about him.'

'We heard rumours.' He smiled at me in an almost unofficial way. I suppose there was a human being buried under him, somewhere. 'This man, Donald Spencer. He never turned up.'

'Do you want him now?'

'The case is closed. Laurence Hopkins had a haemorrhage of the brain, yesterday morning. He died almost at once.'

That quietened me for a bit. Any death is worth a minute's thought. I didn't give him enough thought, even now. No one had ever given enough thought, to Laurence. My mind went over to Donald. They wouldn't want him. They wouldn't want him, ever. I was glad of that, in a detached way.

The Inspector was still asking questions.

'Sarah bought the diamonds out of her savings,' I told him. 'I know she never made a will. You'll have to take my word for it she wanted them sold and the proceeds given to some deserving insurance company.'

He stood up. 'Don't get mixed up in any more murders, Miss Graham. You're the worst liar in the business.'

That was his exit line. He wasn't a bad man. I might have liked him, if he hadn't been official.

After he'd gone, I had a kind of relapse. I couldn't get back to the High Court Judge and the shady art dealer. I kept thinking of Sarah, and Laurence, and Donald. I wasn't allowed visitors, and I didn't mind. There was no one I wanted to see. I lay in bed and thought of the other time I'd been in hospital, after the Jaguar had crashed. Sarah had come then, and Mike had been so frightened of being involved in a scandal that he'd been furious with me, we hadn't spoken for months.

I came out of hospital, in the end. Everyone gets out, one way or the other. Stony drove me back in the new Jaguar, at about five miles an hour. I was very grateful to Stony, for having saved my life, although I didn't seem to have much life left.

People rang up, but Stony was the only one I could bear to see. He had to go back to Canada, with the Jaguar, but he took me for one long night drive before he left. That was a little more like living, again, but I couldn't drive, my shoulder wasn't right.

I hung around the flat for a week, but there was the rent to pay. I couldn't afford the life of leisure for very long. Diagonal found a job I could do for them, in Spain. They were a good firm to work with, as firms go, and I wanted to get out of England, away from everyone I knew who had known Sarah.

I didn't get out quickly enough. Donald came back, as I'd known he would, when everything was safe. There might have been a big scene, but I wouldn't let it happen. I'd had enough of big scenes.

'We're finished Donald, Caput. Affairs end, and this one's ended.'

'I was wrong to leave you at the airport. I shouldn't have done it. But you see, Nancy, I was innocent. I knew they'd never believe it. You wouldn't have expected me to give myself up to the police when I hadn't done anything.'

'I don't expect anything of anyone, Donald. We're alone in this world. We have to look out for ourselves.'

'Nancy, you said you loved me.'

'It's easy enough to love someone. The difficulty is, to keep on with it.'

'I always knew you'd leave me.'

'Then you were right. Good-bye, Donald.'

He went, and that was that, but every time that's that, the pendulum swings, the clock ticks, that will never be that in the same way again.

I was sorry Stony had gone. What I needed now was to drive at a hundred miles an hour until the rushing air washed my mind clean.

I tried to plunge into the arrangements for going to Spain, but I was in a disorganized mood. I put a suitcase on the floor and stared at it for hours before I began vaguely to fill it with the wrong clothes. I should have known by now how to pack a case, I'd done it often enough, there was no excuse.

When the bell rang I didn't know what time it was, except that it was late, and I was almost too tired to answer the door.

I opened it. Mike was there. Of course he had to come. It was what I'd been afraid of, since I'd left hospital. There was no reason why I should pretend to be friendly.

'Hello, Mike. What do you want?'

'I was going to say "Hello, Nancy." But I can't do it on the doorstep.'

'It's too late to come in.'

'I couldn't come earlier. Six curtain calls tonight. What do you think of the show?'

'I haven't seen it.'

'Nancy, you've been out of hospital for a week. You've had plenty of time. Did you read the notices?'

'Mike, I'm tired. I'm going to bed.'

'I've never known you to go to bed at eleven. If you're tired you'd better sit down.'

He went past me, and into the sitting-room.

'You're in a bit of a mess in here,' he said, disapprovingly.

'I'm packing. I'm going away.'

'I envy you, Nancy, always on the move. Not stuck to the same theatre, night after night.'

'I'm busy, Mike. I don't want to see you.'

'But I want to see you.' He stood back and examined me, frowning, as if he was considering me for some minor part.

'I must say, you look a bit of a wreck. Hospital hasn't improved you.'

'Thank you. Now will you go.'

'No. Sit down, Nancy. I've had the hell of a time since you went away. On the first night the only thing that stopped the gallery from rooting up the seats and heaving them at us was pure physical inability to throw them over the distance. And the stalls. What a hand they gave us! It sounded like one old carpenter hammering in his last tack. I didn't think we'd last a week. Then we had a wonderful break. Kit got laryngitis. I hope it's permanent. That woman just has to say three lines, and people begin tearing down theatres and putting up office blocks. So we got Liz back, fresh from her dubious operation. She looked absolutely radiant. It's the only way she can look, she has no other facial expression to offer, but it's all that's needed in this particular work. We're set for a year's run now, at least.'

'I'm glad.'

'You don't look glad.'

'Good night, Mike.'

'Nancy!'

'What?'

'They wouldn't let me in the hospital. They said you weren't allowed visitors.'

'I wasn't.'

'Not all the time you were there?'

I didn't answer.

'It was fair enough, at first, when they were ranting on in that dismal hospital way about danger lists, but later I had the impression there was a touch of keep-Michael-Fenby-out.'

'I didn't want to see you.'

'People in hospitals always go a bit neurotic. Why didn't you want to see me?'

'If you'd really like to know, it was because I told you I'd killed Sarah, and you believed me.'

'I didn't believe that for as much as ten seconds. But you made me so angry, just saying it, still trying to take the rap for Donald when he'd thrown you to the police so he could get away. You got me in a rage. I wanted to shake it out of you. Then you tried to turn that gun against me. The trouble with you, Nancy, is that you've got a shocking temper.'

'Don't start on what's the trouble with me.'

'Are you going to marry Donald?'

'No!'

'Has he turned you down?'

'I don't wish to discuss the matter.'

'Has someone else asked you?'

'That's another matter I don't wish to discuss.'

'Are you going to marry Stony?'

'Go away, Mike.'

'I can't say anything against Stony, now. I think you'd better marry him.'

'Really?'

'He's a very sound man.'

'Yes.'

'He's the only one who's come well out of this affair.'

'Yes.'

'Is he still in England?'

'He went back to Canada yesterday.'

'I'm sure you'll like life in Canada. He's actually asked you to marry him, has he?'

'That has nothing to do with you.'

'I see he has. That finishes it, then. While I was walking up and down the streets, swearing I'd never see you again, he was saving your life. I provided the gun for that maniac to shoot you with, and I left you alone with it, even though . . . Nancy!'

'Yes?'

'I had the hell of a night, thinking you might have killed yourself, with that gun. I ought to have gone back, but I didn't. So you'd better marry Stony.'

'I prefer to arrange my own marriages.'

'Are you going to arrange that one?'

'It isn't anything to do with you.'

'But it is. It doesn't matter if you want to marry someone else, but I regard Stony as having taken out an option, on you.'

'That's a charming way to put it. I'm not going to marry Stony. I'm going away, on a job. I'm going away from everyone I know. I don't want to see any of them, ever again.'

'Except me.'

'You don't want to see me, Mike. You don't like scandal, and I've been involved in enough to make the front page of nearly every newspaper in the world. I'm the kind of person you want to drop.'

'I'd like to drop you out of a window,' he said. He was angry again. 'I take every kind of insult from you, and I'm tired of it. I waited three years to get that divorce from Sarah so that I could marry you, and you know it.'

'I certainly don't know it. You were always mixed up with Addies and Liz's and Judys.'

'You needn't get angry because I chose to fill in the time with beautiful women. I happen to have noticed that you've filled in the time, too, with fake Bulgarian poets and bogus Italian counts and mad motorists.'

'A minute ago you were so keen to marry me off to Stony.'

'But you're not going to marry him. So there's nothing else for it, you'll have to marry me.'

'I'm damned if I will.'

He'd been standing on the other side of the room. He came over to me in a rage and caught me by the shoulders.

'Nancy, look at me.'

'I won't.'

'But you're going to.'

He pushed me back in the chair.

'Now open your eyes.'

'I can't.

'Yes, you can. Don't pretend you're crying.'

189

'I'm not,' I said. I opened my eyes. He didn't care if I looked at him. He wanted to look at me, that was all.

'You're afraid of me, Nancy. That's the trouble, isn't it?'

'You're hurting my shoulder, now.'

He let me go at once. 'I know you think I'm a brute and a bully, but at least you know the worst of me. You ought to. You always bring it out.'

'That's a promising start.'

'I'm serious. You know me, and I know you. If I'm willing to marry the savage, won't you marry the brute?'

'No.'

'I promise you I'll never hurt you.'

'That's not a promise you can keep. You can't change yourself so easily.'

'Then I'll promise to try not to hurt you. I know I've behaved badly, on and off. That's because you always seemed to belong to someone else. When you belong to me I'll never hurt you again, unless you try to run away.'

'You make me sound like a slave.'

'That's it. That's how I want you. Exclusive rights. From the beginning, from the days when I used to order you about my dressing-room, I've wanted it that way. I meant to marry you, then; I was only waiting until I got in a settling-down mood. Then Sarah came along, and I—well, that's the way it was. I made a mistake.'

'It wasn't a mistake, Mike. She was so beautiful. You'd have been happy for ever with her. It was just bad luck, about Peter.'

'Put it that way, if you like. I shouldn't have married Sarah, she belonged to Peter, but that's finished. You shouldn't have loved Donald, but that's over, too. We won't throw the past at each other. You will marry me, won't you, Nancy?'

He waited, but I couldn't say anything at all. I was thinking of Sarah, I was thinking of her with all my heart, for the last time. As Mike said, she was finished. She was like Donald, part of the past that keeps piling up behind us, and pushing us on.

'If you won't, you won't,' Mike said, still waiting. I couldn't find the answer.

'I'll go then,' he said. He was using his arrogant, indifferent voice.

I let him go as far as the door.

'Mike.'

'What?'

He didn't turn, he stood with his back to me, his hand on the door, the old theatrical stance. I had to shake him out of it, somehow.

'If your tie still needs ironing, I'll do it for you now.'

He turned round. I don't know if he saw in my face all I felt, but I saw everything on his.

He'd never kissed me once, not in all the years I'd known him. He kissed me now, and I knew we were both on the right road, at last.